The Judge's Parlour

A 16th Century Pub in a Small Cornish Village with Big Secrets and an Enormous History

Arthur Walters

Matador
9 Priory Business Park,
Wistow Road, Kibworth Beauchamp,
Leicestershire. LE8 0RX
Tel: 0116 279 2299
Email: books@troubador.co.uk
Web: www.troubador.co.uk/matador
Twitter: @matadorbooks

ISBN 978 1788037 440

British Library Cataloguing in Publication Data.
A catalogue record for this book is available from the British Library.

Printed and bound by CPI Group (UK) Ltd, Croydon, CR0 4YY
Typeset in 11pt Minion Pro by Troubador Publishing Ltd, Leicester, UK

Matador is an imprint of Troubador Publishing Ltd

Dedicated to the Devon village of Lydford which gave me so much freedom and enjoyment in my younger years and to the residents past and present who, as custodians, kept and continue to keep it somewhere special.

Prologue

AD 996

As his fellow warriors dragged the ship onto the shore, Felman the "man from the mountains", felt his stomach retch. He had been sick on his journey from the north to where they had rested at Dyflin, but now in the calm river mouth of the Tamar the reality of the raids to come unsettled his bowels.

It had been his father Bjorn, a seasoned warrior as strong as the bear after which he was named who'd taken his fifteen-year-old son to the ships an hour before cast off.

'Bring him back a man, not the weak boy you see stood before you,' he had told the *jarl*. 'Do as you will with him; he is no good to me as he is.'

The *jarl* had instructed him to row, but as it soon became obvious he hadn't the strength, he'd been sent to prepare the meagre rations. At night, men would approach him, but the *jarl* ushered them away.

'Save him until after we land,' he'd joked, 'in case there aren't any women to have.'

But there had been and as they headed inland to

the west, many times Felman watched as husbands and sons were slain, their heads held high on poles, while the women and young children cowered behind whatever cover they could find.

Once the buildings were well alight, the warriors would seek out the prettiest of the hideaways, raping them mercilessly, any resistance ended by a slash of an axe or a sword, or perhaps a thrust of a spear. It mattered not whether these women were alive or dead, as long as the bloodthirsty men could satisfy their needs and relieve their frustration.

On reaching Treforthamm, the ditches and steep banks had offered protection to those who lived there, but tales of freshly minted silver coins had whetted the men's appetites and they were not going to allow earth and stones to stand in their way.

Their first attack had been repelled. The *Berserks* in their bearskins had bitten their shields and after Einar, "he who fights alone", had thrown his spear in dedication to *Odin,* they had charged; spears, axes and razor-sharp, double-edged swords to the ready. But the Saxons were well prepared and many invaders died as, in ones and twos, they ran up the steep bank, misguided in the belief *Odin* had given them invincible powers.

Their feet slipping on loose soil, they clambered back down, many more falling to the spears which pierced their organs and entrails.

And so it was to Magnus "the mighty", to whom they turned.

He instructed twenty or so to form a wedge like the point of a spear and with their shields covering their bodies they slowly and deliberately climbed the bank. The Saxons were able to stop a few but soon they were outnumbered and with losses mounting, they fled to the church in search of their god's protection.

Felman had attempted to join the fighting. After the defeated had run, he'd half-heartedly dismembered three fallen casualties, their hideous screams deadening his senses. Joining the chase, he'd spotted a young girl of similar age fleeing towards the church, her skirts billowing like the sail of his longboat. Catching her, he'd grabbed her blonde tresses, dragged her to the ground and pinning her by the throat, raised his axe. Resigned to her fate, she'd spat in his face, daring him to carry out his will, her contemptuous expression showing no fear. He'd hesitated, her beauty reminding him of Brynhild "the fighter", the girl he admired back home. Ignoring the hardness in his trousers, he'd risen to his feet. Wiping her defiant saliva from his cheek, he'd licked his fingers, smiled and reluctantly returned to the melee.

That night, he'd prayed to Freya, the Goddess of fertility, begging for the safety of the young woman. He'd watched as the flames leapt from the church, the smell of burning flesh filling his nostrils, hoping against hope she'd not perished.

The following year they returned, Felman, now a seasoned warrior, hopeful of seeing the girl alive. But this time they moored in the TauVechan and headed inland to the east to the village of Hlidanford, where many were slain and buildings destroyed. At night, camped by a white waterfall as high as a ship was long, Felman prayed their morning's journey would take them west, but it was not to be.

Instead, the next day, his fellow warriors plundered the abbey in TauVechanStoke, the pleas of the unarmed monks falling on impervious ears. As he set sail for home, Felman questioned his being, swearing that one day he would return and make good his countrymen's wrongs.

CHAPTER ONE

6 May 2016

'I'm so sorry Caroline. I still can't believe it, not Gareth; he was such a kind and generous man.' Brendon Gallagher, a wiry, unassuming, short back and sides, dark-haired sixty-year-old, was stood in the dimly lit public bar of The Judge's Parlour, a sixteenth-century unspoilt country pub in the village of Lingtree. It was originally a coaching inn, a welcome overnight stop for wealthy travellers journeying across the moor for holidays in the Cornish seaside destinations prior to the building of the railways, or perhaps to attend business meetings in the larger mining towns of Camborne and Redruth, or possibly to pay stannary taxes in the county's financial centre of Truro. However, whatever the individual's purpose for enduring the bumpy and uncomfortable coach ride, few would have been bothered by the bar's low ceilings, whereas for Brendon, his six-foot-six height meant him regularly lowering his head to avoid striking the original oak beams. He'd had the same problem as he'd opened the door from the entrance porch into the lobby; the left-hand door to the public bar offering yet a further challenge.

'Thank you Brendon,' replied Caroline Pettit, acknowledging his words with a forced smile. 'None of us in the village has come to terms with it yet; it's not the sort of accident you'd expect to happen in a sleepy place like this.' She stared through her glass of white wine, her eyes beginning to water. 'I don't understand why he was in the castle. Like you, he said he would never go inside again. I keep seeing him laid out...' Failing to hold back the tears, she hastily wiped her cheek with an already sodden handkerchief. 'We'd been married nearly forty-one years; it's not how I want to remember him.'

Appreciating Brendon's silence, she managed to regain some composure. She looked up at him.

'Thanks so much for coming; Gareth would have been pleased you made it; I just wish he could have been alive to see you after all these years.'

'I'm sorry,' he replied. 'My work means I travel a lot and time in this country is rare.' He bit his lip. 'I really regret—'

Caroline saved his embarrassment. 'I know Brendon.' She touched his arm. 'It's been a long time for all of us.' She looked around the crowded bar. 'Some of us moved on after school while others...' She picked out the two men, one with long hair, the other shaven headed, dressed in unpressed, double-breasted, dark coloured, ill-fitting suits, stood by the table laden with sandwiches, sausage rolls and canapés, enjoying at least their fourth free pint, '... decided to stay or come back.'

Brendon smiled. Forty-seven years had passed since

he'd first met this petite, blue-eyed, still slender, although now weather-beaten and physically farm hardened, sun-bleached blonde.

He'd wanted to be more than just great friends with Caroline, but it was Gareth who'd won her over. She may be "pushing" sixty but there would be many a man who would happily step in where her late husband left off.

'I know what you mean, Caroline. I sometimes wish I'd chosen a different path… you know, met someone, settled down and had kids, but on the other hand—'

'You wouldn't have had the excitement of working for The Ministry.' She smiled. 'Gareth often wished he'd done something different with his life but farming was in his blood and goodness knows what his dad would have done if he'd sold the farm; turned in his grave several times I should think.' She shrugged. 'Ah well… c'mon, I'll get you another drink and then I'd better circulate. You're not rushing off are you?'

Brendon shook his head. 'No, I've booked a room here. I've decided to stay a few nights, try and catch up with everyone and visit the old haunts.'

'Perhaps we could have dinner tomorrow night. The kids are off back up country and really there's little I can do until the farm is sold. A couple of lads have offered to help out until I decide the future.'

'Which is?' enquired Brendon.

'I've got no idea to be honest,' Caroline replied, a sad look in her eyes. 'The farm was Gareth's life and I just fitted in where I could. Neither of the kids ever showed any interest in it, so I suppose the obvious thing is to sell, but then I'd be letting down Gareth and his forebears.' She sighed. 'Ah well, what will be, will be. Large whisky, is it?'

Brendon nodded. 'Thanks Caroline and yes, dinner would be good.'

~

The last time Brendon Gallagher had been to Lingtree was to arrange his mother's funeral. Both adopted parents had died within two months of each other just over ten years ago. He'd moved to Lingtree when he was eleven and had little memory of the years before then as being an unwanted orphan had taken its toll. His adopted father had been a detective chief inspector in Surrey, but had transferred to Cornwall to take up a senior role investigating unsolved serious crimes. However, in the years since his last visit little had changed. Several new houses had been built on the sides of the mile-long main street, many of the old ones had been renovated to modern-day standards and were now occupied by "new money" families, whilst some of the untouched ones had been passed from one generation to the next, their owners unable to afford renovations.

The two petrol stations had closed many years ago, defeated by cheap supermarket fuel eight miles away. The one in the centre of the village was now a first-storey private residence, the workshop below turned into a double garage with dark brown stained wooden doors, whilst the forecourt, which had once proudly sported both a four-star and a two-star petrol pump, just an underused concrete parking area. The other station on the outskirts had tried to carry on as a village store but sadly the supermarkets had won once again.

Despite several changes of ownership, the sixteenth-century Judge's Parlour with its quaint public bar and lounge bar-cum-restaurant had survived and continued to offer good ale, quality pub food and cosy, if not particularly modern accommodation. Situated on the southern edge of Bodmin Moor, Lingtree attracted an abundance of visitors in the summer; some appreciating sultry walks over the heather and bracken-covered tors which in winter were shrouded in a cold, damp, penetrating mist, the well-worn paths replaced by bottomless, muddy bogs, whilst others preferred to explore the history of the remains of the medieval castle and the adjacent Norman church, or enjoy the excitement of a demanding stroll through the renowned Lingtree Gorge, allegedly as deep as any in the South-West. Folklore says it was the hideout of the infamous Dobbings family, an incestuous bunch of robbers and murderers. However, Brendon took all this beauty for granted; after all, as a kid, to him and his mates it was just an adventure playground, something to have fun in but not really valued.

Alone in bed on his numerous journeys abroad, he would lay awake, awareness of the possible threats to his life temporarily dismissed as he recalled the uncomplicated freedom he'd enjoyed as a youngster growing up in the countryside, unencumbered by the restrictions of adulthood and city life. It had been fun, spoilt only by the loss of his best friend Alan.

~

'Don't be scared, you prick, it ain't a fucking pike; it's hardly going to bite you!'

Having had his twelfth birthday, Jim was the eldest. Stocky, scared of nothing, willing to try anything, on leaving school he should have joined the Special Forces or the Marines. Instead, he'd get a job in a hardware store situated seven miles away in Chilstoke, a popular town with a twelve-thousand population and still be working there over forty years later. His social life would involve beer and the occasional whisky whereas his wife of twenty years would prefer luxurious home comforts paid for by the money left over from the odd occasion he settled his bar tab!

'It's all right for you, smartarse; you're not the one trying to get it off the line. You know I hate touching the fuckers,' replied Alan, his old-fashioned cane fishing rod held upright in one hand, while his other was frantically trying to grab the ten-inch brown trout which, having taken the illegal bait, was wriggling frenetically a few inches from his face in a last ditch attempt to escape.

'Then why come fishing, you twat? What were you expecting to catch, a fucking cold?'

Pete, a pasty looking, but tall for his age, eleven-year-old, was always keen to offer his encouragement, despite the fact he was pretty useless at anything practical. After leaving grammar school he would go on to university and then qualify as an accountant. He'd work for several years in London, pass all his exams and then set up a business employing twenty people in Melkthorpe, a town half the size of Chilstoke and eight miles from Lingtree in the opposite direction.

Eventually he'd sell out to a national company, end up with a "bob or two" and buy The Old Brake House in Lingtree, a six-bedroom property in four acres of land a couple of miles from The Judge's Parlour and along the lane which led to Caroline and Gareth's farm. After losing his husband to AIDS, he'd have unfulfilled spare time and *evolve* into a loyal drinking partner for Jim.

'Give it here Alan, you're fucking useless.' Brendon grabbed the line and carefully unhooked the fish, its resistance now all but ended. Deftly, he bent the head back, cleanly breaking its neck, an art he would carry on in later life, albeit rarely on fish. He pulled the remains of the earthworm off the barb and threw it into the river, its *raison d'être* fulfilled.

He and Alan lived next door to each other in bungalows built in the sixties by a local builder, a stone's throw away from the granite cross war memorial bearing names of those who died in the First and Second World Wars, the Falklands and Iraq. Their respective parents got on well and often socialised together. Within six months of meeting, Alan and Brendon had become best mates.

Unfortunately, unlike Jim and Brendon, Alan, who was rather small for his age, was not particularly good at juvenile country life although this never stopped him trying to be part of everything; sadly it was this eagerness to impress which would end his life early.

Once the "worth keeping" trout was safely deposited in Jim's fishing bag (there was no way Alan was going to take it), they packed up their gear. It had been a wet afternoon, the ten *Kensita* cigarettes had all been smoked and the light was beginning to fade. His rod carefully dismantled, Brendon thoroughly and painstakingly washed the clingy, stinking fish scales off his hands in the cloudy, muddied water. As he shook them dry, Jim shouted his challenge.

'Race you girls to the bridge,' he barked. 'Last one home's a dick head.' With that, he grabbed his bag and rod and disappeared up the steep grassy bank to the narrow carved-out path which ran a few metres above the river.

The waters of the gorge were in full flow. The eagerly anticipated January snow on the high tors of the moor had all but melted and the first two days of February had brought heavy rain. The gorge was closed to visitors at this time of year, the paths deemed to be too slippery for "townies" wearing posh trainers instead of non-slip walking boots. In thirty years' time, health and safety would decree the Trust, the long-term custodians of the beauty spot, install handrails and fences to ensure nobody lost their footing and fell into one of the many deep crevices and cauldrons, but for now, last autumn's greasy, rotted leaves fallen from the many trees towering over the sunken chasms made for exciting races.

The three lads chased after him, Brendon leading the pack ahead of Pete and Alan. At their age they saw no danger and as they reached the steepest part of the footpath just before it dropped down beneath the road bridge, it became a sprint finish.

Jim's false start was enough to see him home in the lead, although Brendon wasn't far behind. Pete and Alan finished together. Panting heavily, their strained gasps forming a steamy mist in the chilly, damp air, the four of them paused for a couple of minutes to catch their breath, then walked slowly to the paint-bare, unimpressive, wooden entrance gate next to the ticket kiosk where the retired Mr Philpots would sit all day, collecting money from the paying visitors, but not from the village youngsters.

'Get on in,' he would say, as though instructing a black Labrador to follow the game into the bushes, 'before anyone sees you.'

Ensuring they avoided the four strands of barbed wire stretched above the gate in a half-hearted attempt to keep out any trespassers, they took it in turns to climb over, jumping easily down the other side. As they picked up their fishing gear which Jim who had been first to go, was supposed to have caught as it came flying as high overhead as he mates could toss, Alan shook his shoulder-length hair.

'I'm soaked,' he exclaimed, 'and fucking cold.'

'Shouldn't wear your hair so long, you big girl's blouse,' joked Jim, who preferred a crew cut, or rather his mother did. 'You might be able to run a bit faster then.'

'Bollocks,' replied Alan, 'at least I've got some you skinhead.'

'I'm not, I'm a Cavalier. I'll show you if you want,' said Jim, laughing as he reached for his trouser zip.

'Yuck, I don't want to see your cheesy knob thanks and anyway, it's Roundhead not skinhead,' said Brendon confidently. 'C'mon, let's get home; I'm starving. Mum says I can have chips tonight.'

'Lucky bastard. My mother's on one of those healthy diets she saw in the newspaper, so we all have to be on it.

Pork chops and cabbage with boiled potatoes.' Jim looked genuinely sad but his physique suggested he wasn't starving.

'Cheer up Jim,' encouraged Pete, 'at least you're getting fed. My parents are both working late, so I've got to get my own sandwich; jam again, I expect.'

'Boring,' chirped Alan. 'Let's go.'

Brendon looked at him, his head cocked to one side. 'Hang on, if you're bored, how about after tea we meet in the churchyard and chase out the ghouls, the ones with the axes and swords?' he suggested, waving his arm around in a fencing motion.

The others exchanged glances.

'Don't be daft Brendon, it'll still be raining. My mum will never let me out,' claimed Pete.

'But you said your parents won't be home 'til late,' countered Brendon. 'You're just shagging scared.'

'No I'm not,' argued Pete. He looked at Alan, desperately hoping for moral support.

Alan pursed his lips, his head to one side. 'I'm up for it,' he said. 'I'll tell my mum we're going to Jim's house so she'll let me out despite the weather and time.'

'So will I… I mean, tell my mum I'm round Jim's. She won't know,' confirmed Brendon, 'and Jim, you can say you're round mine if you like.' He, Jim and Alan stared at Pete.

'Oh… oh… okay,' he stuttered, desperate not to lose face. Pushing his shoulders back he announced, 'Half past six then, at the gates of the graveyard and don't be late.'

~

At precisely six-thirty, Pete stood alone in the rain and the dark by the tall, wrought-iron gates. In the gloom, the eastern end of the church was only just visible, but the four pointed finials on the corners of the steeple stood out like Saxon arrowheads against the thick black moisture-laden cloud. To his right, the row of tall fir trees waved in the wind, every now and again offering a view of the medieval castle, its thick, stone walls hiding its barbarous secrets. Five minutes later none of his mates had shown up.

'Where are you, you bastards?' he half shouted. 'I know you're hiding in there and you think I'm afraid to come in on my own, but you're wrong.' There was no answer. He waited another five.

'Right, I'm going home if you don't come out.' The silence felt unbearable. Another five. 'That's it, I'm off you shitheads.' As he turned to go, he heard a scraping sound, like something heavy being dragged along a loose gravel surface. 'Fuck,' he muttered under his breath. He wanted to go home, to take off his wet clothes and watch television, but he knew he'd get so badly ridiculed the next day by Brendon in particular, he'd hate himself for ages.

'Right, I've… I've… had enough. I'm c… c… coming in so l… l… look out when I find you,' he stuttered, plucking up every ounce of courage he could muster before pushing open the inhospitable, cumbersome gate. It creaked noisily on its hinges.

'I mean it, you'll be in trouble,' he shouted rather less convincingly than before. 'It's obvious you're hiding behind one of the gravestones, so you might as well come out now.' He desperately wished he'd brought a torch, but the only one in his house needed new batteries. He began to shiver, partly because of the cold, but more because of the prickly fear creeping down his back. He took a few steps forward. The scraping sound could be heard more clearly; it was coming towards him along the church path directly in front of him.

'I know where you are; I can hear you so there's no point in pretending,' he said nervously, his voice shaking as much as his body. 'F... f... f... fuck's sake guys, it's not funny any more.' The scraping noise stopped. Pete screwed up his eyes, trying to see through the rain and moonless sky.

'Tha... tha that's it, you pussies. I'm going home. I won't forget this you cu... ' He shut up, unable to release his last expletive. For one brief second the moon broke through, shedding a dull grey glow on the gravestones and sarcophagi. Lying on the ground, no more than a few yards in front of him, he saw the outline of a large man, a glint of light reflecting off an iron helmet, its frontispiece covering the nose of a bearded, tussle-haired head. A raised arm was wielding an axe, the handle much longer than the one his dad used to chop the kindling for the fire. In his other hand, Pete could just make out a severed head dangling by the hair.

As the moon returned to its hiding place, the raised arm drew back, as if preparing to launch the axe in Pete's direction. It wouldn't be the last occasion he'd fill his pants, but it would be the final time he couldn't blame it on sphincter looseness caused by an over-active sex life.

Fortunately, the warm sensation running down the inside of his leg stirred him into action. His sport's teacher would never have believed how fast he could run; neither could Pete. Charging through the unlocked front door at home, the water dripping off his saturated hair and duffel coat, he ignored the shouts of his father and headed straight for the bathroom. Despite his best intentions and best aim, he missed the toilet bowl and spewed all over the bathroom floor. Hearing the retching, his mother rushed in. Holding her nose, any feelings of sympathy were instantly extinguished by the sight of undigested white bread stained red by the jam, spread all over the six- month-old pale cream carpet. Pete was grounded for the next week. He never mentioned what he saw to his mates whose mothers had stopped them from going out that night, but it stayed with him and he swore that one day he'd get even with Brendon for suggesting they meet, however long it took.

~

Despite the occasional *upset*, life as kids was there to be enjoyed. Regardless of the lawful season, they fished all year round in the gorge. In the summer they swam in a moorland pool created by damming a section of the River Ling as it meandered its way between the gorse and bracken. On bikes they explored the country roads barely used by motor vehicles and if they wanted to "hang out", provided it wasn't raining, they'd gather at the old castle, seemingly landlocked between the church and The Judge's Parlour.

All that remained was the thirteenth-century keep, the stone of the outer boundary walls having been "robbed" years later for local building projects. Like many other castles built after the Norman Conquest, soil piled around the keep's three-metre-thick lower stone walls gave it the appearance of standing regally on a natural grass-covered mound. From the outside, it looked like a two-storey building, but inside two further floors sunk into the depth of the earth. From roofline to internal ground level was a drop of approximately forty metres, enough of a fall to kill any man, or child for that matter. The roof and floors were long gone, so to enable the keep to be opened to the public, a metal landing was installed stretching out from the second-storey entrance arch and supported by several horizontal steel beams sunk deep into an interior wall. This led to a spiral staircase, allowing access to the former dungeons below.

Before the building of a jail in Bodmin, the castle's purpose evolved from an outpost to protect King John against potential uprisings, to a prison and it was rumoured that the infamous Judge Fredricks held court there, sentencing inmates to be hung, drawn and quartered if found guilty and in some cases not guilty, of tin mining offences. However, none of this history meant anything to Alan, Brendon, Jim, Pete and occasionally Gareth when he could get out of working on his parents' farm. It was just a place to climb walls and from the very top, watch the steam trains and occasional fancy diesel engine run along the Great Moorland Railway line on which they placed old pennies to squash them and bet on how many head or tail imprints were left on the rail. Dr Beeching would never know how his callous plans would spoil their fun.

Reaching their "personal" viewing area entailed scaling three metres up an internal wall to the bottom of an original stone staircase. All but Alan found the footholds easy to use. Sometimes he would be left to work them out on his own, whereas at other times the lads would virtually haul him up. Once at the top, to gain the best possible view from the front, a walk along the unguarded fourth-storey, one-and-a-half-metre-wide walls had to be negotiated. Provided you didn't look down, this proved straightforward, but a glance to the dungeon floor from this height could scare even Jim, hence why Alan normally stayed in the relative safety of the staircase.

There were other challenges to be faced in this cold, uninviting granite "play area". A half-metre-wide, uneven stone ledge ran from the metal landing around three walls to a deeply splayed Norman-style window at the front of the building and anyone who didn't accept a dare to clamber along its formidable surface, temporarily lost all credibility. Perhaps that's why Alan went to the keep on his own the day he fell to his death.

It was a hot summer's day in the middle of school holidays. Gareth had been given a couple of hours off by his demanding father and the five had met at the sports field about a half-mile from the village centre. Once they'd lifted one set of the "very, very occasionally used for local football derbies" metal goalposts from the hedge and slotted the uprights into the pipe-lined holes in the ground, they enjoyed an energetic "kick around". After about half an hour of "three and in", Alan announced he had to "pop" home for a few minutes. Thinking he was knackered and needed a shit, the others made fun of him as he cycled away from the field. The "piss-taking" together with the names they'd called him the day before when once again he didn't make the climb to the top of the castle, were words they would live to regret, for two of them in more ways than one!

CHAPTER TWO

7 May 2016

'Thanks Brendon.' Caroline took the large glass of Chilean Chardonnay.

'Not an "ABC" moron then?' he joked as he sat down opposite her at the white linen covered restaurant table in The Judge's Parlour. He sipped his glass of Shiraz.

She smiled. 'Never been one for fads. Gareth used to laugh quite openly when he heard the "city darlings" tell their husbands or partners they wanted "ABC… Anything But Chardonnay" in their wine glasses. He always wanted to tell them to try it first, rather than be a connoisseur based on something they'd heard on the telly. Same with the bottled cider everyone suddenly started drinking.' Caroline looked down at the table, hiding her sadness. When she looked back up, her eyes had moistened. 'He would say loudly so everyone would hear, "If you have to fill the glass with ice before drinking it, then there can't be much flavour in them imported apples; not like our coxes!"' She took a large swallow of wine.

'He always was one for speaking his mind,' encouraged Brendon.

She nodded, falling silent as she recalled how her late husband had never had a seriously bad thing to say about anybody; that is until just a few weeks before he died. It was Brendon who broke the awkwardness.

'I thought yesterday went really well... sorry, I mean as well as any funeral can go. He had a lot of friends.'

'Thanks,' agreed Caroline. 'It was good to see. Shame the vicar got Gareth's name wrong though.' She faked a smile.

'I wasn't going to mention that,' apologised Brendon. 'I heard he's reasonably new; is that right?'

'Not particularly,' dismissed Caroline. 'Moved here eighteen months ago, same time as the pub was taken over by the Polsons. Not easy to learn everything about everybody in that short time I suppose, but names...?' She shrugged. 'Anyway, enough of that. How's your room?' she enquired, eager to change the subject. 'Which one are you in?'

'Room five, one of those down the village end of the pub. It's more of a family room but all the others were full apparently. Didn't charge me extra though,' Brendon replied, pleased for the diversion. 'I slept well, other than the occupants in the room a few doors up the corridor were a bit noisy.' Spotting her knowing look, he hastily added. 'No... no... not in that way, Caroline, honestly.'

'In what way then?' she asked, meeting his eyes over the rim of her glass.

He frowned. 'Well, I don't want to sound melodramatic, goodness knows I get enough drama thank you, but it sounded more like screams of pain rather than... than... er... pleasure, almost as though someone was being... um... tortured.' He hastily swallowed some wine.

'Really?' asked Caroline, scoffing at his suggestion. 'What room were they in, the one with the four-poster bed and furry handcuffs?'

'Very funny Caroline. I was actually being serious.' He picked up the red leather-bound menu. 'Anyway, what are you going to eat?' He hadn't really expected her to believe him, but what he'd heard had played on his mind. He'd tried to convince himself he'd been dreaming, but the agonising caterwauling had stuck with him.

'I'll have the pan-fried scallops please, not that I know of an alternative way of frying anything other than in a pan!' They laughed together and for a split second it was as if they had gone back to a time before Gareth had intervened in Brendon's attempts to woo this beautiful female. If she had chosen him instead of her farmer boy, then how different life would have been... for both of them.

~

'Ere, have you seen that young maid who's just moved into Farm Cottage' asked Gareth as the five of them lay on the sheep-grazed grass beside the moorland river, drying themselves in the warm sunshine. 'Proper pretty she is.'

'The one with the long blonde hair you mean?' asked Jim.

Gareth grunted his agreement.

'She ain't that good Gareth, not much of a milker,' said Pete, a wide grin covering his face.

'I wouldn't mind seeing her naked,' added Alan.

'Wouldn't do you any good; you ain't even had a hard-on yet,' scoffed Jim.

'I have too… honest.' His reddening face suggested otherwise.

'Bit out of our league I reckon,' contributed Brendon. He rolled over onto his front and pulled out a strand of thick, vetiver grass from the clump he'd been using as a pillow. 'Heard her talking to her mother, very posh and "okay ya",' he said, chewing and crunching the fresh green fibre.

'Get on bey. You don't want get put off by some bleddy "green wellie" lingo; after all, you'm still talks to me my luvvers!' beamed Gareth.

'That's 'cos you're as thick as cow shit,' blurted Jim, 'and anyway, I find "green wellies" exciting.'

'You wouldn't if you'd been wearing them all day; your feet would stink like that cheese Gareth's mother makes,' remarked Brendon.

'Nothing wrong with Mum's cheese, you wanker; best in the village I'll have you know,' replied Gareth indignantly. 'Much sort after that is.'

'It's the only fucking homemade cheese in the village, you twat. Some say it tastes like your dad's knob!' Brendon began laughing uncontrollably. Alan, Pete and Jim joined him, while Gareth jumped to his feet.

'You saying my dad tastes like a bit of old cheddar? How would you know?' questioned Gareth indignantly, screwing up his eyes to fake anger. 'I'll make you pay for that, you prick.' He jumped on Brendon, kneeling astride him and trying to turn him over.

'More like that new stuff we had the other night, camisole or something,' choked Brendon, initially resisting Gareth's efforts, but eventually giving in to his superior strength. The two boys faced each other, Brendon on his back, Gareth holding down his wrists.

'Give in, you tosser,' shouted Gareth, 'or I'll break your fingers.'

'You win,' conceded Brendon, a massive smile covering his face, 'you're far too strong for me you sheep-shagging lump of lard.'

Calling Gareth a lump of lard was somewhat unfounded. Helping his dad lift bales, shear sheep and other farm work had given him above average strength for someone his age; fortunately, he'd never fully tested it on his mates. Added to his blonde curly hair and bright blue eyes, he was probably the best looking of the five.

He fell off Brendon and rolled onto his back. 'Pussy,' he said as he stretched out his legs.

'You wish,' suggested Pete. 'And Brendon, it's camembert, not camisole.'

'Thank you Pete. I knew it began with c.'

'Bit like you then,' acknowledged Alan, unafraid of any physical assault which may follow from Brendon. Fortunately his mate was too tired to launch an attack.

'I'll take that as a compliment; after all, I know how much you'd like some!'

They all laughed.

Jim jumped to his feet. 'Who's for another swim? Last one in's a massive pussy.' He tore off in the direction of the pool created by the dam of stones and turf, unconcerned as he trod barefoot in some sheep droppings.

'Must be worse things in life,' said Brendon, 'and "green wellies" would give you a foothold!'

As it turned out, the posh maid with the long blonde hair wasn't so posh after all and when they were both nineteen, Gareth and Caroline married in the local church, the expected child already beginning to show. The groom had three best men; but for the "accident", it would have been four!

~

Their meal over, Brendon and Caroline moved to two well-worn armchairs beside the roaring log fire in the virtually empty lounge attached to the far end of the restaurant, the majority of diners having long since retired to their beds or homes. Had it not been for the fact that Caroline had just lost her husband, the sight of the two of them sat sipping brandy, deep in private conversation, could have seemed to the world as though it was their second or third outing after meeting on an Internet dating site.

There were clear signs of past feelings for each other. The last fortnight had taken its toll on Caroline. There had been the post-mortem, the funeral arrangements, the protocol of the wake and the future to deal with and she was glad to temporarily put it all to the back of her mind and enjoy the company of a man she trusted and if she was honest, still loved. Had it not been for the baby, her choice might have been different.

'Another brandy?' enquired Brendon, keen for one

himself. It had been a long time since he'd had a break from routine and he intended to make the most of it.

'I shouldn't,' she replied through dreamy, blue eyes. Getting out of his seat, Brendon caught the attention of the pretty young girl wiping glasses behind the restaurant bar. As she looked up, he mouthed, 'Two brandies, large ones please.' Returning to his chair, he asked, 'What time's Ellie picking you up?'

'When I ring. She told me it would be good for me to relax and you know she's always liked you.' She smiled then added, 'Not that she's seen much of her godfather.'

Rubbing the back of his neck, he looked away. 'I'm sorry. I've never forgotten her birthday but it's not always been easy to send a card from some of the countries I end up in.'

She momentarily stared at a burning log spitting on the fire, before gazing back at him. 'It can't have always been easy.'

Shrugging his shoulders, he sighed. 'It does have its challenges at times, but hey ho, it's what I get paid for.' The waitress arrived with their drinks. 'Thank you. Please have one yourself and add it to my bill.' She acknowledged him as she picked up the empties. He raised his glass to Caroline. 'Cheers.'

'Cheers Brendon. Here's to the future.' If she was feeling any sadness at her loss, for the moment it seemed totally forgotten.

Over dinner, they'd chatted about the various housing developments Brendon had seen in his walk around the village. Plush, new, stone-faced detached houses with brown-stained wooden window frames, brand new four-by-fours and unnecessarily large German luxury vehicles parked in the road. Despite the buildings "fitting in", apparently Gareth had been staunchly against the loss of open land to outsiders, but there was no way of defeating the planners and in fairness, with the exception of one or two who wanted everything changed to accommodate their arrival, most of the newcomers were happy to go along with the old village customs and ways.

'And what about you Caroline?' Brendon had asked. 'What do you feel?'

'You can't stop progress,' she'd replied, 'although I agreed with Gareth about the compulsory purchase of land for the new quarry, especially as the reopened and extended railway line will cross the old Corpse Way. Things like that should remain sacrosanct as far as possible.'

Brendon's eyebrows had risen. 'The railway's reopening?' he'd queried, obviously surprised by the news. 'I never thought that would ever happen, not that it should have been closed in the first place, hindsight being a wonderful thing of course. So where's the quarry going to be?'

'In the valley, just up from the start of the public part of the gorge. They're going to build a siding about two hundred yards from the viaduct on our... I mean my land, or rather they want to.'

'What do you mean, want to?'

'Gareth refused to sell to the developers and the council are struggling to apply a purchase order as one of our fields has an Iron Age burial ground and all the heritage organisations are up in arms about it. Enquiries could go on for months, if not years and delays aren't welcome.'

'I see. So what's so important about the quarry?' he'd asked.

'The Crown's surveyor has discovered exceptional deposits of tin and as it, the Crown that is, has exclusive mineral rights to all the land around here, they've decided to extract it.'

'Bit like the old stannary law regards tin and forestry then. They'll be bringing back Judge Fredricks next to oversee it,' Brendon had joked but it hadn't drawn a laugh or smile from Caroline. Instead, she'd stared at him through half-closed eyes, appearing to want to speak, but keeping her words as thoughts. It would be one reason he would lay in bed awake that night, puzzled by her reaction, regretting not querying what had caused it, but understanding why he hadn't pushed just yet to find out. Not once during their evening together had Caroline mentioned how Gareth had died. He knew it was an accident, at least that's what she'd told him the coroner had decided when she'd rang to tell him about the funeral, but she hadn't offered any more information. No doubt she would eventually talk to him about it, but for the moment, she had a lot on her plate and he wasn't going to upset her.

Another reason for his lack of sleep was the repeat of the muffled screams, whilst a third was her totally unexpected innuendo.

Finishing her brandy, Caroline looked at the grandfather clock in the corner of the lounge. It was just after midnight.

'Time to ring Ellie,' she said, her speech attractively slurred. 'My eyes are going to need matchsticks to keep them open soon.'

'I'm sorry, I didn't mean to bore you,' apologised Brendon uncomfortably.

She touched his hand. 'You'd never be able to do that Brendon, never in a thousand years.' She held his eyes and added. 'If Gareth had died a few months ago, I wouldn't be ringing Ellie to collect me, but it's a small village and...' she flashed a glance in the direction of the bar, 'there are ears and eyes everywhere and gossip travels quickly!'

Ellie appeared within fifteen minutes of her mum's telephone call. As soon as the "younger, smooth-skinned, taller version of her mother" female entered the lounge and saw Brendon, her face lit up and beaming, she gave him a massive hug.

Staying for a drink, they exchanged news, something there hadn't been time for at the wake. Ellie continuously said sorry for having to go back to work so soon after the funeral. However, her job as managing director of a large jewellery manufacturer meant she couldn't be away for too long as it was currently in the middle of a takeover bid for another firm and she had to travel abroad for discussions. She'd been helping her mum with the funeral plans and so had already been absent for six days. Skype and emails could only replace personal business contact for so long.

'I'm a big girl now,' she said, as Brendon apologised for his sporadic contact and lack of input in her life, although he quickly added she seemed to have done rather well without him. Strangely, she virtually dismissed his sympathy for the death of her father.

'Daddy and I didn't always get on,' she explained, sipping her vodka and tonic, 'especially once it was clear I wasn't interested in taking over the farm. Not that I was his first choice of course; that was brother Nathan's birthright, but as you're aware, he much preferred the RAF.' Lowering her eyes from Brendon's, she added cynically, 'I suppose you know he's a flight lieutenant now.'

Brendon did know. He'd spent quite some time talking to Nathan after the funeral and had been surprised how much the bloodshot-eyed officer had drunk. His unbuttoned formal shirt collar and loose tie wasn't what Brendon had expected to see from a senior ranked member of Her Majesty's Armed Forces. Although he'd put this down to the occasion and also the not particularly recent breakup of Nathan's ten-year marriage, it didn't account for his aggression.

'Fucking village,' he'd said, swaying and supporting himself on the bar. 'So fucking narrow-minded, deserves whatever it gets.'

'Which is what Nathan?' Brendon enquired, totally bewildered by this comment.

Cautiously planting his empty whisky tumbler on the bar, he'd waved Brendon away.

'Got to go for a leak; talk later.' But they didn't; in fact Nathan never returned from his pressing requirement. Brendon assumed he must have gone home to his mother's.

On leaving university, both Nathan and Ellie had been exceptionally focused on their chosen careers and neither had offspring of their own. In fact, according to Caroline, despite her daughter's beauty, she'd never had a serious relationship.

'Enjoys the money and status too much,' she'd informed him. 'Doesn't want anything or anybody to get in her way; a chip off her father's block I suppose.'

'Right Mum, time to get you home by the look of it,' Ellie joked as she noticed her mother's eyes beginning to close. 'Must have been a good dinner.'

'Very,' agreed Caroline, lifting herself slowly to her feet. 'Very nice indeed.' She smiled at Brendon.

Taking her mother's arm, Ellie led her through the restaurant to the door to the entrance lobby. Directly opposite, the door to the public bar was propped open; presumably the heat from its open fire proving a little too much.

Turning to Brendon, Caroline put her arms around him and kissed him full on the lips.

'Will I see you tomorrow?' she asked as he held the door open.

'That would be nice,' he replied.

'Coffee at the farm then. Shall we say eleven?'

'Eleven it is,' he confirmed. 'Perhaps you could show me the site of the quarry and siding.'

'No problem Brendon. We could have a walk around our old playgrounds.' She grinned, ushered out by Ellie who had already said her heartfelt goodbyes.

Brendon stared at the door. His job with MI6 put him into many challenging situations, but none had confused him in the same way as his reunion with Caroline.

'Can I get you anything else, sir?' He jumped, startled by the waitress' question.

'Er... er... is it too late for a nightcap?' he asked, his mind disorientated by Caroline's comment.

'Not at all. We've still got several locals in the other side. They'll be here for a while longer yet drinking with the landlord.' She looked a little embarrassed. 'One of his occasional male bonding sessions.'

Brendon heard the raucous shouts coming from the public bar. He hadn't noticed them when deep in conversation with Caroline, but now the sound of male voices was loud and clear.

'In that case, another large brandy please.' He followed her to the bar. 'Would you care to join me?'

'Thank you sir, that's kind but I've got to serve and wash up the empties. The landlord wants to drink rather than work, if you see what I mean.' She smiled apologetically as she pushed a clean glass against the optic. 'Just pop your head around the corner if you want another.'

'This'll be me thanks.' Warming the glass in his hands he returned to the lounge. The waitress disappeared through the doorway between the two bars. As he sipped the drink, he heard a female's scream.

Sounds like more than just a male bonding session, he thought to himself, but hearing no further cries, he finished his brandy and made his way to bed.

CHAPTER THREE

8 May 2016

'Sugar in your coffee?'

'No thanks Caroline... oh and no milk either.'

'Any more mysterious screams in the night?' she asked.

'Funny you should...' Brendon stopped himself.

Caroline frowned. 'What's funny Brendon?' she quizzed.

'Nothing really. I think... I think I must have been dreaming that's all.'

He hadn't, but he wanted his first port of call to be the landlord; however, breakfast was busy and he hadn't had a chance to discuss it after, as the landlord had returned to his living accommodation, the former stables block opposite the pub, immediately after service. Brendon had sat in the lounge reading yesterday's *Telegraph* in the hope Clegg would return, but when the grandfather clock had chimed a quarter to eleven, Brendon had given up waiting, walked to his car and driven to Caroline's. He'd catch up with Clegg later.

'Okay,' she said, but Brendon guessed it wasn't. She passed him an open biscuit barrel. He shook his head whilst patting his stomach.

'The pub serves a helluva breakfast; full works and cooked by the landlord himself,' explained Brendon. 'Waited table as well.'

'No staff?' She sounded surprised. 'From what I heard a couple of girls in the village were virtually falling over themselves to work there after the last one left,' she remarked. 'I'm told Phil has fingers in other pies and whipped her off to bigger and better things up country. Apparently his partner, business one that is, has a small chain of hotels providing "live-in" accommodation and better wages than down here.'

'Interesting; can't blame them though I suppose. Lingtree always was a bit of a dead end...' Brendon could have kicked himself. 'Sorry Caroline, I wasn't thinking.'

'Don't be so daft. I know what you meant and anyway I'm sure if Gareth hadn't taken the farm over from his father, he'd have probably moved away himself,' she reassured him. Smiling, she continued, 'Right, after coffee, I'm going to take you to see where they want to quarry. Oh... I forgot to tell you, there are archaeologists there as well.'

'Archaeologists?' he queried. 'Presumably that's because of the burial ground.' Frowning, he scratched the back of his head. 'Hasn't it been dug before?'

'Not that I'm aware of, at least not in our time. Perhaps you're thinking of the old Norman fort,' suggested Caroline, 'you know the one near the castle. You all offered to help with the dig but kept mixing up the burnt corn with the soil and the boss man asked you to leave.'

'Ah, that's right, of course it was,' he acknowledged, laughing as he recalled how they'd thought it would be great fun but then immediately regretted volunteering. 'Grown men scratching around with builders' trowels and putting black soil in small plastic bags. And poor old Alan... ' He fell silent, momentarily staring at the ground. Caroline caught his hand.

'C'mon, drink up, let's go and see how the archaeologists are getting on. The fresh air will do us good.' She steered him towards the back door. 'Grab your jacket; we'll take the shortcut through the woods.'

Brendon put down his mug on the breakfast bar-cum-island in the middle of the recently refitted farmhouse kitchen. As he'd followed her in, Caroline had told him the worktops and doors were all handmade from a genuine oak tree Gareth had felled himself. 'A carpenter in Chilstoke got it cut to size at the wood mills in Melkthorpe. It wasn't cheap but... well, I like it. '

As they walked past the closed doors of the shiny, recently built, impressive steel-clad barn next to the original, tired looking, open-fronted stone ones, she nonchalantly confirmed Ellie and Nathan had left first thing and she was now on her own again.

~

It was late spring and the trees and hedgerows had not long been in leaf. There was still a damp morning chill but as they climbed over the hedge and joined the route of the old Corpse Way, the sun-warmed air led Brendon to wish he'd left his jacket behind.

Continuing their walk, they crossed a wooden footbridge over the River Ling; here its long passage to the sea unhurried and tranquil. After ascending several roughly laid granite steps they passed the Old Mill from where years ago the flour would have been taken to be loaded onto railway wagons for sale in nearby towns and far off cities. The waterwheel having long rotted away, it was now a private residence, recently purchased by a demanding village newcomer. A few metres more and the second arch of the defunct Great Moorland Railway viaduct loomed above them; a massive granite monument to local Victorian stonemasons who risked their lives constructing the additional five arches stretching out across the breadth of the valley where the Ling lost its leisurely flow and began its chaotic journey through the depths of the gorge.

'Hasn't changed at all,' he commented as he wiped the sweat from his brow. 'I used to love the early morning five-mile runs.' He took a deep breath, savouring the smell of wild garlic.

'Really?' enquired Caroline. 'What stopped you today then?'

He ignored her mocking, distracted by the bullet case lying on the side of the stony, unmade single-vehicle-width track.

'Nine millimetre, like they use in a Glock 17,' he muttered to himself as he rolled the case inquisitively around in his fingers, his brow furrowed, 'or an MP5.'

'Poachers or rough shooters I expect,' said Caroline,

unperturbed by the find. 'There're quite a few gun owners in the village.'

'But you wouldn't use this for hunting,' he explained, scanning the nearby fields and woods. 'Unless it's not animals you're after!'

'Sorry Brendon, what are you saying?' she asked, rather puzzled.

Shaking his head, he dismissed her question. 'Just me going back into work mode,' he assured her. He slipped the spent cartridge into his trouser pocket. After another hundred metres, through a gap in the hazel and hawthorn hedge, Brendon spotted half a dozen white tepee-style tents. 'Ah,' he exclaimed, 'I guess that's the archaeologists' camp. Let's see what they've been up to.'

~

'We were given five weeks max,' Frank Hatcher, the man who approached them volunteered as they leant on the closed, five-bar wooden entrance gate to the field in which the tents were erected. Roughly fifty metres further into the field, several young men and women were busy with shovels and trowels. A bright yellow JCB digger was parked beside a large mound of rocks and soil.

'Could do with longer, especially as we've also been given permission by the Trust to locate the tunnel in the gorge,' continued Hatcher. He smacked his lips together. 'No doubt partly filled with water, but I reckon we might be able to cope if we can find it.'

'Is that the tunnel which was always said to lead to the castle?' asked Brendon as he summed up this man with long, straggly hair, unkempt beard and gold-rimmed spectacles. He guessed he was in his late sixties and judging by his khaki shorts, knee-length socks and work boots, he wasn't in the *Indiana Jones* mode. 'I thought it was just an old wives' tale.'

'Possibly, but you never know. No smoke without fire and all that. With the lack of rain this spring the river's a bit lower so it might throw up something. Anyway, the dig's nearly over so last chance to find out in the next fortnight.' Hatcher's eyes lit up. 'Should prove extremely exciting.'

'I'm sure,' agreed Caroline, 'and hopefully your time here has proved fruitful?'

'Oh very, my dear, very much so,' he beamed. 'Bones and pottery everywhere, not all Iron Age either. Anglo-Saxon bits and pieces as well. Excellent dig, absolutely excellent. Must get back though. Good to see you. Goodbye.' Hatcher hurried away, eager to return to his finds.

'Well, good luck,' Brendon shouted after him. 'I'll be interested to know how you get on, particularly regards the tunnel.' They turned to walk back towards the unofficial start of the gorge. 'It always fascinated me as a kid.' Quietly, so only Caroline would hear, he added, 'Just folklore, same as the Dobbings family who supposedly lived there centuries ago.'

Caroline smiled; the slightest shake of her head unnoticed by Brendon.

A walk of a few hundred metres led them to the wire stock fence above where the River Ling began to flow into the narrow cleft of the gorge, the water speeding up as it fell headlong into the depth of the high-sided valley.

As kids, entry could be gained to the river virtually anywhere, but in recent times, like the installation of handrails and barriers, the Trust had fenced off two miles or so of the area which hadn't originally been accessible to paying visitors.

'Over here Brendon, the fence is broken.'

'Broken or deliberately damaged?' he asked as they climbed through the narrow gap onto a muddy path leading gradually down to the official one, fifty metres below.

Caroline grinned. 'I couldn't possibly say; can't be responsible for the latest crop of village kids. Mind yourself on the barbed wire.'

The river was as just as Brendon remembered. In places the rushing water made a thundering noise as it cascaded down the chasms and ravines hollowed out through the rock over the centuries. Occasionally, the flow would swirl in deep, foaming circles, sucking in anything that dare fall in its way. Since the gorge had been opened to the public, two people were known to have lost their lives in the unreachable depths and no doubt many more might have perished in the past, perhaps stumbling in the dark, or drunkenly stepping off the unprotected bridges on their return from the pub.

Despite all the dangers he'd faced during covert trips abroad, he still felt a tingle run up his spine as he recalled the times he and his mates had fearlessly run along the narrow paths. It was a tingle he'd experience later that day as he and Caroline made love in her bed.

'Have you been in the castle since you've been back?' she asked him as they sauntered casually along the well-maintained paths.

'No, I need to though. It's been a long time but I have to face my demons eventually I suppose.' He took a deep breath. 'I haven't been in there since... since... the day we found Alan's body.'

CHAPTER FOUR

17 August 1969

'What the fuck's he doing, building the bog or something?'

It had suddenly dawned on Jim that Alan had been gone for far longer than it would take any man or boy to move their bowels.

'I was beginning to wonder as well,' agreed Pete. 'Do you think we should go and look for him?'

'It's not like him to miss out on a kick around,' confirmed Jim. 'You know how mad keen he is on football; even believes he's going to play for England one day!'

'Yeah, right, and I'm Jimmy Greaves,' exclaimed Gareth.

'How the fuck do you know who Jimmy Greaves is, you sheep-shagger!' mocked Brendon. Immediately he regretted his words. 'Ow, that hurt; get off me you mad sod.'

Gareth lay on top of him, having knocked him to the ground with a well-executed judo trip.

'Serves you right. I'm gwain to make you suffer for

that.' Holding down one arm, he started tickling Brendon's ribs, something he knew would really upset his friend.

'Get off you fucker or I'll—'

'Or you'm what? It takes a man, not a maid's blouse to stop me.'

'C'mon you two, you know it'll end in tears,' interrupted Jim. It was a phrase his mother often used when he had a rummage with his dad.

'Give in little bey?' enquired Gareth. By now, Brendon was already in tears, not of pain but of laughter.

'Yes, yes, you win. For fuck's sake get off me you great lump of lard.'

Gareth released him and lay down beside his crestfallen mate. 'I've told you before, don't mess with muscle.'

'Muscle, my arse,' sneered Brendon. 'That's not muscle, that's fat.'

Gareth sat up. 'Do you want some more then?'

'Bring it on,' sniped Brendon, jumping to his feet.

'Enough.' Jim glared at them both. 'We need to go and call on Alan, make sure he's not stuck on the bog!'

The ridiculous possibility of Alan's bare arse firmly lodged in the loo seat caused all four to burst into simultaneous uncontrolled laughter. Brendon offered Gareth his hand and pulled him upright.

Alan wasn't at home but neither were either of his parents.

'Must of gone out for tea or something,' suggested Pete. 'C'mon, I've got enough for a bottle of Corona. Providing you like dandelion and burdock I'll share it with you.'

'I'm with you Pete,' responded Brendon.

'And me, Pete,' chirped Jim.

'Bleedy thirsty me,' announced Gareth.

It was the next day before Jim and Pete heard about Alan.

~

'Must have fallen from somewhere up there guv, possibly the top of the wall.' Standing beside the grotesquely misshapen corpse, Detective Constable Williamson pointed skywards towards where once the pitched roof of the keep would have kept the rain off the floors below. However, the ground under the policemen's feet was now wet, the damp soil the source of the liberally splattered mud on the young body lying in an abnormally crippled posture.

Shaking his head, Detective Chief Inspector Davies focused on the hideously twisted, blood-covered neck.

'It's not just a fall that's responsible for this mess, Constable. Something or somebody's had a go at the throat. See the tear marks.' He lifted a piece of torn green-coloured clothing. 'In fact, it looks as though he's had flesh ripped from all over.'

He carefully rolled Alan Sumner face up.

'Oh my God!' exclaimed Williamson. It was more than he could take. Retching, his arms against the wall to support himself, he vomited in a corner of the dank dungeon, the stench of rat faeces increasing the dizziness.

'Are you all right lad?' enquired the chief inspector.

When it came to dealing with suspicious deaths,

Detective Chief Inspector Davies could definitely be described as a "battle-hardened" copper. During his twenty-five years in the force, he'd seen enough spilt blood to keep the transfusion service going for months, but even he felt his stomach tighten as he peered at the remains of the torso and horribly mutilated face. It was as though a pack of wolves had partially feasted.

'I've been better thanks, Guv.' It was Williamson's second year as a detective and although he'd seen many a road traffic collision during his previous four years in uniform, this sight was worse than any mangled body trapped in a seatbelt-less car. Aged twenty-six, he still had much to learn.

Davies turned to the uniformed sergeant stood on the metal landing.

'Don't let the parents in just yet Jones. Wait until the coroner's examiner's been and had a go at piecing together some of the mess.'

~

It had been Brendon and Gareth who'd discovered the body.

After downing the bottle of Corona whilst sat on the hedge on the opposite side of the road to the small "only room for two customers at a time", well-stocked, pre "best before era" village store, they'd concluded Alan must definitely have gone out and after another hour, they'd decided it was time for their own tea.

'Cheers guys; see you all tomorrow,' shouted Jim as he ran off home.

'Not if we see you first, tosser,' the other three replied in unison. It was their customary and well-used farewell.

'Think I'll see if Alan's back,' said Brendon as he got to his feet and prepared to depart in the opposite direction to Jim. 'Cheers for "Chivers"'

'Bye luver boy, give him a kiss from us.' Pete sure did have a strange sense of humour, although as he grew older and found success, it became evident that kissing a male was far more enjoyable to kissing one of the other variety. It was when his husband of eleven years had died from AIDS shortly after moving back to Lingtree, that he'd turned to drink and his old mate Jim for evening comfort.

'Don't you fucking include me in that, I ain't no queer bey,' joked Gareth, as he wrapped his arms around Pete and pretended to give him a snog.

'What if he does, lard-arse?' retorted Brendon. 'Afraid you might like it!' He laughed. 'See ya tomorrow.'

However, he would see Gareth again that evening, as finding Alan's parents at home with no knowledge of their son's whereabouts, Brendon took it upon himself to go and look for him. He met Gareth still sat opposite the shop, the crafty fucker having kept the shilling he had in his pocket until after the others had left.

'Where you gwain Brendon?' Gareth asked, his mouth full of liquorice.

'Alan's mum and dad are home but he's not,' replied Brendon, 'so I thought I'd go and look for him. Mum said my tea won't be ready for another hour.' He eyed the liquorice stick longingly as it slowly disappeared into Gareth's mouth. 'Got any left?' Gareth bit off a length and passed it to him.

'Are you gwain to search in the castle?' asked Gareth. Brendon nodded, his mouth also enjoyably full. 'Okay, makes sense s'pose; I'll come with 'ee.'

Twenty minutes later, they made their joint decision not to visit the castle again.

'Oh fuck Gareth, that's him, isn't it?' They were stood on the landing, eyes transfixed on the red mess spread on the floor. 'He was wearing a green shirt wasn't he?'

Mouth wide open, the remnants of Gareth's liquorice crept down his chin with the rest of his drool.

'I feel sick.' Gareth's vomit shot out over the railing, closely followed by Brendon's. Eventually he managed, 'We'd better go and tell his dad.'

~

The inquest confirmed the cause of death was a fall from the top of the castle walls. The tearing of flesh was considered to have been done after Alan died, as the main blood loss had come from the one-inch split in his skull. The majority of bones were either broken or fractured and one leg had become partially detached, as though an attempt had been made to drag it away. A calculation suggested the body had hit the ground head first in excess of fifty miles per hour. As regards what tore at the flesh, this was left open but was assumed to be a stray dog, although some of the bite marks didn't totally match those normally left by a canine attack.

~

'Mum says I shouldn't have dared him to go and climb on his own,' admitted Brendon. 'It's all my fault.'

It was the last day of August, two weeks after Alan's fall. The four of them had tried to carry on, but kicking a football or riding their bikes seemed so pointless. Jim and Pete, eager to satisfy their morbid curiosity, explored the reopened castle several times, but to Gareth and Brendon, it was now a place where the sight of Alan's mangled, blood-covered body would haunt them forever.

'How the fuck did she know?' queried Jim as the four of them lay on the sun-scorched grass of the cricket field, 'I've never said anything to my mum and dad.'

'I woke up screaming,' apologised Brendon. 'I couldn't help it. I keep seeing him, every night and I can't always get back to sleep.'

Looking sheepish, Gareth nodded. 'Me too. It fucking scares the shits out of me and I've seen loads of dead lambs attacked by foxes, but I don't dream about 'em. Even saw a calf squashed by its mother but Alan— '

'Fucking wimps,' sneered Jim. 'It wouldn't have frightened me none.' He laughed. 'Bit of blood and guts never hurt anyone. Just like the pictures in my war comic. Must have been a spectacular fall... head first probably.'

Gareth and Brendon glared at him.

'Shut your mouth Jim, you twat, or I'll shut it for you!' It was Pete, his face bright red. Whether or not he could have carried out his threat even he doubted, but it had the desired effect.

'Bollocks. I'm bored,' proclaimed Jim, attempting to dismiss the embarrassment of Pete's "put down". Jumping to his feet, he picked up his bike. 'Anyone coming?'

The others ignored him.

'Sod you lot then.' He stuck up two fingers as he rode out the gate.

Pete returned the gesture. 'Good riddance I say.'

CHAPTER FIVE

Caroline held him close. She kissed him gently. 'Brendon, that was so good; I'd forgotten what physical love could feel like.'

Whether this was a compliment or more likely she needed his comfort, at this moment he couldn't care. They'd finished their walk through the gorge and although he had fully intended to revisit his castle nemesis, the warmth of her hand as she'd accepted his help climbing the mossy bank to the road, had sparked something he'd never forgotten.

Sweating in the damp heat as they made their way along the narrow cleft carved out by the water forcing its way on its journey from its humble beginnings on the moor to its proliferate outlet into the ocean, they both knew the choice she'd made to marry Gareth and stay in the village, thereby missing out on what the rest of the world had to offer, was never the right one. Caroline had hinted at this on the several occasions they'd met since Brendon left for university to study foreign languages. He'd passed A level French and German at sixth form and consequently it seemed a natural route to follow. Now fluent in Russian and Arabic, as well as passable in Mandarin and Swedish, he'd no regrets in joining The Ministry, but it had meant leaving behind the only girl he'd ever cared deeply for, not that his job encouraged long-term relationships.

'Yes, I know the exit is just a few hundred yards away, but not being seen by the staff at the gate is far more exciting,' he'd said as he'd almost dragged her along. 'It brings back good memories.'

'For you maybe, but you aren't wearing these shoes.' She may have been struggling for grip in her lightweight sandals, but she wasn't bothered. She had already planned to take him back to her bed without visiting the castle; there was plenty of time for that. She had a desire and Brendon was the one who could fulfil it.

They lay back, Caroline pulling the duvet over them. For Brendon, it hadn't been his "A" game; he'd come too quickly to rate it that highly, but his gentle kissing and caressing of her breasts and nipples and exploration of her soft, smooth body had ensured she'd responded noisily to his loving thrusts. She'd shouted his name as her orgasm engulfed her and he'd wanted to tell her how much he loved her, but knew it was probably best left unsaid. It had been a long time since he'd been with a woman and he was relieved he was able to give Caroline so much pleasure.

Facing him, she smiled. 'It wasn't Gareth's forte you know… I mean lovemaking. I think he spent far too long with sheep and cows to realise there is such a thing as foreplay.' She kissed Brendon's forehead. 'He was never the greatest of lovers, not like you.'

Brendon felt his face flush. Lying in the bed of a childhood friend whose coffin had only just been laid to rest was one thing, but to hear his widow speak so openly, greatly increased the guilt consuming his mind and his body.

Moving to the edge of the bed, he threw back the duvet.

Sat up, he admitted, 'This shouldn't have happened Caroline, it's unfair on Gareth.' His head in his hands, he stared at the Persian carpet covering all but a narrow border of the dark-stained wooden flooring. Caroline shifted to him, her arms around his chest. She ran her hand through his hair.

'Don't say that Brendon,' she insisted, as she kissed the back of his neck. She sighed. 'Look... ' she hesitated, sighed again. 'If it helps, Gareth and I haven't made love in over ten years.' She pushed her head against Brendon's shoulders. 'Oh God, this isn't easy to say about a man you've spent the best part of your life with, but, but I never really loved Gareth... I mean... I loved him, but... not deeply... not in my heart.' Brendon felt her tears run down the middle of his back. He lifted his head.

'What do you mean? I thought you were happy.'

Caroline pulled him back onto the bed. She propped herself on one elbow. 'Honestly,' she asked, 'you really thought that?'

He looked at her, shook his head. 'Perhaps not,' he accepted. 'But I always convinced myself you were.' He shrugged. 'Okay, I know you sometimes said things to me that suggested otherwise, particularly after you'd drunk the champagne at Ellie's twenty-first, but I just assumed they were spur of the moment comments, you know—'

'They weren't,' she affirmed. She reached to the

bedside table for a tissue. Wiping her eyes, she continued, 'Gareth and I were fine; well, we were for the first thirty years. He was kind, hardworking, good at his job, enjoyed socialising at the pub and he provided well for me and the kids, not that we ever had much spare cash. Anything we ever did have always seemed to disappear into buying things for the farm, or reducing the overdraft...' She paused to look at Brendon.

Reassuring her, he rubbed her arm with the back of his hand. 'Go on.'

She gazed at the ceiling. 'Despite how I felt, things carried on going well. Beef and lamb prices were good, the kids were successful in their careers and Gareth seemed at his happiest and then... and then something happened.' She fell silent.

'Caroline... ' She continued to stare at the ceiling, tears pouring down her cheeks. 'Tell me Caroline, what something happened?' enquired Brendon, frustrated by her reluctance.

Without warning, she threw herself out of bed. Rushing towards the bathroom, unbothered by her nakedness, she shouted, 'Please go Brendon. I'm sorry, but I can't say any more.' The door slammed behind her.

After five minutes of asking if she was all right and being told she was okay, but would he please leave, Brendon dressed, shut the front door quietly and drove back to the pub. As he sat alone at a table in the corner of the dimly lit bar, his mind worked overtime trying to make sense of the afternoon. In addition to languages, he had the equivalent of a degree in psychology, but at this moment, it might just as well have been a degree in basket weaving, the good it was doing. Over his second pint, he decided that if it took a few days to find out what had triggered Caroline's upset then so be it. He also still didn't know exactly what had happened to Gareth. Caroline didn't appear to want to volunteer the information and nobody had even mentioned it at the funeral. Taking a long draw on his beer, he decided it was time to find out.

CHAPTER SIX

'Not been here long you understand,' Phil Clegg the landlord explained. 'Brewery asked me to look after the place until a new tenant could be found. The previous ones...' his brow furrowed, 'well, let's say they left very suddenly.'

Brendon was sat at the bar, the "dressed for the part in white shirt, red tie with gold clip and pressed black trousers" landlord having accepted his offer of a drink once he'd finished busying himself stocking up the chilled drinks' cabinet. The lunchtime trade finished, it would be another hour or so before the locals came in for their early evening refreshment. With just the two of them, it was an ideal opportunity for Brendon to try and learn more.

'I see,' replied Brendon. 'Weren't they doing very well then?'

Clegg shook his head, the grey in his short, gelled up hair, exposed by the bright sunlight shining through the small south-facing window. 'Totally the opposite.' He took a swig of his red wine. 'They were the rising stars. Brought the pub back off its knees after the previous couple... or rather odd couple virtually killed all the trade.'

'Why odd?' enquired Brendon, his interest aroused.

'Not really for me to say, but between you and me, two gays running a pub isn't the best thing.' Clegg finished his wine. 'Another… on the house?'

Brendon emptied his glass. 'Cheers.'

As Clegg pulled the beer, he smiled at Brendon. 'I know, bit of an old-fashioned attitude, but I've been in the pub trade for fifteen years or so, the last ten as a temporary replacement when the brewery unexpectedly loses a tenant or manager.' He placed Brendon's pint on the bar and reached for the wine bottle, 'and in that time, I've seen successful pubs and unsuccessful ones.' He poured his Cabernet. 'In my humble opinion, husband and wife make the best team.'

It wasn't a view Brendon agreed with, especially as his local in North London had been run perfectly well by a same-sex couple, but he wanted information from the man leaning on the counter opposite him.

Clegg yawned before asking, 'Are you married Mr Gallagher?'

'Call me Brendon, Phil, and, in answer to your question, no I'm not. How about you?'

'Used to be,' he confirmed, 'but the wife got fed up with the licensed trade and ran off with one of my best customers.'

Brendon took a swallow of his beer, smiling inwardly at how the landlord had just blown his own argument. 'So the "odd couple" as you put it, wrecked the business and then the next tenants built it up but left in a hurry. Any idea why?'

Clegg topped up his glass. He smirked. 'Said they

didn't like the feel of the place, silly buggers. Said they sensed a "presence".' He laughed. 'Reckoned the place was haunted.'

'And is it?' Brendon queried, recalling the screams he'd heard, at least thought he had.

'Don't be silly Brendon, no such things as ghosts,' asserted Clegg.

'Of course not,' agreed Brendon. 'Having said that, I have been hearing some strange screams during the night. Seem to come from the other end of the corridor to my room.' He watched the landlord closely.

'Must have been dreaming sir,' he replied politely, his face expressionless. 'Now then, if you will excuse me, I ought to go and have a word with the chef. He'll be wanting to get on. Can I get you another drink before I disappear?'

Brendon looked at his three-quarter pint. 'No, I'm fine thanks; don't want to spoil my dinner.'

Clegg nodded. He turned as he made his way to the hallway. 'Fresh liver and onions special tonight if you're interested Mr Gallagher. Really sweet and tasty.' He left Brendon alone.

~

'Oh, sorry sir, I'm still a bit clumsy.'

'Not a problem. I'm sure it'll wipe off,' Brendon reassured the pretty, dark-haired waitress dressed in a white blouse and black slacks. 'I've had much worse spilt over me.' He rubbed his shirt sleeve with the cloth napkin. 'It's your first night, isn't it?'

'That's right,' she replied, relieved by his calmness. 'Trying to earn some money so I can go travelling after my A levels.'

He glanced around, quickly taking in the other diners. Two tables of four casually dressed males, their conversation limited; a table of two males and two females chattering excitedly, three helium balloons wishing "Happy 40th" tied to the back of the chair of the woman with the low-cut dress and ample breasts and a further three tables of couples, one with two "suited and booted" businessmen exchanging papers, another with a young couple their eyes locked on each other and on the third, an elderly man and woman with little to say, boringly staring at the window or fireplace.

'Looks as you could do with more help.'

She nodded. 'Yes. I was told Jan would be showing me the ropes, but apparently she didn't turn up to serve breakfast this morning.' She spotted the man waving at her from the table with the balloons. 'Excuse me, I'm needed. Enjoy your meal.'

'Thank you; I'm sure I will.'

Brendon wasn't a lover of offal so had chosen "traditional beer-battered fish and chips" one of his favourites when he was back in England. It looked delicious as he spooned the tartare sauce from the small, stainless steel bowl which he'd saved from ending up in his lap. Sipping his "not overpriced" Marlborough Sauvignon Blanc, he wondered what Caroline was doing. As much as he'd enjoyed their lovemaking, he was still surprised by how she'd welcomed him into her bed so soon after the funeral, but he was far more puzzled, at least for the moment, by the way she'd reacted about Gareth. He'd received the same lack of information from Jim and Pete when they'd walked in shortly after the landlord had abruptly ended his and Brendon's conversation. He'd offered to buy them a drink but although they'd accepted, it seemed to Brendon it was with some reluctance and the conversation which had followed, was strange and unsettling.

~

'Cheers Brendon.' The three of them raised their pints.

'Cheers boys.' Silence followed their tasting. Brendon broke it.

'Sorry we didn't have much chance to talk at the funeral. There were a lot of people there. Great to see Gareth get such a good send-off.'

The other two remained silent. As trained as Brendon was in interrogation, he wasn't expecting to need his skills when talking to his childhood mates. Eventually Jim spoke.

'How long you staying Brendon?' he snorted, brushing back his shoulder-length, unkempt greasy hair from the top of his collarless shirt.

'Er... a while yet.' It wasn't the friendly reunion chat Brendon had envisaged. 'I'm due a fair amount of leave, so I thought I'd make up for lost time.' He laughed. 'So, what have you two reprobates been up to then?'

The accused swallowed their pints.

Pete thumped his empty glass on the bar. 'Married are you? Got family?' he asked.

'No to both questions.' Brendon's palms felt clammy. 'Why do you ask?'

'Just wondered,' Pete replied.

Jim's glass joined Pete's. He climbed off his tall stool. 'Going for a fag. You coming, Pete?' Pete nodded as he put his tobacco and papers in the side pocket of his light green, Musto shooting jacket. The front door closed behind them.

For a moment, Brendon sat motionless, staring at the row of optics behind the bar, a strange, cold shudder trickling down his back.

'Sorry I had to dash.'

Brendon jumped. He hadn't heard Clegg walk in.

'Got involved with a delivery. Should have been here this morning. Ready for a reload?'

Focused on the upturned spirit and Vermouth bottles, Brendon shook his head. 'No, I'm fine thanks Phil.'

'Are you all right?' observed Clegg. 'You look as though you've seen a ghost.' Putting down the crate of fruit juices, he shrugged. 'Mind you, pretty likely in this place. I see them all the time after a couple of bottles of wine.' Laughing, he added, 'Locals reckon I'm losing it.'

Still distant, it was a few seconds before Brendon responded, not registering how the landlord's opinion of the supernatural had changed dramatically since his earlier put-down.

'Sorry Phil, it's been something of an odd day.' He glanced at his glass. 'I think I'll leave this and go for a walk. The fresh air will do me good and I need to make my peace with the castle.'

'As you wish Mr Gallagher, but be careful. Can be

rather slippery in there if the Trust hasn't swept up the muck left by the birds.'

'I will be,' replied Brendon, not giving a second thought to the caution. He closed the door quietly behind him.

'Going for a walk in the castle?' grunted Pete as Brendon walked past. He was sat next to Jim on the picnic-style bench outside the front of the pub under the swinging sign of a seated man wearing a red frock coat and sporting a long, fair-haired wig.

'That's right Pete,' he replied as he carried on by. 'Thought I'd go and have a look at where we used to climb; still gives me nightmares when I think about it.'

'Shouldn't have thought you'd be scared of anything, not with what you do for a living,' commented Jim, raising his voice to ensure Brendon heard him. 'I imagined you James Bond types were all macho and 'ard, at least that was what Caroline had hoped for today... macho and fuckin' 'ard.'

'And big,' scoffed Pete. 'Not the tiny weaner she said you were.' Holding up his hand, he waggled his little finger. The two locals grinned at each other, Jim's rotten teeth filling his face.

Brendon turned. 'What the fuck do you think you're saying?' He glared at them, his eyes half closed. 'What the hell's happened to you both?' he shouted, visibly shaking.

'Nothing the matter with us that another pint won't put right,' said Jim, unperturbed by Brendon's raised voice. 'C'mon Pete, my round.' He picked up his tired looking leather coat.

Standing, they nodded at Brendon.

Pete pointed at the castle. 'Be careful in there. Can be really slippery at this time of year… really slippery.' He followed Jim back inside.

Brendon wiped his forehead. He felt mentally shattered as he sat on the empty bench, the stale smelling ashtray on the table in front of him adding to his nausea. He shook his head, struggling to believe the conversation. Virtually smashing holes in the screen of his mobile, he tapped in Caroline's number. The call went straight to voicemail.

'Caroline; it's Brendon. Ring me when you get this message; we need to talk.' He pressed "end" and stomped off along the main street in the direction of the moors. His castle demons could wait another day.

~

However good the meal, eating it without Caroline's company had spoiled the taste. He'd looked at his phone several times as he ate, hopeful the screen would say "missed call" but there was nothing. The large brandy following the bottle of white had made him feel even more depressed and consequently he'd contemplated driving to Caroline's house, in the hope it would raise his mood. He was desperate to know how knowledge of their liaison had got back to Pete and Jim, but fortunately he was sober enough to decide it wasn't worth risking his licence. The likelihood of a police patrol was probably zero, but he could hear his two ex-childhood friends in the public bar and bearing in mind their attitude towards him, he couldn't ignore the possibility of one of them making a phone call to the local constabulary. He decided it was time for bed.

'Goodnight sir, sorry about your sleeve,' said the waitress as she spotted him leaving the restaurant by the doorway leading to the hall and the staircase.

'Not a problem.' A small tartare sauce stain was nothing compared to the day's other upsets. 'Good night… er… sorry what's your name?'

'Melanie sir, after my grandmother, not that I met her or either of my parents.'

'Sorry to hear that.' He would have liked to have empathised more, but not now. Assuming she meant she was also adopted, she'd turned out okay. 'Goodnight Melanie. See you in the morning?'

'Not tomorrow sir. The landlord's serving breakfast.' She smiled. 'Sleep well sir.'

'Thank you Melanie; I'll do my best.'

Brendon felt particularly tired. After his "chat" with Pete and Jim he'd at times had trouble keeping his eyes open. Obviously good ale and fine wine had had their effect.

He slept soundly, undisturbed by any screaming. He was sure Caroline would ring in the morning; if not, he'd drive over to her. Unfortunately, the early events of the following day meant it would be noon before he'd arrive at the farm and by then it would be too late.

CHAPTER SEVEN

9 May 2016

'Sorry sir. This area's closed off to the public. You'll have to go the long way round if you need to go by.'

The police constable obviously wasn't local; the shortest "long way" round was a walk of at least five miles, unless of course you wanted to get more than your feet wet in the fast flowing waters of the gorge.

'What's going on, officer?'

Brendon had been served breakfast by a non-conversational landlord and having not heard from Caroline, he'd decided to take in some fresh air and walk up the "not ideal for low sprung cars" back lane to her farm.

'Police business sir.' The officer pulled himself to his full height. 'Now then, if you'd like to go back up the hill to the village, I'm—'

Producing his Ministry of Defence identity card immediately ended the rebuttal.

'Ah… sorry, I didn't realise.'

'No reason you should have done, Constable. Now then, who's your SIO?'

'I am,' said a firm yet feminine voice from behind him. Turning, Brendon faced a fresh-faced, thirty-something, neatly groomed, fair-haired female wearing a dark pinstriped tailored trouser suit. 'And who wants to know?'

He showed her his ID. Her wide blue eyes scanned it thoroughly.

'I see,' she acknowledged, 'and why would The Ministry be interested?'

'They're not,' he confirmed, 'but as I was passing—'

'You thought you could interfere,' she interrupted, shaking her head. 'Well, unless you've got scuba gear in your pocket Mr Gallagher, I suggest you do as the constable politely asked.'

Brendon held up both hands. 'Okay, okay, not a problem, I'll leave, but first can I ask what's happened here?' He glanced round at the three police vehicles and another which he assumed was an unmarked one. 'It's obviously not a fishing trip.'

'Very funny and yes you can ask, but no, you won't get an answer. Now then—'

Before she could finish, the head of another uniformed officer appeared over the bridge parapet.

'Sarge, I did my best to hold on, but the current's too strong. The body's been swept off downstream like a bullet out of a gun.' He climbed into the road, his trousers soaked. 'Jennings thinks he should be able to pull it out a bit further down though.'

'Shit, I'll have to come in.' She looked at her feet. 'It'll cost the taxpayer a new pair of heels though.'

Ignoring Brendon, she swung her leg over the metre-high stone parapet.

'Abrahams, you stay here; chase up the DCI. He'll probably want to take a look and get some more officers. Jones, you come with me; Jennings will need all the help he can get.'

The officer, who'd just returned, threw a pissed-off look at Abrahams, before obediently following his sergeant. As their heads disappeared, Brendon heard her shout, 'And get rid of that nosey MoD bloke.'

Abrahams smiled at Brendon. 'Sorry sir, you heard the boss. I think you'd better move on.'

'Fair enough.' He turned to go then stopped. 'Look Officer Abrahams, is there any reason I shouldn't continue in the direction I was going; after all, I'm hardly going to affect the crime scene am I?'

The young constable checked around, considering the request for a moment. 'I suppose not. There's no sign of any funny business up here; we think the body's come from upstream, based on where it was first seen, so go on then, but be quick.' He lowered his voice. 'And if another copper stops you, say you started from that direction, okay?'

'Okay and thanks.' Brendon set off, grateful for the help. Walking past one of the cars, he noticed an elderly woman sat in the back. She shouted to him.

' 'Ere, what's gwain on? Time I was getting 'ome. How long's you'm gwain be?'

Brendon bent down by the open window. Immediately a black and white spaniel jumped on the woman's lap and tried to welcome his face with its tongue.

'Get back you silly bugger.' She pushed it to the other side.

'I'm sorry but I'm not a…' He paused, glancing over

his shoulder at Abrahams whose attention was now focused on the events on the other side of the parapet. 'Not long Mrs… Mrs…?'

'Monkton,' she informed him; 'like I told the other one and this is me dog Dolly.' She pointed at the wall the sergeant and constable had climbed over. 'That's the way we used to get in as kids, saved us paying at the gate.'

'You're local then?'

'Lived here all me eighty years m'dear. There's nothing I doesn't know 'bout Lingtree.'

'Did you find the body?' he asked, guessing that was the reason she was sat in the car.

'Of course. Thought it was a bullock at first 'til it rolled over in the water. Bleedy 'orrible sight. All bloated and missing 'alf its face.' She crinkled her nose. 'Probably reeks and all.'

'Any chance you know who it is?' It was a long shot but worth a try.

'With that mangled face, you'm joking ain't you?' Brendon wasn't, but nothing ventured! 'I tell 'ee what though, even with my bloomin' eyes, I'd say 'ee weren't from round 'ere.'

Brendon raised his eyebrows. 'How can you be so sure?'

The woman looked at him with a hint of disdain. 'Nobody wears clothes like 'ee had on in this village; every bugger would bleedy laugh at 'im!'

Brendon smiled, surmising the woman had not only lived in the village all her life, but had probably never ever left it either, not that he remembered her! He saw another police car approaching.

'Thank you Mrs Monkton, you've been very helpful.' The car drew up beside him. As the uniformed officer opened his door, Brendon calmly said, 'This is Mrs Monkton and her dog Dolly. She found the body. I'll leave her with you.' He waved and continued his walk to Caroline's.

CHAPTER EIGHT

'Will she be all right?' asked Brendon as the paramedics closed the left-hand rear door of the bright yellow ambulance.

'It's too early to say Mr Gallagher,' replied the senior of the two. 'It looks like someone thought she was dead, or if they didn't, then they wanted to give her one helluva kicking.' It was a blunt synopsis, but the amount of blood on the kitchen floor and the numerous bruises on the parts of Caroline's body which were left uncovered by her bra and pants, confirmed his theory. Skin under her fingernails suggested she'd tried to defend herself.

'Are you coming with us?' enquired the younger paramedic as he climbed in. Brendon shook his head.

'No. I'll come and see her later. There's nothing I can do at the hospital and I need to talk to the police.' He turned to the senior one. 'Look after her.'

'We'll do our best, but we can't guarantee anything.' The second door closed.

Brendon watched as the ambulance disappeared down the partially gravelled drive to where it joined the unmade lane. Turning left, after two-hundred metres or so, it would emerge onto the main road between Chilstoke and Melkthorpe. He'd dealt with death many times, but like the loss of his adopted mother and father, this was "close to home" and he wished there was something he could do. But there wasn't and now he wondered whether if he'd done what the police had told him, he would have gone back to the pub, driven to the farm around the main road and arrived a good half-hour earlier. The blood on Caroline's facial wound had not long started to clot, so whoever had hit her had only just left before he'd knocked at the door.

He'd rung the police and ambulance immediately and then did as much as he could to stem the bleeding from the facial cuts as he'd comforted the unconscious Caroline. The paramedics had been grateful for what he'd achieved, but the police detective now stood in the farmhouse doorway, hadn't been so welcoming.

'So, we meet again so soon Mr Gallagher.' Detective Sergeant Pearson, the copper he'd met at the gorge incident was the first to arrive after his 999 call. She winced as she walked towards him.

'It looks that way, Sergeant. Thank goodness you were so close,' he acknowledged. 'Did they kick you off site for not wearing boots?'

'Very funny,' she sniggered. 'Lowest form of wit, you know?'

He smiled.

Removing one shoe, she massaged her heel. 'If you must know, DCI McKenna took over from me and not that it's any of your business, it appears the man in the river had been shot, so it looks as though we have at least one murder on our hands.'

Brendon didn't appreciate her prognosis, but she was right. He hoped to God it wouldn't become the two she was expecting.

'I see.' Rubbing his chin, he asked, 'And why are you telling me this? An hour ago you virtually told me to piss off.'

'Hmm, yes I did, didn't I?' She smiled. 'Not one to bear grudges I hope?' She pulled her shoe back on, her pained expression suggesting she'd be more comfortable in a pair of slippers.

He shook his head. 'I'm not with you.'

She folded her arms. 'Let's just say that I was probably a teeny weeny bit hasty.'

'Okay, so does that mean I can have a look around the house? I was… I mean still am a very close friend of Caroline.'

'Yes you can, but put these on.' She handed him a pair of powdered gloves. 'And mind where you tread, particularly in the kitchen. It's a crime scene and forensics will go ballistic if you interfere with anything, as of course will I.'

He began pulling on the gloves, still puzzled by this hard-nosed female's change in attitude. Walking into the kitchen, it all came back to him.

'Chloe Proctor,' he muttered. 'Colin McKenna worked with me on the Chloe Proctor case shortly before she took her own life. I'm right, aren't I?'

DS Pearson nodded.

'He must have told you.'

'Correct Mr Gallagher and he also instructed me to allow you to help, bearing in mind the events of the last couple of years.'

Her comment regarding the past meant nothing, Brendon was only interested in the present. There was no suggestion of a forced entry, so assuming Caroline had locked her doors then it was possible whoever attacked her was already in the house. Opening the door wearing just her underwear was unlikely and the thought she may have been undressed by her assailant wasn't something he wanted to contemplate.

Blood splattering covered the sink and floor cupboards and whatever had been used to hit her had done so with considerable force.

'No sign of any weapon in here so I'll get uniform to search the grounds,' said Pearson as she wandered around the kitchen. 'Meanwhile, we'll have a look in the other rooms, not so messy.'

There was no indication of a struggle in either the lounge or minimally furnished dining room, or the small downstairs study. The laptop on the corner desk was switched on.

'Right, let's see what she was looking at.' Pearson tapped the left mouse and a page of farms and smallholdings for sale filled the screen.

'Perhaps she was thinking of selling,' offered Brendon. 'Her husband died from a serious accident, so she might have been looking at prices.'

'Could be,' agreed Pearson, 'and yes I did know about her husband.' She clicked on history; it was empty. 'Strange. Not something I ever bother doing, how about you?'

'Sometimes,' replied Brendon, 'if I remember.'

Upstairs yielded nothing helpful either. One of the

three bedrooms was neat and tidy presumably Ellie's, whereas the larger one in which they were now stood, had a "lived in" look and was roughly how Brendon recalled it as he and Caroline lay naked together. Her silk dressing gown hung behind the door and clothes were piled on the back of the ancient rocking chair Caroline and Gareth had bought when Ellie was born.

'I used to sit in that when feeding her,' Caroline had told Brendon as she'd unfastened her bra. 'Gareth and I took it in turns to rock her to sleep.' She made no mention of having done the same with Nathan.

On entering the smaller, third bedroom, the police sergeant had voiced her disgust.

'Who lives in a shit hole like this?' she'd exclaimed loudly, as she covered her nose with her hand. Although her outburst was perhaps a little excessive, Brendon had to agree the room was indeed in a mess. Dressing table drawers and wardrobe doors were wide open, the duvet hung off one side of the bed and the large yellow stain on the faded white shagpile rug beside the bed suggested someone hadn't made it to the bathroom. An empty whisky bottle lay on its side on the floor. He guessed Nathan must have carried on drinking after leaving the wake.

'Brendon, are you still with us?' Pearson's question startled him.

'Sorry,' he said, his eyes staring blankly at the pink floral-design duvet cover. 'Mind elsewhere for a moment and all that.'

'Recognise the bed do we?' she asked. If it wasn't for his credentials, then he would be an obvious one to put on her list of "possibles", but for now, she had to accept her boss' opinion.

He flashed her a half-hearted smile. Her mobile ringing broke the awkwardness.

'Yes Guv… okay Guv… about fifteen minutes then. Bye.' She slipped the mobile back in her pocket.

'The boss is on his way. The pathologist is coming from Truro but won't get to the gorge for another hour, so he thought he'd join us. It'll be a nice chance for you two boys to catch up.'

~

'Brendon, how are you?' As he climbed out of the car, Detective Chief Inspector McKenna presented well in his light grey tailored suit and yellow tie despite the mud-covered wellingtons. Although not as tall as Gallagher, his broad physique suggested he wasn't someone to be messed with in a dark alley at any time of the day. His crew-cut and two-inch scar on his cheek added to the effect.

Shaking the held-out hand, Brendon acknowledged the welcoming smile.

'Well thanks, Colin, and yourself?'

'Good considering all the crap flying round. Financial cutbacks don't help with resources in cases like this, but… ' He shook his head. 'Anyway, you don't want to hear about that.' His smile left him. 'I heard about Chloe. Brave decision, euthanasia that is, but grateful relief I guess.'

'It was,' agreed Brendon sighing deeply, 'but it left a few unanswered questions. Still, that's history and your gorge body and Caroline's beating are what are important now. Any ideas on the identity of the dead man?' he asked, recalling Mrs Monkton's observation.

'None whatsoever and it ain't going to be easy,' McKenna responded. 'Not much face left, no report of anyone missing and... ' he shrugged his shoulders, 'no teeth.'

'What, none?' inquired Pearson. 'You mean his mouth was rotten?' She found it hard to believe.

'I think what your Guvnor means Detective Sergeant Pearson, is that they'd been extracted. Am I right, Colin?' To Brendon, it was nothing unusual. 'Hands removed too?'

McKenna nodded. 'Yep, so no fingerprints, not that he might have a record anyway, so it all depends on DNA.'

'And that might not be on record either,' considered Pearson. 'So no one's missed him; bit odd Guv.'

'Correct, Sergeant. And the way he's dressed, he doesn't appear to be local.' He turned to Brendon. 'I gather our lady with the dog told you the same.'

Brendon smiled. 'She did and by the sound of it, she was right. How long was he in the water?'

'Until the pathologist arrives we can't say for sure, but judging by the wrinkled skin and bloated stomach, I would guess several days. He had a bullet hole in his head though, so we need to know whether he was dead before his last swim which is probably a fair assumption, or whether he was still alive and drowned, which is most unlikely.' McKenna turned his attention to the hall and staircase of Caroline's house. 'So what's been going on here then?'

'Vicious assault of a female aged about… ' she looked at Brendon for guidance.

'Fifty-nine, Colin. I knew her… shall we say quite well.'

'Quite well or very well?' asked McKenna.

'The latter,' confirmed Brendon, 'we grew up together as teenagers and we… err… renewed our acquaintance at the funeral of her late husband a couple of days ago.'

'And in her bed,' added Pearson, somewhat sarcastically.

'I see.' McKenna shrugged. 'None of my business Brendon, but presumably you are aware of how Gareth Pettit died?' Brendon's expression told him otherwise. McKenna looked at his watch. 'I'm going to have to shoot back to the gorge shortly, got to see the pathologist. Perhaps I could bring you up to speed later. Meet at the pub, The Judge's Parlour, do you know it?'

'Staying there.'

'Good, you can buy me supper. See you at six.' He headed to the front door. 'Right Pearson, fill me in here, I hope we haven't got another fucking murder on our hands.'

A white forensic-team van passed Brendon as he walked back along the rhododendron bush-lined lane. He searched "Plymouth City Hospital" on his mobile's Internet, but the 3G signal was coming and going. He'd have to find the number back at the pub.

CHAPTER NINE

'Cheers Brendon. How long's it since you last bought me a beer?'

Appreciating his pint's distinctive flavour, Brendon took a few seconds to answer. 'Nearly three years. It was roughly six months after Johnson retired.'

'I'm not sure he'd have seen it as retirement in fairness.' McKenna shrugged as he placed his glass carefully on a beer mat. They were sat at an old, square, farmhouse style table in the public bar by the exit to the reception and toilets. 'Saw him last year at our wedding.' He spotted Brendon's raised eyebrows. 'I married Julie... you know Julie Ransom; she was one of the detective constables working on the case. She's a sergeant now; went back to uniform.'

'Ah, right, with you. Give her my love then.'

'Will do.'

Brendon supped his beer. He was pleased for McKenna. They'd become good friends whilst working together on the murder of Grant Marshall, or rather the investigation of his partner Chloe Proctor. It was never officially discovered who carried out the killing but although McKenna had his suspicions, friendships did not mean discussing the workings of The Ministry. Eventually McKenna had given up probing and as a consolation, had happily accepted his rapid promotion.

Having contacted the hospital, Brendon confirmed Caroline was still unconscious and although her condition hadn't deteriorated, it hadn't improved either. McKenna told him forensics hadn't found anything to lead to her attacker. They were checking the bloodstains to see if any belonged to someone other than Caroline.

'So Colin, tell me about Gareth.'

McKenna observed him closely. 'What do you know?'

'Bugger all, other than he was found in the castle, a place he and I swore we'd never go in again after what happened. I assume he'd had some sort of accident but no one, not even Caroline, seems to want to talk about it.'

McKenna glanced around the room. Seated at the bar, occasionally talking to young Arnold, the acne-faced barman, were Pete Grayson and Jim Evans. They'd been eyeing the copper and MoD employee since the two of them sat at their table.

'Who're your friends?' McKenna enquired, nodding towards Jim and Pete.

Brendon told him their names. 'We grew up together, were great mates until... until... we lost Alan Sumner; kinda changed things. Gareth and I found him mangled and partially torn to bits on the floor of the castle. That's why we said we'd never go in there again.' He drained his pint. 'We wanted to forget, but despite everything I've seen since, it still haunts me.' Brendon felt the blood rush from his head.

'Are you all right Brendon?'

'I'm fine, just someone walking over my grave I guess.' He paused as Jim shuffled past him, probably on his way to the gents. Brendon avoided his stare.

'Don't look like great mates to me,' commented McKenna, his empty pint glass in hand. 'Sit tight, I'll get you another drink; it seems as if you could do with one.'

McKenna was back within a couple of minutes. 'Other than those two and the vicar, we're the only ones drinking; everyone else seems to be eating.'

'What you mean is, where's our wild boar burger and chips?' He took his beer, his eyes on the bar where David Soby, in dog collar and sports jacket, his fair hair neatly parted on one side, had a moment ago joined Pete. 'Thanks Colin. Sorry about the food; I'll chase it up in a moment.'

'Not a problem.' McKenna sunk some of his beer. 'So what happened to your friendship?'

'After Alan's death, the four of us stayed friends but somehow it was never the same. It was as if Jim and Pete blamed Gareth and me for Alan's death.'

'Were you there... you know, when he died?' asked McKenna, sitting back in his seat.

Brendon shook his head. 'Not really... ' he hesitated. 'But it was us who found him shortly after.' He looked away. 'I know we taunted Alan about his fear of heights and things, but that was all of us.' Spotting Jim returning he waited until he was back on his stool. Nodding towards them, he told McKenna, 'As for now, they don't even want to talk to me.'

'Envy?' queried McKenna.

Brendon shrugged. 'Unlikely,' he replied. 'More disturbing at the moment though is that they knew about me seeing Caroline the other day.'

A wry smile crossed McKenna's lips. 'It's a small village, Brendon, and gossip travels quickly.'

'Yeah, you're right I suppose,' he conceded. He leaned forwards. 'Now then, you were going to tell me about Gareth.'

An hour later, their meal finished and the offer of a third pint turned down by McKenna, Brendon walked with him to his car parked in the public car park across the road from the front of the pub.

'How long are you staying?' enquired McKenna.

'Not sure. At least until I know Caroline's outcome. I'm on an indefinite sabbatical, reward for my outstanding performance in the Middle East apparently,' he replied before adding sarcastically, 'which probably means imminent retirement.'

McKenna held Brendon's arm. 'Look, I can't ask you officially, but you came here for the funeral, so with luck no one would suspect you.'

'Suspect me of what?' asked Brendon, his brow furrowed.

'Spying... well... rather keeping an eye open.' McKenna unlocked the door of his car. 'What I've told you tonight isn't something I would normally discuss with anyone outside the force. Until this morning, I had four suspicious deaths on my patch in the last two years. Now it looks as if I might have at least one definite murder and I'm sorry, but it could be two. It's a small village, everything's out of proportion.'

Brendon looked at him then gazed up at the castle, its square, symmetrical shape, eerily silhouetted by the distant setting sun, casting a shadow over the low slung Judge's Parlour nestling comfortably beside it. He imagined Gareth's body lying face down in the mud, recalled Alan's mutilated neck and limbs and then thought of Caroline lying in intensive care, presumably attached to an array of medical support systems. After the funeral, he'd hoped for a rest, for relaxation and for help to get over the mental traumas his job had continually thrown at him over the last God knows how many years. Had these reflections not immediately been replaced by the sudden mental infusion of how Caroline had felt as he entered her, how he'd held her close and the way she'd shouted his name as she'd climaxed, he would have felt incapable of agreeing to McKenna's request. He turned to the detective.

'Okay Colin, I'll see what I can learn, but only if you keep me informed of any progress with the body in the gorge and Caroline's attack, however small or irrelevant you believe it to be.'

McKenna slapped him on the back. 'Deal, good man.' He passed Brendon his card. 'Right, home to Julie and hear what she's been up to. Thanks for supper.' Shaking hands, he closed the car door, started the engine and waved as he drove off, guilty that he hadn't told Brendon what had happened to the previous landlord and landlady. They were now in a police safe house, having been released from the psychiatric hospital three months ago. It was unlikely they would ever return to the force, but they knew the risk when they went undercover. McKenna's conscience was clear; at least they were still alive.

'Night.' It was Jim.

Whilst talking to McKenna, Brendon hadn't noticed Jim and Pete sat outside the pub having a smoke on what they probably considered was their own private bench. He walked past, intent on ignoring any baiting. As he entered the pub's porch, Jim's loud comment caused him to pause.

'Off to pull your tiny weaner, are you? Nowhere to shove it any more s'pose.'

Brendon swallowed hard, resisting the temptation to confront them. If they knew what he was capable of doing, what he'd done to many men and women in recent years, they might not be so cocky. But he was on a sabbatical and this wasn't business. Gently he closed the solid oak door and took the stairs to his bedroom.

As he lay awake, he reflected on what McKenna had told him. He slept soundly, the screams going unheard.

CHAPTER TEN

10 May 2016

'Will you be staying long sir? Only I have to know how many rooms I have available. Busy time of year the bank holiday.'

Brendon finished pouring his tea. 'A few days yet Phil. A close friend of mine was hurt yesterday and I need to know she's okay before I leave.'

'Ah yes, nasty business.' The landlord picked up the empty cereal bowl. 'Nice girl Caroline. Just after her terrible loss as well.' He stacked the bowl on top of the other in his hand. 'I heard you found her. Has she woken up yet?'

'Er, I don't know. I'm going to ring the hospital in a moment.'

'Well, wish her all the best. Something we can't do for the other body they found. Sounded really messy that one. No face and a bullet to boot.' Phil shook his head. 'Really messy business. Makes you wonder what the world's coming to.' He walked towards the kitchen door. 'Anyway, you take care now. Don't want an unpaid bill, do we?' He laughed as the door swung closed behind him.

Leaving his tea, Brendon hurried back to his room. He'd ring the hospital, but not until after he'd spoken to McKenna.

'Brendon, how are you this morning?'

'Good thanks Colin.' Brendon missed out on the "niceties"; how Colin was feeling wasn't immediately important. 'Have details of Caroline's assault and the body in the gorge been released yet, you know, to the press?'

'Press conference this afternoon. We wanted to get the pathologist's preliminary report on the dead man first. In fact, I'm about to leave to attend the post-mortem. Regards Caroline... ' He hesitated. 'We've decided to try and keep quiet on that one until— '

'You know if it's a murder enquiry,' interrupted Brendon. 'It's all right Colin. It hurts, but I can handle it. So no press at the gorge bridge?'

'Nope. We had "road closed" signs up pretty quickly. Pearson's an efficient young lady, well trained you see.' Brendon sensed Colin's smirk. 'To most it was just a traffic incident. Anyway, why do you ask?'

'The landlord was talking about it this morning. Knew the gorge victim had been shot and also Caroline was unconscious.'

'Perhaps the landlord chappie overheard us talking.'

'He wasn't there last night,' snapped Brendon loudly, openly agitated by Colin's lack of concern. 'It was that young dough-bake, Arnold or whatever he's called.'

'Brendon, for goodness' sake, calm down. It could have been Arnold or even your friends or anyone else for that matter. I know we were tucked in the corner but—'

'But we never mentioned the guy was shot,' argued

Brendon. 'Not even Mrs Monkton knew that. Yes, I gave you the empty bullet casing, but that doesn't mean anything.' The other end of the line fell quiet. 'Colin... Colin... are you still there?'

'Yes, I'm still here Brendon... ' He paused. 'Look Brendon, I've got to go, but I'll come and see you this afternoon. Uniform have been making enquiries around the village, but I want to have a chat with the landlord and have a look at the guest book. I'll be there about two. Okay?'

'Okay Colin,' Brendon agreed, before asking, 'Has anyone got hold of Caroline's son and daughter, Ellie and Nathan?'

'Still trying Brendon. Apparently the daughter's in Tanzania trying to tie up some takeover of a mineral mine and her mobile's not functioning. Regards the son, the RAF says he's on manoeuvres in the Med but they will let him know as soon as convenient. Not straightforward, I'm afraid.'

'Thanks Colin. Sorry to be a pain,' apologised Brendon, slumping on the unmade bed. 'I know you're doing everything you can, but even the tiniest things seem to be getting to me at the moment and they shouldn't be; it's not as though I'm not used to dealing with pressure.'

'But this is personal Brendon and personal is different,' reassured McKenna.

'True I suppose,' accepted Brendon. 'I guess you're right.' He sighed. 'I'll see you later then.'

'Will do.' As Brendon was about to switch off his phone, McKenna remarked, 'Be careful Brendon, we don't want number six.' The line went dead.

'Or seven,' thought Brendon, picturing Caroline lying

in hospital. He sat forward on the edge of his bed, staring at his mobile. Being careful was routine but McKenna's words sunk deep, deep into his mind. He lay back, his head on a pillow.

~

'Sorry Mr Gallagher, I didn't realise you was in here. Would you like me to come back after I've done t'other rooms?'

Brendon sat upright, shaking his head. He looked at his watch; ten past eleven. He'd been asleep two hours.

'No, that's all right Grace, come on in. Just felt a bit tired that's all.'

'Are you sure you'm feeling okay Mr Gallagher? You looks very pale.' Grace was the chambermaid; a portly, grey-haired lady in her fifties who also cleaned the bar and restaurant. They'd passed the time of day a couple of times as she'd gone about her business.

Brendon smiled. 'Honestly, just tired, but thanks for your concern.' He stood up. 'I'll get out of your way.' Hesitating, he turned to Grace who'd begun tidying the tea and coffee tray.

'Grace.'

She put down the saucer. 'Yes Mr Gallagher,' she acknowledged, straightening her back, as though standing to attention.

'Brendon, please. I think I've been staying here long enough to drop the formality.' It wasn't something he'd offered the landlord a second time. Grace blushed; she seemed uncomfortable with the suggestion. 'I understand,'

82

he said, returning her smile. 'Anyway, I wanted to ask you if you ever hear or see anything strange in the pub.'

She looked puzzled. 'Like what Mr Gallagher?'

It was Brendon's turn to feel awkward. 'Well… like… err… screaming.'

'Sorry Mr Gallagher.' She laughed. 'I knows they say room nine is haunted 'cos of the stonework they used to build the fireplace, but I've never in the four years I've worked 'ere seen a ghost or such like.' She mimicked a shiver. 'I'd run a mile if I did.'

'So nothing during the night?'

Her lips pursed, she shook her head. 'I'm gone by lunchtime. Used to 'elp in the evenings, waitin' table and things but the new landlord says 'ee don't need me, although I knows they gets a bit busy and non residents complains.' She shrugged. 'But that's up to 'ee. Now then, best get on or my old man will be the one complaining he ain't got no dinner on the table.' She smiled politely and disappeared into the en suite, saucer and cup in hand.

Intending to ring the hospital from outside, he stopped at the top of the stairs. About five metres further down the corridor, the door of room nine stared back at him. He looked over his shoulder. Grace had four more rooms to clean before she got to this end. Cautiously he edged his way along the narrow passage, at this time of day lit only by the emergency lighting and the natural light coming from the top of the stairs. Pausing twice to check Grace was still fully occupied he faced the door, checked once more he was alone then reached for the handle.

'Can I help you Mr Gallagher?'

Brendon instantaneously spun round, ready to negate anyone who might be about to infiltrate his space. It was the landlord.

'Sorry Mr Gallagher, didn't mean to startle you,' he said, totally lacking sincerity.

'Er, been here a few days,' explained Brendon, the hairs on the back of his neck relaxing, 'and realised I hadn't had a good look round. Hope I'm not causing any problems.'

'None whatsoever Mr Gallagher. You only had to ask, I would have given you a guided tour.' He nodded towards room nine. 'Unfortunately this room's occupied and my guests gave me strict instructions they didn't want to be disturbed.' He pointed in the direction of the stairs. 'Now then, if you would like to come down, I'll show you the kitchen and storerooms and once Grace is finished we can view the unoccupied bedrooms.'

Brendon shook his head. 'Thanks, but not necessary. I think I need some fresh air. Perhaps I could have a look round later.'

'As you like Mr Gallagher.' He looked at Brendon sternly. 'Now, if there's nothing else, I must get back to my work.'

'Yes of course Phil; sorry to have troubled you.'

Brendon walked alone to the stairs, sensing the landlord's eyes following his every step. Before descending he turned; Clegg hadn't moved. After acknowledging each other politely, Brendon sighed deeply, careful not to slip on possible loosened carpet. He'd read more than one book on paranoia and it was beginning to worry him.

Sat in the hydrangea, dogwood and buddleia enclosed rear garden, his back to the castle, he rang the hospital.

'Are you family, sir?' asked the friendly but "jobsworth" voice on the other end.

'No, but I'm the one who found her and rang for an ambulance. My name's Brendon Gallagher, I'm a close friend.'

'I see, sir. Hold on just a moment please.' Drumming his fingers impatiently on the green plastic garden table, it was a full two minutes before the "up my own arse" voice returned. 'She's still in intensive care. Not woken up but breathing on her own. Can I help you with anything else, sir?'

'No, that's fine. Thanks for your help.'

'My pleasure, sir, have a good day. Goodbye.'

Brendon turned his head and gazed up at the side of the castle. He felt his stomach tighten. He knew he had to go back and he knew now was as good a time as any, but that didn't make it any easier. Eyes wide open, once again he imagined Alan's badly distorted and blood-covered body and he saw Gareth, his decapitated head split open, weirdly smiling as the flies explored every inner enclave of the bird-pecked sockets.

~

'The pathologist reckoned he must have died around 5 a.m. It was the hottest day of the year so far and he wasn't discovered until the first visitors found him at just after three in the afternoon,' explained McKenna. 'Apparently Caroline just assumed he'd gone off on another of his walks. He'd been suffering from mild depression according to his wife, not that he'd been to the doctor and walking the moors helped him control it.'

Brendon recalled Caroline had said something had happened to stop things going well but she hadn't made any mention of depression; however, he didn't interrupt.

'Anyway,' continued McKenna, 'by the time I arrived, the castle had been closed off and the body covered with tarpaulin to try and keep off the worst of the flies. The head had detached from the neck and was lying a full ten metres from the torso. Both legs were broken, all internal organs were crushed and crows had had a go at the eyes.'

It wasn't a subject which Brendon would have chosen to discuss whilst eating, but they'd been served during the conversation and McKenna seemed totally unperturbed by the content. To him, it was just another gory crime scene. It would have meant nothing to Brendon either, had it not been Gareth they were discussing. McKenna ended up eating both portions of chips.

'Anyway, to cut a long story short,' concluded McKenna, 'based on the findings of the pathologist the coroner returned an "open verdict" although suicide was the likeliest cause of death.'

'I see,' said Brendon, now understanding why Caroline hadn't wanted to discuss the death with him. He frowned. 'Was there a suicide note?'

'Nothing found.'

'And what were the findings?'

'The pathologist felt the injuries were conducive with a fall from the top of the castle walls, the head having been ripped off by contact with one or more protruding ledges on the way down; not that any evidence of contact was found.'

'And that's it?' enquired Brendon, surprised that Gareth would have gone into the castle in the early hours, let alone have climbed to the top in the dark and jumped off. It certainly wasn't the Gareth he'd known.

'Just about.' McKenna took a deep breath. 'As I said, there was nothing to confirm the head had hit something on the way down. We had an abseiling group from Truro check all the inside walls, but they discovered no blood, nor lumps of flesh or strands of hair.'

Brendon shook his head, one eyebrow raised. 'Are you saying the skull was ripped apart, not just decapitated?'

McKenna crossed his arms. 'Look Brendon, I'm just a copper, not a pathologist.' Lowering his voice, he leaned forwards. 'It didn't appear in the formal report but all four limbs had chunks of flesh torn out of them, as though some wild animal had had a go, but as I said, nothing was found either on the walls or the floor.'

Brendon dropped his knife on his plate and stared at the table; it was a while before he spoke.

'Why was all this detail withheld... from the report I mean?' The question was rhetorical; he knew why.

'Because it was the same thing as happened to your friend Alan and it was decided not to cause the fear and irrational behaviour all over again.'

'You mean the slaughter of all dogs within a five-mile radius and incessant fox hunting?'

'That's right Brendon and from what I've been told, the stigma still remains even now with the elderly residents.'

Sitting on the damp castle floor, the smell of stale urine from one dungeon corner clogging his nostrils, Brendon cried openly. Climbing the bank to the entrance had been easy, but entering through the Norman archway had taken an unexpected effort. It was as though the castle didn't want him there and had created its own force field. As the tears ran down his cheeks, he realised his chief of staff's imposed sabbatical was a necessity not a reward.

~

'So Mr Clegg, you haven't had anyone leave without paying or not collecting their property?'

'Not in the time I've been here Detective Chief Inspector McKenna,' replied the landlord. 'Our prices don't attract the sort of guests who do runners.'

'I see, sir, bit too posh are they?'

'Something like that.'

'Do you mind if I look at your guest book?'

'Not at all, I've nothing to hide.'

'Why would you, sir?'

Clegg regarded him closely, shrugged then passed him the open book from the office shelf.

'Thank you, sir.'

McKenna laid it on the desk and scanned the first page. A couple of minutes later he handed it back. It hadn't been any help other than he was able to confirm room nine was currently empty.

'Do you recall seeing anyone drinking or eating alone

over the last month or so, you know, someone looking anxious, out of place, anything unusual?'

Clegg quickly confirmed what McKenna already knew, namely it was a ridiculous question.

'We get loads of single people in here Chief Inspector, particularly at lunchtime. Reps, walkers, cyclists, tradesmen. Apologies, but I don't ask them if they're going to go missing after leaving here,' he responded sarcastically.

'Who said anyone had gone missing?' queried McKenna, eyebrows raised.

Clegg smirked. 'Why else would you be asking? It's not every day you find a body in the gorge with a bullet through the head, is it Chief Inspector?'

'News travels fast.'

'It's a small village.' He reached for the handle of the office door. 'Now, if that's all, I've got a brewery order to sort out.' Clegg pulled the door open.

McKenna stopped in the doorway. 'Did Caroline Pettit upset anyone the day of her husband's wake?'

'Think you'd be better asking your friend Mr Gallagher that one, don't you?' sneered Clegg. He followed McKenna out. 'After all, he seems to know her... rather intimately shall we say?'

McKenna met Brendon in the car park. He was sat on the wing of McKenna's car. 'Nice man "mine host",' McKenna announced cynically.

'Can be when it suits him. Did you glean anything useful?'

McKenna shook his head. 'Nothing of any help, although according to the guest book, room nine is empty.'

'I thought so, so why didn't he let me go in there?' puzzled Brendon.

'Perhaps it was in a mess, perhaps he'd forgotten to get whoever was staying to sign the book, or perhaps he's just not one for sharing.' Smiling, he leaned against the car. 'Look Brendon, there's probably nothing sinister going on in that room, so don't get wound up about it.'

'But I heard screaming,' Brendon countered, frustrated by McKenna's put-down. 'It reminded me of… of… '

'Of what, Brendon?'

Brendon shook his head. 'Of nothing,' he conceded. He peered up at the castle. 'It's just that bloody building; it… '

McKenna put a sympathetic hand on Brendon's shoulder.

'I know you've probably had some tough times lately and no doubt you've seen some horrific sights, but there's no point in letting this get to you.' He took a deep breath. 'We'll find out who assaulted Caroline and we'll find out whose body was in the gorge and who put him there and as sure as hell, we ain't going to let a pub landlord and a few customers get to us,' he reassured him.

Brendon smiled. 'You're right Colin… I'm being ridiculous… thanks.'

'No problem.' McKenna checked his car was locked. 'Right, time to show me where you found the bullet casing; it's not too far, is it?'

CHAPTER ELEVEN

'About here; it was lying on top of some dead leaves.'

The walk from The Judge's Parlour past the possible site of the Anglo-Saxon mint, had taken twenty-five minutes.

'Hmm, strange place if you were rough shooting,' said McKenna surveying the lane. 'Visibility over the hedges isn't good and little likelihood of seeing anything much on the path I would have thought. Could just have been dropped here though I suppose.'

'Wrong calibre for hunting rabbits or foxes,' advised Brendon.

'Roughly matches the hole in the back of our unknown person's head.'

This was the first Brendon had heard of the location of the entry wound.

'Where did the bullet exit?' he enquired.

'Through his lower jaw,' confirmed McKenna. He saw Brendon's knowing expression. 'That's what the pathologist thought as well.'

'Any evidence of his wrists being tied?'

McKenna nodded. 'Bruising on the forearms.'

'Executed?'

'That's what it looks like.'

'So whoever killed him, shot him whilst he was probably knelt, cut off his hands, removed all his teeth and disposed of him in the river. Not exactly a spur-of-the-moment job.'

'Absolutely spot on,' concurred McKenna. 'The pathologist confirmed he was dead before entering the water. Very little of the river in his lungs.'

'But why for God's sake? And is it connected to the attack on Caroline?' Brendon linked his hands on top of his head. 'What the fuck's going on?' Before McKenna had a chance to answer, a third voice joined their conversation.

'Apologies for interrupting you, gentlemen.'

The two of them hadn't heard the man approach from behind. They turned together. It was the archaeologist Brendon had spoken to the day he'd walked with Caroline. Judging by the mud-stained clothes, washing facilities were limited at the campsite.

'Can I help, sir?' enquired McKenna.

'Are you the pathologists?' asked Frank Hatcher, but before either of the two could answer, he instantly withdrew his question. 'No, of course you're not, it's too soon and anyway, you haven't any bags. So silly of me, sorry, only rang twenty minutes ago.' He started to walk back the way he'd come.

'Just a minute sir. I may not be a pathologist but I am a policeman.' McKenna flashed his warrant card. 'Perhaps I can help.'

'Not unless you can examine dead bodies or rather the remains of dead bodies,' he shouted, dismissing the offer with his hand and carrying on walking. McKenna and Brendon hurried after him.

'Mr Hatcher.' At the sound of his name, the archaeologist stopped and turned.

'How do you know my name?' He studied Brendon through his gold-rimmed spectacles. 'Ah… yes, you were the gentleman I spoke to the other day… you were with the woman who owns the land.' He frowned. 'Got attacked or something. We were all questioned about an hour ago. Nasty business, really nasty.'

'That's right Mr Hatcher, Brendon Gallagher and this is Detective Chief Inspector McKenna. He's investigating the assault.'

'And the dead man in the river?' inquired Hatcher.

McKenna nodded.

'Was he murdered? Everyone's saying he was. Any idea who did it?'

'Can't say too much just yet, sir, but we're working on it,' McKenna assured him. 'Now then Mr Hatcher, what's this about some dead bodies?'

Hatcher took off his specs, wiped them in a soiled handkerchief. Slipping them back on, he pointed in the general direction of the dig.

'Young Sam found them in a ditch.' He saw their puzzled look. 'Beside the burial ground. Not part of it, you see. Weren't very deep. Not sure why he was digging; says he was drawn to that spot, but he's only a student so we have to make allow— '

'But assuming you were expecting to find bones and remains, why have you contacted a pathologist?'

'I didn't… well, not directly that is Detective Chief

Inspector; it's what someone at your Melkthorpe police station did,' replied Hatcher as though it was an everyday occurrence.

'Still not with you sir.'

Hatcher shook his head in despair, clearly irritated by McKenna's lack of understanding. 'Because the bones were recent, not the sort of thing you expect to find when excavating an Iron Age site.' He let out an exasperated sigh. 'Damn nuisance. Everything's had to stop. It's not as though we have months to complete the project.' He turned to go.

'Just a minute,' instructed McKenna. 'How many bodies were there?'

'Two adults, a male and a female according to our so-called expert osteoarchaeologist, plus two children, probably a boy and a girl,' he replied, scratching his head. 'Now then, I really must go; don't want our unwelcome guest to miss us.'

As Hatcher strode meaningfully away, McKenna turned to Brendon. 'That's interesting,' he commented as he took out his mobile. He selected a speed-dial key.

Brendon waited impatiently as McKenna spoke with a colleague. 'Thanks Billy… it's as I thought… no that's fine… find out who the pathologist is and make sure he or she gets a copy of the report to us as soon as. Cheers.' He pocketed the phone.

'Are you going to share, Colin?' pressed Brendon. McKenna smiled.

'Sorry Brendon.' He rubbed the back of his neck, pausing for a while before continuing. 'About four years ago, we had a seriously cold winter with unprecedented snowfall. Lingtree was literally cut off for a couple of weeks and food and animal supplies had to be flown in by helicopter when the weather allowed. Only people to benefit were the landlords of the pub. They'd not long filled up their walk-in freezers so did a roaring trade as residents' fridges and larders emptied.

'On the day the snow started, a family by the name of Henderson set off from their home in Penzance to visit friends fifty miles the other side of the village. They were intending to stay there for New Year,' he explained, 'but they never arrived. Their car was found abandoned in snow just before the gorge bridge; you know where you met DS Pearson the other day?' Brendon nodded. 'Despite several searches,' continued McKenna, 'both during the snow and then again after the thaw, no bodies were ever found.'

'Nothing at all?' queried Brendon.

McKenna nodded. 'Absolutely nothing,' he confirmed. 'Luggage was still in the car. No coats had been left in it, so it was assumed they'd tried to finish their journey on foot and possibly fallen into the gorge where strong currents might have swept them into an underwater cavern which couldn't be found by divers. Why they would have been on the back road, particularly bearing in mind the weather conditions, rather than the A30, God only knows.'

'So what was the verdict?'

'Eventually "death by misadventure"… ' McKenna paused. 'I say eventually as the coroner wasn't happy there hadn't been foul play, but at the same time, bearing in mind the weather conditions, it's unlikely anyone else could have been involved.'

'None of the locals knew anything?'

'Nope, apparently not. Obviously they were all interviewed, the pub landlord and customers who drank regularly in particular, as that would have been an obvious place to head for, but no… absolutely nothing.' He shrugged. 'The case file is, in effect, still open which I guess might now become active again if the bodies your friend Hatcher found can be identified as the missing family.'

'Were you the SIO?' asked Brendon.

McKenna shook his head. 'DCI Johnson, the same one— '

'As worked on the Proctor case,' interrupted Brendon. 'So he had two unsolved mysteries on his hands then?'

'Might be able to put him out of his misery on one of them now,' speculated McKenna. His phone rang. 'McKenna… Hi Jenny… no useful forensics in the house at all… okay… weapon…? Possibly didn't use one… How is she…?' He glanced at Brendon. 'Right I'll tell him, he's with me now. Have you got hold of her children?' McKenna's eyebrows rose. 'Oh, well fair enough… oh, Jenny… you might want to dig out the Henderson file, there's a possibility someone in the office is going to need it… yes, that's the one. I'll be back in a couple of hours. Cheers.' He looked at Brendon. 'Did you get the gist?'

'No change with Caroline and nothing in her house of any help?' guessed Brendon.

'Correct and still unable to contact the kids,' confirmed McKenna. 'The girl's somewhere out in the back of beyond and the boy is working under radio silence. On some manoeuvre or other.'

'I'm not sure it's a manoeuvre, more like a mission if

he can't be reached,' surmised Brendon. He ran his hand through his hair. 'Forensics found absolutely nothing, no weapon, no signs of a burglary?'

'Apparently not, I'm afraid. Doctors think the wounds could have been inflicted with fists and feet... someone in one helluva rage. We have to rely on Caroline and there's no guarantee she'll—'

'I get the picture,' snapped Brendon.

'Sorry Brendon, mouth kicked in ahead of brain.'

~

That evening Brendon decided to eat in the bar again. Sat at the same corner table he'd shared with McKenna, he wouldn't go unnoticed but at the same time he wouldn't be too conspicuous to the local drinkers. He was feeling much better now. When he and McKenna had introduced themselves at the archaeological dig and viewed the four bodies laid side by side in what had obviously been shallow graves, he was overwhelmed by a weird vision of four naked bodies, their sickly red torsos split wide open from throat to groin.

'Are you all right Brendon?' McKenna had asked. 'You look as though you're about to faint.'

29 December 2012

'Daddy, why has the music stopped?'

'Shush Lizzie, the man's going to tell us about the weather,' replied her father.

'The Met Office issued the following weather warning at 16.30 hours GMT,' a posh voice announced on the car radio. *'The snow now falling over Devon, Cornwall, Somerset and Dorset will become heavy, particularly over the moors where blizzard conditions are expected. Falls of up to thirty centimetres are likely during the next six hours and extensive drifting will occur in the strong winds. Fresh snow landing on already frozen roads will cause hazardous driving conditions and the police have asked motorists not to travel unless their journey is absolutely necessary. A further update will be made as more information becomes available.'* The voice became less formal. *'Now, we return you to "Drive time" with Simon Mayo and guests.'*

Ian Henderson turned off the radio.

'Dad, why have you switched it off?' asked Sam, his twelve-year-old son. 'I like the music on that programme.'

Ian looked at his wife Kate. Seeing her worried expression, he tried to make light of the reason. 'The snow's sticking to the windscreen Sam, so it's a bit difficult to see and listen at the same time. It's a grown-up thing.' What he really meant was, *If this fucking snow carries on like this, we're going to be in trouble.*

'Okay, I see. It's like my old primary school teacher. She couldn't write on the board and teach at the same time, so she used to tell us to be quiet and get on with our work.'

Kate nodded and forced a smile. 'Something like that Sam.'

'Oh well, never mind.' He picked up his mobile and selected his current favourite game involving numerous Father Christmases trying to climb up slippery roofs and dropping their sacks of presents down the chimney. It was a free one he'd found on the Internet and then fortunately downloaded, as there hadn't been a phone signal for the last half an hour. It was one of the reasons Kate had lost patience with her husband, the other being the fact he'd insisted on ploughing on through the deepening snow, desperate to prove to her and the kids his vehicle was invincible.

'You know it's why I spent so much of my army compensation on doing it up,' he'd told her the first time the wheels had begun to spin on the icy surface. 'Air diff locks on each wheel means it can go anywhere.'

However, as the dark red Series 2 Land Rover Discovery made its way gingerly past the turning for the Hang Tor Reservoir then up the sloping bend to the humpback bridge over the now defunct GMR railway line, Ian began wishing he'd taken more notice of his wife of fifteen years.

Peering out the front passenger window, Kate saw the large building set in spacious grounds to her left.

'If only that was a pub, we might have been able to spend the night there,' she muttered to herself.

Had she and her family been passing twenty years or so ago, it would still have been a hotel and although it would have been several days later before the weather allowed them to continue their journey, they would at least have arrived safely at the holiday cottage they were due to share with their friends, or given the circumstances, more likely to have returned home.

Reaching the top of the bridge, Ian paid little attention to the "Priority to oncoming traffic" sign; there being little likelihood of anyone else being on the road. After travelling downhill for a further one-hundred metres, the road began another steep ascent. Sliding from side to side, tyres spinning, the Discovery somehow continued to make forward progress. Ian ran the back of his hand across his forehead, wiping away the beads of sweat. Had he been alone, sleeping in the car wouldn't have been an issue; as compared to many places he'd slept whilst serving abroad, a roof over his head would have been a luxury. However, there was no way he could expect his ten-year-old daughter, plus son and wife to spend the night freezing to death. If only he'd thought to put in some food and blankets, but as usual, he was too pig-headed to take the advice of the BBC weather girl before setting out.

'We'll be all right luv; it's only a bit of snow and these days they give out a warning as soon as a hint of a flake is spotted,' he'd reassured Kate as they threw their bags in the boot.

Her frown told him she didn't agree. 'Living in Penzance is one thing Ian, but you know how different the weather can be on the moors at this time of year.'

He did, but as they drove past The Jamaica Inn on Bodmin Moor and the snow had only just started, the light covering on the A30 hadn't offered much of a challenge. Eager to try out his restored Discovery on the back roads, he'd "shut off his brain" and left the main road. 'We'll join up again later with the dual carriageway which by then will be gritted and cleared,' he'd informed her confidently before becoming totally lost on the unclassified roads. Old vehicles didn't come with complementary satnav.

However, a mile later, not even modern technology would have helped.

Sliding down the hill, trying to avoid the temptation of applying the brakes, he steered the SUV into a deep snowdrift causing the back end to spin sideways. 'That's it, that's as far as we're going. The tyres are useless in this weather.' Ian Henderson thumped the steering wheel with both hands, trying to make out it was the Land Rover's fault. 'We're well and truly stuck.'

'I told you we should have turned back, Ian,' his wife snapped. 'What the hell are we going to do now?'

'Mum, I'm scared, I hate the dark.'

'It's all right Lizzie, there's nothing to worry about,' her mum reassured her, leaning over the back of her seat and reaching for her daughter's hand.

But Kate knew there was plenty to fear in the height of a blizzard. In the restricted beam of the headlights, she could just make out the stone parapet of the bridge no more than three metres away. They were stuck, probably miles from their destination.

'C'mon Lizzie, this is like a big adventure on the telly, it's real exciting.' Sam was a big fan of Bear Grylls. Eagerly grabbing the door handle he asked, 'Does it mean we're going to have to walk in the snow, Dad?'

Ian nodded.

'Cool!' exclaimed his son, swinging his door wide open. Large, icy flakes immediately blew into the car.

Ian looked at his wife. 'It's either that or stay here and shiver. There has to be somewhere soon. I'll get the coats from the back. Right kids, everybody out.'

~

Thirty minutes later, the children wet and exhausted by the effort of fighting their way up the steep hill through the thickening snow, Kate read "Welcome to Lingtree" as a much relieved Ian brushed the layer of fresh, pure white powder off the sign.

'I told you we were probably somewhere near here,' he exclaimed. 'There's bound to be a place to stay.'

'I hope so, Ian,' she replied, shaking her head.

~

'I've a couple of doubles you can have… £60 a night each, take it or leave it.' It wasn't the "bonhomie" welcome expected from the landlord of a cosy country pub, but at least his bar was warm and dry, heated by the logs burning fiercely in a large, open, stone fireplace.

The two locals sat on stools had nodded politely. The odd stare the greasy, long-haired one, dressed in a full-length leather coat, had given the children hadn't gone unnoticed by Kate; instinctively she'd drawn her offspring closer.

Ian looked at his wife. She shrugged.

'We'll take them, thank you,' he confirmed. 'Are you serving food? We haven't eaten since breakfast.'

The landlord glanced at his locals. They smiled, giggling like nervous teenagers. 'I'm sure my partner could knock you up something,' he replied, his grin revealing gleaming white teeth. 'In fact, he's in the kitchen right now.'

'The kids will be happy with sausage and chips but

perhaps you can cook Kate and me something a little more substantial.'

Once again, the landlord looked at his regulars. 'No problem.' He raised his eyebrows. 'Our speciality might be nice by the way.'

Tight-lipped, the two men stared down at their half empty pints.

Lifting the counter flap, the landlord pointed to the hallway. 'I'll show you your rooms first. Been empty for a while, so they might feel a little bit damp. I'll put on the heating so they'll soon warm up.'

The Hendersons followed the dapperly dressed individual as he led them to a small office marked reception. Reaching through an open hatchway from the hall, he lifted two keys off a rack screwed loosely to the wall. The rack, roughly made from a half-metre-square piece of MDF, contained three rows of three hooks, the numbers one, two and three written underneath the top row, four, five and seven, under the middle row and eight, nine, ten on the lower one. All but room ten had a key and a large blue plastic fob hanging on the hook. 'This way, the staircase is just here.'

Ian noticed the guest book on the desk. 'Don't you want us to sign in first?' he enquired as the landlord turned away.

Without looking back, he replied, 'No need, we don't usually bother. Now, if you'd like to follow me. '

~

Fifty minutes later, Ian hurried Sam and Lizzie back to their room. Feeling the radiator, he sensed it was beginning to produce some heat but the air still felt damp and unwelcoming. Save for the area taken up by a large, open, bare stone fireplace with a heavy wooden mantelpiece, the end wall of the building was plastered and although no doubt originally painted white, like the bar below, the colour was now a nicotine brown. The firebox, although blocked off with a metal plate, was not well insulated and felt almost icy to the touch. The small window opposite the door rattled as the howling wind continued its insatiable swirling of the falling snow. Pulling the sun-faded, dull red damask curtains tightly together, he managed to get them to overlap, cutting out as much of the draught as possible. Tucking up Sam and Lizzie in the double bed, the heavy duvet, pillows and under sheet surprisingly well aired, Ian leaned over and kissed their foreheads. 'Goodnight kids, sleep tight, see you in the morning.'

'Where are you going Daddy?' asked Lizzie, her eyes beginning to close.

'We'll be in the bar having a drink and something to eat. The man said our food would take a while as he had to get it out of the freezer.' He pointed to the floor. 'This room's right above us, so be warned, we'll hear you if you don't settle down.' He raised his eyebrows at Sam. 'No television and no games or I'll take your phone away. You need your beauty sleep after that walk up the hill.'

Sam immediately sat up. 'That was exciting, Dad, especially when we opened the door to the pub and saw those men sitting there.' He waved his arm in the air, an imaginary weapon in hand. 'I thought about taking them out with my machete but it might have been a bit messy just before tea!'

'I'm sure Sam. Now then, both settle down… I'll leave the bedside light on; it's not very bright.'

'Goodnight Daddy, see you in the morning.'

'Night Dad, I'll look after Lizzie, make sure she stays safe and all that,' said her brother, snuggling back under the duvet.

As he closed the door, Ian Henderson couldn't possibly have known it would be the last time he'd kiss his children goodnight.

~

Kate was sat in the bar, her third large glass of Merlot beside her on the well-worn oak table. She was reading the book she'd found on the hallway table near reception. Ian sat down opposite, glad to take the weight off his legs.

She glanced up. 'It's all about the pub and the old castle next door. Apparently Judge Fredricks,' she pointed to a portrait in the book, 'used to come here in the seventeenth century to sit in judgement of people accused of breaking stannary laws.' Seeing her husband's furrowed brow, she explained, 'It relates to tin and forestry. He was a nasty bit of work apparently as, after hanging the guilty, they used to have them drawn and quartered as well.' Puzzled, she looked enquiringly at her husband. 'Does drawn mean what I think it does?'

Ian laughed at his wife's look of disgust. 'If you mean did they remove all their insides after cutting them in four, then yes, you're right.' He pursed his lips. 'Though I'm not sure in what order!'

'Really, that's vile. Who could do such a thing?' For a moment her husband's mind flashed back to the Middle East, his brutally butchered comrades, the smell of the hospital ward. He drained the rest of his beer.

'Anyway,' continued Kate, 'it goes on to say that some of the stone from the castle was used to rebuild one of the pub's bedroom fireplaces… room nine apparently and that this judge bloke regularly haunts it in the form of a snarling rabid dog-like creature!'

'Grrr! Glad I'm not in that room then,' replied Ian, not having noticed the screw missing from the top of the metal number on the kids' bedroom door which had allowed it to swing upside down.

'Me neither, but you shouldn't be so cynical. Don't knock what you can't disprove.'

'No dear, sorry,' apologised Ian sarcastically.

'I hope they hurry up with the food, I'm starving. This wine's making me hung… ' She paused, her eyes following the long-haired local as he brushed past their table, his full-length coat flowing behind him.

She looked at the picture, then back to the strangely-clad figure. Glancing behind him, he turned and made his way up the stairs. She shook her head.

'Are you all right Kate?' asked Ian, concerned at his wife's worried expression.

She frowned. 'Must be the wine.'

'What do you mean… what must be the wine?'

She looked at him blankly. 'Nothing. Just being silly.' She smiled. 'Thought I saw a ghost, that's all.'

He laughed. 'What do you mean, you saw a ghost?'

'Oh never mind. Just a bit tired, my imagination. No more wine though.'

'Are you sure?' he asked, eyebrows raised. 'I'm going to have another.'

She was sure. Kate just wanted food and her bed.

~

It was a further forty minutes before they were served their food by the bald-headed landlord.

'Sorry to keep you waiting, had a bit of trouble getting the liver out.' He placed their plates in front of them and then collected a condiment tray from the wide grey slate windowsill. 'Enjoy your meal.'

'Thank you,' acknowledged Kate. 'We're definitely ready for it.'

As the landlord made his way to a stool beside the two locals, the long-haired one having briefly visited the kitchen after his return from upstairs, Kate cut a slice of the liver.

'This meat's lovely, it tastes very fresh. I'm surprised it's been frozen.'

'Perhaps it's the landlord's way of getting us to drink more...' whispered Ian. 'You know, delays serving the food by saying it's frozen. He was quick enough with the kids' sausages. Hmmm, I haven't had liver and onion for ages... good choice Kate; it's so tender, so young.'

'Sorry darling, can't bear touching offal at home, but it's nice to have it out once in a while.' Her supper finished, she returned to the book. A few seconds later, she screamed hysterically.

'Kate… Kate. What's the matter, what's wrong?' Ian followed her eyes. She was staring at the ceiling, the part of her face not splattered with blood as white as the snow outside.

'Kate, are you all right? Kate… shit, what's that?' He wiped the top of his head, then his eyes, felt the warmth trickling down his neck. Overhead, an ominous red blemish had begun to engulf the years of tobacco-smoke-stained plaster.

'Oh my God Ian, the kids are in the room above here, aren't they?' she shrieked.

Together, Kate and Ian Henderson ran to the stairs. Ian shoved his wife to one side as they fought to reach the first floor's dimly lit, musty smelling corridor.

Ian stopped, his senses telling him the worst. Bright light shone from under room nine's door. Hesitating, he shook his head violently. 'No, this can't be happening.'

'Ian what is it? Why have you stopped? Let me get past, let me get to our children.'

He forced her back. There was no room to pass. Kate's screams deafened the air.

Desperate to know, but dreading what may lie beyond, Ian pushed the heavy wooden portal, forcing it open, the room number swinging from side to side as his bladder finally lost control…

~

Steadying himself, Brendon had shaken off the misty image. Assuring McKenna he was fine he'd returned his attention to the graves. As suggested by Hatcher, these were located just inside the field gate, a good ten metres away from the nearest archaeological trench. When asked what had made him dig, the "young" Sam told them for some unknown reason he'd had an urge to start moving the soil in the ditch running close to the hedge.

'It was as if someone was calling me,' the matted-haired youth, dressed in a T-shirt extolling the virtues of "making love rather than war", had told them. 'Like a voice in my head.' He'd thrown away the thick spliff when the two of them had first approached. However, whatever his reason, the decision had proved fruitful.

Digging graves any deeper without a mechanical digger, an aid the archaeologists were using to loosen the occasional granite rock covering the burials and cremations they'd so far discovered, would no doubt have been impossible.

Whilst the Iron Age graves contained trinket and weapon remains, the four shallow ones offered only bones and four pairs of wellington boots, the latter probably indicating the family were prepared for the snow. Clearly the bodies were of two adults and two children, a fact later confirmed by Brian Roundtree, the Home Office pathologist.

'Can't say how long they've been here but certainly a couple of thousand years less than those over there,' he'd joked as using a two-inch paintbrush, he painstakingly cleared the loose earth off one of the taller of the four. 'Will know more once they're back at the lab. Probably take a couple of days though provided the cavalry gets here shortly.'

Hatcher had been relieved when Roundtree told him

they should be able to clear the bones by early tomorrow, but not so happy when McKenna had said forensics may want a few days to examine the graves and surrounding area.

'Someone will have to pay for this delay,' Hatcher had exclaimed, pacing a couple of steps left and then right, obviously unconcerned for the feelings of any potential relatives of the presumed Henderson family. 'And we were doing so well.'

As Brendon and McKenna parted, the chief inspector was unaware of whether he would be allocated this case. He felt he had enough on his plate with Caroline's assault and the gorge body, but he'd thought it likely he and DS Pearson would be, especially as shortage of resources had increased every detective's workload. On the positive side, it might throw some light on the three other suspicious events McKenna had discussed with Brendon the evening he'd told him about Gareth's death.

Two years ago, we found Jess Withers, the forty-three-year-old managing director of Causeway Enterprises, dead at the bottom of an old tin mining shaft in the middle of the moor.

March 2014

'Mr Withers, welcome to Lingtree and to The Judge's Parlour.'

'Thank you very much. You must be Fred, we spoke on the phone,' replied the short, well-groomed, overweight man dressed in a tailored blue blazer, open neck shirt and chinos.

'That's right. My partner Bernard and I are the landlords, have been for the last few years.' Fred, a slightly effeminate, bald-headed man who always wore a red bow tie with his white short-sleeved shirt, immediately sensed he'd get on with his newly arrived guest, not that he'd do anything to upset his partner. They'd been together too long, although that didn't stop him flirting with any well-to-do male.

'Now, if you'd just like to sign the guests' book,' he continued, 'I'll get your key. We've put you in room eight, one of our newer rooms. Very charming and comfortable with a balcony overlooking our splendid garden. Nice on a pleasant evening with a chilled glass of our best Pinot Grigio.'

Jess Withers smiled. 'Thank you, not that I drink. Had to keep my head clear over the past several years; been building my business.' He passed the pen and book back to Fred. 'That's why I'm still on my own I'm afraid, bit of a bore you see.'

'Oh, surely not,' simpered Fred. 'We'll have to see what we can do to liven things up for you.'

'A rest and some moor walking is all that I need, thank you,' replied Jess Withers, already fed up with this sycophant. He picked up his holdall. 'If you could just show me to my room, I'd like to freshen up.'

'Of course... of course. This way.'

Fred swaggered up the stairs, turned left at the top and led his guest to his room. Walking over to the wooden-framed patio doors, he threw them wide open. He took a deep breath.

'You see Mr Withers, such a gorgeous room to enjoy all the delights of the countryside.' He stepped out onto the balcony decking. 'And you have a wonderful view of the castle as well as our beautiful beer garden. Some of the delightful plants are just beginning to bud. We've a very good gardener you know.'

'Yes, I'm sure that you have and I'm sure it's very nice, very nice indeed,' Withers acknowledged, tossing his bag on the bed. 'Now if you will excuse me, I'd like to get changed.'

'Of course, of course,' repeated Fred, 'no problem.' He tapped the bed as he crossed to the bedroom door. 'Very comfortable, tried it myself once; slept like a log.'

'I'm sure you did,' commented the exasperated guest. 'Now, if you wouldn't mind?'

'Of course, of course.' Stood in the doorway, Fred announced loudly, 'Dinner between seven and nine and breakfast seven-thirty to ten, unless of course you'd like a little something in your room.'

Jess Withers shook his head. 'The restaurant will be fine thanks.' He virtually pushed his host out as he closed the door.

After dinner that evening, Withers was comfortably seated in the public bar with a cafetière, reading the business pages of the previous Sunday's *Times* newspaper when a voice from behind interrupted him.

'I see you like a bit of share dabbling then.' It was Pete. He and Jim had been sat on their stools surveying the only other person in the room for the last thirty-five minutes.

'Sorry... hmm... did you say something?' asked Jess Withers, removing his reading glasses.

'I said... I see you like a bit of share dabbling,' repeated Pete, climbing down off his stool. 'I'm into it a little meself.'

'Ah, right... with you now. My apologies.' He put down the paper. 'In answer to your question, no I don't dabble, no time you see, but I follow the market... like to know what my competitors are doing.'

'You own your own company?' asked Pete, plonking himself on a low stool at the table. 'Which one's that then?'

'Causeway Enterprises... we're responsible for keeping the River Severn dredged... well, us and a few others. But we've been very successful over the last four years.' Had it been a different subject matter, it's unlikely he'd have given Pete the time of day, but talking about the way he'd built his company from a three-man business to one employing sixty staff and finally getting a listing on the stock exchange, was something he was happy to boast about to anyone.

'I see Mr... Mr... ?'

'Withers and you are?'

'Pete and this is my mate Jim.' Pete pointed to his "mate" who was currently engrossed in deep conversation with Arnold, the young barman whose face was still covered in acne. Jim had no interest in finance.

'Pleased to meet you Pete.' He nodded towards Jim, but didn't proffer his first name.

'And you Mr Withers. So how many co-directors do you have?' Pete enquired, hoping he might scrounge a pint.

'Just the one, though he's more of an accountant really. It's me that's done all the hard work. Without me, the company would fold.' There was no humour in his voice; modesty wasn't a trait. 'Now, if you'll excuse me, I'd like to read the rest of the paper. It's been nice meeting you.' He lifted his coffee cup, his little finger raised.

'Are you staying long?' Pete asked, getting up.

'A few days, perhaps more. I want to take in some "letterboxing" while I'm here.' He buried his head in his paper.

Five days later, after not returning from a planned walk over the two highest tors, Brown Willy and Rough Tor, his body was discovered by the local Moor Rescue Group at the bottom of a twenty-foot-deep shaft which somehow or other he'd managed to fall into head first. The pathologist, who was lowered in on a rope, confirmed Withers' stomach had been penetrated by an old cow's bone from one of several animals which had met their end in the shaft and consequently he'd bled slowly to death. The coroner had no choice but to return a verdict of "death by misadventure", adding that perhaps Mr Withers had lost his way in the dense mist which the army firing-range warden, located in his stone hut on Merlin Tor, testified had descended unexpectedly in the afternoon, blotting out the bright sunshine.

'Couldn't see me 'and in front of me face Your Lordship. One moment 'twas bright and sunny and next thing it was fuck... apologies, thick fog.'

The "letterboxing" guide found beside his body showed no reason why he should have been wandering on that part of the moor.

Unfortunately, without his direction, the share price of his company plummeted and three months later his business went bust; the insolvency practitioners said it was unlikely shareholders would get back their money.

Seven months after the death of Jess Withers, an eighty-five-year-old local disabled resident called Michael Enscale, lost his life when fire engulfed his house.

October 2014

'I'd be a fucking idiot if I didn't sell,' proclaimed Michael Enscale from his wheelchair parked by the bar as he sunk his eighth pint, his food-stained fawn cardigan soaking up the dribble running down the side of his dimpled glass. 'Ten thousand pounds per acre is what I'll be asking and I won't accept a fucking penny less.'

'I've told you before Dad, you'll never get that and once it's gone, you won't be able to buy it back again. They ain't making no more land you know.' Simon, his twenty-seven-year-old, unmarried son who lived with him in his house in the village a couple of hundred metres from the pub, wasn't of the same opinion. 'And anyway, 'tis only a fucking rumour at the moment.' He swallowed the last of his pint. ''nother one please Brenda.'

'Only if you both stop swearing; there's diners next door and the way you're both shouting you'll be putting them off their puddings,' Brenda the ponytailed landlady replied with good humour.

'Don't you tell me to stop swearing woman. If me boy and I want to have more beer, then we'll say whatever we fucking wants.'

Brenda thumped Simon's glass on the bar and leaned over as far as she could. 'Now listen here Michael Enscale, you may have lived in this village all your life and you may have made some money selling off your farm when you decided to retire, but that doesn't give you the right to use the language you want in my pub.' Brenda's goodwill had been stretched too far.

'Fucking previous queer boys didn't care what I said. Think they liked a bit of dirty talk,' he sniggered, meeting her stare. 'You just don't like cripples, that's your trouble woman.'

'Dad, for goodness' sake, shut your mouth. I want another drink.'

'Do what he says Michael, there's a good chap.' The calm and patronising interjection by David Soby who, until a moment ago, had been in deep conversation with Jim and Pete the only other customers in the public bar, failed to pacify the inebriated, irate man in the wheelchair.

'Don't you fucking tell me what to do you fucking hypocrite. I've heard you talking to that young waitress from up the road, telling her how you'd like to feel her tits and give her a fucking good seeing to in your vestry, you dirty cunt. Sticks your fingers up 'er short skirt every time she comes near you.'

'Right, that's enough.' It was the firm, no-nonsense voice of Graeme, Brenda's six-foot-plus husband. He'd been in the kitchen when his wife had come rushing out to get him. 'Out of here Michael and think carefully before you try and come back again. Simon, take him home will you?'

'But I isn't the one who's been swearing, Graeme.

It ain't fuc… sorry, it ain't fair if I can't have another,' pleaded the son with the gelled-up fair hair and red and white checked shirt.

Graeme looked at his wife; she nodded.

'Looks like it's just you then, Michael.' He began wheeling him out.

'Give me your keys Simon, I'll see him home,' offered the vicar. Simon picked them up from beside his phone on the bar.

'You ain't taking me fucking nowhere you fucking pervert,' protested Michael Enscale, wiping the saliva from his narrow, slimy lips with the back of his hand.

'Try and stop me. You're too drunk to crawl let alone operate a wheelchair,' the vicar joked as he steered Michael Enscale through the open doorway.

'You ain't heard the fucking last of this you bunch of wankers. You wait until they gives me my money. They ain't got no fucking access for their fucking great lorries without my land. I'll see you fuckers in… ' His voice faded as the vicar wheeled him home.

Brenda pulled Simon's pint.

'Thanks Brenda.' Sipping his beer he mumbled. 'I wish he'd hurry up and die.'

He had no idea that within the hour his wish would be granted.

~

'I'm so sorry Simon, I should have left him the keys, but I thought he might lock you out.' The vicar was sat on the concrete and wood bench outside the village hall, his arm around the young man whose father had just burnt to death in his own home. 'He would have been killed by the smoke before the flames got to him,' said Soby, as if these words would make the orphaned son feel better. Betty Enscale, Simon's mother, had died of breast cancer when he was just ten years old. His father had never remarried, although he'd had many short-term housekeepers look after him.

Fifty metres away, the immediate area taped off with blue and white tape, the fire brigade had managed to gain access to the smouldering property. The ambulance crew had departed leaving the charred and unrecognisable remains of Michael Enscale seemingly welded to his wheelchair. The undertaker was on his way and, supervised by two police officers, would be responsible for removing the body from the front hallway.

The next day, the investigating officer said the cause of the fire couldn't be definitely identified, but as it started near a night storage heater it was likely an electrical fault, although no trip switches had been thrown. His front exit cut off, Michael may at first have tried to escape via the door in the kitchen, but this had been locked and he'd had no keys. It had been Jim Evans who'd called the fire service, having joined Pete Grayson outside the pub for a smoke after returning from a long visit to the gents shortly after the vicar had wheeled Michael Enscale home.

'Dunno what's wrong with my fuckin' guts tonight; must have been something I ate!' he'd declared as he rolled up a fag.

He'd spotted the fire as it caught hold, but allegedly hadn't reacted immediately as he and Pete had taken a while to discuss whether Elsie Keel, who lived in the Old Bible Christian Chapel on the other side of the lane, had lit a bonfire that afternoon and the smoke was still drifting over the road. Had they not both been inebriated, their discussion may have been many minutes shorter.

Although his father's house was insured, Simon didn't want it rebuilt, but instead ended up living in a luxury, three-bed static caravan, situated on the parcel of land he'd inherited from his father. It had neither mains water nor electricity, but Pete Grayson was more than happy to let this fit young man use his toilet and shower facilities once Simon had walked the mile or so to his house. A petrol generator provided the power needed to run the caravan lights and the laptop Simon mainly used to watch his regular fix of porn. Allegedly, his mental health had been affected by the loss of his father and although he was made redundant from his job as a mining engineer in Camborne, his lifestyle wasn't affected; his BMW four-wheel-drive was often seen outside various nightclubs and brothels around the county.

'Must have inherited a fair old sum,' suggested Brenda and Graeme as they chatted with some of the locals, the ones who rarely visited the pub.

Our final cause of concern was the double death of Linda Collier, a blonde-haired, attractive and flirtatious thirty-year-old and her next door neighbour, Harry Elliot, a thirty-one-year-old wannabe extrovert. They lived in separate, one-window-fronted cottages, part of a row of three in the centre of the village and were both married; Linda to Paul, Harry to Laura and the two couples were said to be close friends, too close for Linda and Harry as it turned out. Neither couple had children and they usually spent most weekends drinking together in The Judge's Parlour.

November 2015

'Bitter for you Paul and gin and tonic for the luscious Linda.'

'Cheers mate.' Paul raised his glass, his large hand enveloping the straight pint glass.

'Yes, cheers Harry,' said Linda, her fingers teasing the palm of Harry's hand as she took her drink. 'Cheers Laura.'

'Cheers everyone. It's seems to have been a bloody long week.' Laura took a large swallow of Prosecco. 'Have to get another bottle in a minute, my love.'

'You're going for it,' remarked her husband.

'Looks like you're in for a good time later mate,' chuckled Paul, smirking at Harry.

'He should be so lucky. A few more glasses and I'll be out for the count. He'll have to wait a while longer yet,' announced Laura, shaking her head. 'Too tired for all that business.'

She wasn't joking. The last time she and Harry had made love, or had sex as she put it, was Valentine's night and that was only because whilst doing her bedtime stretches, he'd crept up behind her. Bent over naked, she hadn't enjoyed it, but she hadn't stopped him from finishing. Unrolling the well-lubricated and reasonably filled condom from his shrinking prick, he'd thought of

Linda next door and how exciting Paul's sex life must be. The sound of their creaking bedsprings penetrating the party wall as Harry had undressed had aroused his virtually redundant cock and the two bottles of red had given him the courage to remind it that it wasn't just for pissing out of. Fortunately, the K-Y jelly had made penetration comfortable.

'Not funny,' Laura had said as she climbed into bed beside him. 'You know how I feel about sex.' He did and as she turned off her light, he felt his cock begin to stir. Linda could be rather noisy when reaching her climax.

'So Paul, how's the driving going? Been far this week?' Harry asked, sitting down and taking a large slug of beer.

'Aberdeen. Flipping long way in an artic, but it pays well.' Paul belched. 'Oops, sorry ladies.' He rubbed his pronounced belly, the cotton holding on the buttons of his denim shirt stretched to its limits. 'Seems like I'm going to be on that run for the foreseeable future, so no chance of being home other than at weekends.'

Harry caught Linda's wink out of the corner of his eye. There had been a fear Paul would be transferred to short haul, meaning he could be at home most nights. Laura didn't always do late evening shifts, but it was unusual for her not to do at least three a week until 10 p.m.

It had been after a drunken night at the pub when Brenda and Graeme had had one of their regular "lock-ins" that Harry had discovered Linda was quite happy to extend her sexual favours to not just her husband.

As he'd returned from the outside gents, she'd met him by the reception.

'Just going out for some fresh air, fancy joining me?'

she'd asked grabbing his hand and virtually dragging him up the three stone steps to the garden. Ensuring they were alone, she wrapped one arm around his neck, clamped her lips on his and with her tongue exploring his mouth had reached for his zip.

'Christ, you're a big fucker, no wonder Laura can't cope with it.'

Whilst in Harry's real world he knew he wasn't anything other than average, her words had the desired effect and within seconds, he gasped as his cum shot over the grass. He hadn't said a word, but as she wiped her hand on a tissue pulled from her jeans pocket, she'd whispered,

'There, that's better, isn't it? My five fingers are far more enjoyable than yours, aren't they?' She did up his zip. 'Next time Laura's working, come round. I've got a hard-working mouth and a really moist fanny.'

He did and as a primary school teacher and churchwarden, she was exceptionally good at helping him learn. Even when he and Laura had had a sex life, it was usually him on top and although he'd use language his colleagues in the council planning office would never have expected to hear from him, it received no response from her. The only way he could bring her to a noiseless orgasm, was by wrist-numbing rubbing of her clit.

Linda was so different. Often dressed in stockings and suspenders, she loved oral, "doggy", on top, in fact all the stimulating lovemaking scenarios Harry had wanked off to when quietly watching late-night soft porn movies. However, despite this, "dogging" as opposed to "doggy" had never crossed either of their minds which is why it should have been considered strange they were found dead on the back seat of Harry's Volvo, having died from carbon monoxide poisoning. They were both naked, Linda sat astride her lover. They were parked in Lingtree Woods, a well-known "dogging" spot on the edge of Lingtree Forest, a large acreage of forestry land open to the public. An anonymous passer-by had telephoned the police and when the first copper arrived, the car engine had still been running. Blue oily smoke was pouring out from a hole in the exhaust pipe underneath the car and one rear window was slightly open.

The coroner decided on an 'open verdict' as the pathologist could not categorically state the gases inhaled through the window would have been sufficient to poison the occupants. It was, however, assumed that, as there had been a ground frost that night, the engine was running to drive the heater which the police confirmed was set on its highest output. The cold may have been a contributory factor to their deaths and was probably the reason there was only one other "participant" in the vicinity.

~

Brendon sipped his beer and tucked into his pie. Although not keen on offal, he found the small amount of fresh kidney enhanced the flavour of the lean, unique-flavoured steak. Jim was sat alone at the bar, finishing what Brendon guessed was probably his third pint. They hadn't spoken or acknowledged each other.

'Another please Phil,' Jim ordered, 'and a large whisky, blended will do.'

Phil began refilling the pint glass from one of three traditional handpumps, careful to ensure the beer came to a reasonable head. The locals weren't slow in coming forward if there was the slightest hint of their favourite pint beginning to lose its appeal.

'Pete not coming in tonight then, Jim?' the landlord asked as he pressed a tumbler against the spirit optic.

'Should be in later, Phil, with a bit of good news I hope. Won't be drinking blended shit then I can tell 'ee.' He smiled, his rotten teeth appearing green in the coloured, lacklustre overhead bar lights.

Phil placed the whisky glass next to the pint.

'How come?' Using the pen on the food order pad, he added the drink to Jim's ever increasing tab.

'Had a bit of luck on the stock exchange I hear. Made a bit of a killing.'

'Like he did with Causeway Enterprises?' asked Phil.

Jim nodded. 'S'right.' He glugged his beer. 'Something to do with "Put Options" he said, not that I understands it.' He tapped his back trouser pocket. 'Everything I've got is in me wallet.'

'And nothing comes out of there very often,' commented Phil.

'Very funny landlord.' The door opened. 'Ah Pete, me old friend. Was it good?'

Eyeing Brendon, Pete slid onto a stool and slapped his copy of *The Telegraph* on the bar.

'Evening Jim, evening Phil. Pint please.' He lowered his voice. 'Ten grand less expenses,' he whispered.

'Fuckin' 'ell,' exclaimed Jim. 'That was a fuckin' good tip that posh bastard from London gave you.' He scratched his head. 'Wish I'd had some spare but missus takes most of what I brings 'ome.'

'Expensive tastes still?' enquired Phil putting Pete's handled glass in front of him.

'Bleedy jewellery channel and that fuckin' online bingo. Lucky we've still got a house.' He downed his whisky. 'Your shout then Pete.' He passed his glass to Phil. 'That one's done thanks Phil. I don't want the flavour of me triple-sized single malt ruined.'

The three fell silent as Brendon made his way to the bar.

'Yes please Phil.' Jim and Pete stared at him. 'Can I help?' he asked, meeting their eyes. They looked away, but once again he felt the uncomfortable cold shudder run down his back.

'Cheers Phil.' He returned to his table. He sat down as Melanie appeared from the direction of the kitchen. She picked up his empty plate.

'Can I get you anything else Mr Gallagher?' she asked, tucking the salt and pepper pots into the condiment rack.

'No, that's fine thanks.'

'How's your lady friend? Has she woken up yet?'

Brendon observed her curiously. Everybody seemed to know everything. 'Still no change.' He noticed the scratches on the girl's neck. Pointing to them, he asked, 'What happened to you?'

Embarrassed, Melanie looked across at Phil. She covered the scratches with her free hand. 'Oh… err… nothing really. Had an argument with my cat.' It was more a suggestion than an answer.

'Have you put something on it, you know… antiseptic?'

She shook her head. 'It's nothing… honest.' She looked again at Phil. 'Best get back to the kitchen. Quiet in here tonight but the restaurant's busy.'

As she turned to go, Brendon asked, 'Is Jan not back yet?' Melanie ignored him and headed off.

'Gone to work at my business partner's hotel,' shouted Clegg. 'No ties here and wanted to earn more money. Nothing to worry about Mr Gallagher.'

Brendon hadn't been worried, but the fact Clegg mentioned it seemed to make it a cause for concern.

'Parents happy with that?' he asked. Pete and Jim stared at him.

'Old enough to make up her own mind,' replied Clegg. The bar door opened. A couple in their forties entered. 'Good evening sir, madam, what can I get you?'

Brendon held Jim's and Pete's stares for a moment then returned to his beer. He wasn't sure how old Jan was, but it hadn't struck him she was more than sixteen.

Aware that a further influx of customers, three couples and a group of five middle-aged women fresh from the village aerobics class by the look of their red faces and tied-back hair, would be keeping the landlord busy for ten minutes or so, Brendon decided to visit room nine, the room Clegg had not been keen to let him enter. Finishing his beer, he glanced around, checked Pete and Jim were engrossed in conversation, then walked nonchalantly towards the hallway leading to the reception office, kitchen and toilets.

Reaching the office, he checked behind him then leaned in through the hatchway and unhooked the key to room nine. There were no other keys on the rack.

Presumably, the rooms were occupied by some of the diners he could hear chattering loudly in the restaurant. After another quick glance round, he climbed the stairs two at a time.

Once on the landing, he surveyed the shadowy lit corridors to his left and right. They were empty and there were no sounds coming from any of the rooms. He crept to room nine, passing the door to room one, his shoulder brushing the uneven, yellowing white-emulsioned wall as he threw glances behind him. Hesitating outside the door, he carefully pushed the key into the lock. Another quick scan confirmed the all clear. Grasping the door handle, he turned the key. A loud click, the door gave a fraction and as he began twisting the recently polished brass knob, he heard the creak of a floorboard a split second before feeling the thud on the back of his neck.

CHAPTER TWELVE

11 May 2016

'Mr Gallagher… Mr Gallagher… are you all right?'

Through hazy eyes, Brendon saw the soft, smooth skin of Melanie's frowning, concerned expression leaning over him as he lay on the bed. His head hurt like hell, his hand immediately confirming the warm and wet sensation on his forehead wasn't sweat.

Melanie dabbed it again with the damp, bloodstained white towel. 'Thank God you're all right; he thought you were dead when he found you.'

Sitting up, he gazed about the room. It was room five, his own room. Puzzled, he focused his mildly misty eyes on hers.

'How the hell did I get here?' he asked, squinting as his vision began to clear.

'Mr Clegg found you at the top of the stairs. He thinks you must have tripped and knocked your head on the fire extinguisher,' she explained, dabbing gently. 'He's moved it now so no one else has the same accident. He said he should have listened to Grace. She was always saying it was dangerous.'

Brendon rubbed the back of his neck. 'How come I hurt here as well then?' His mind was muddled, uncertain, totally confused.

'Whiplash Mr Clegg said; same as in a car crash. Your head jerked back when you hit the extinguisher.'

'Really. I see.' But he didn't. 'How did he know it hurt? After all, it's my head.'

She giggled, lighting up her face. What a difference a smile can make thought Brendon as Melanie continued to dab, the undone top two buttons of her blouse revealing her youthful cleavage.

'Your hand was holding it silly, when he found you on the floor.' She examined the towel. 'Bleeding's stopped at last. Can I get you a drink; a brandy or something?'

He shook his head, immediately regretting it. The pain seared through his skull. Lying back, he closed his eyes. 'No, I'll be fine thanks and thanks for looking after me.'

'Not a problem, just pleased you're okay.' She folded the towel. 'Mr Clegg said if you still have a headache in the morning, he'll take you to A & E. Says there might be a risk of concussion and you could need stitches.' Crossing to the door, she pointed to the bedside table. 'There's some ibuprofen there if you want it.' She turned the handle. 'Now, are you sure you don't want anything, anything at all?'

He controlled the urge to shake again. Instead he raised his hand. 'No, I'm good thanks.' He began to yawn. 'A good sleep that's all I need. I'm really tired.' He closed his eyes.

'I'll say goodnight then Mr Gallagher. I'll see you in the morning.'

'Goodnight Melanie, see you at break…' He frowned. 'If you're up here, who's looking after the dining room?'

Laughing, she replied, 'The dining room closed four hours ago; it's one o'clock in the morning.' The door clicked behind her.

Brendon looked at the bedside alarm clock. Even the red LED numbers glared uncomfortably back at him; five past one. As much as the pain was making him confused, he knew it had been just after eight-thirty when he'd made his decision to visit room nine. Rubbing his neck, he was convinced he was struck from behind, but the blood and cut on his forehead clouded his certainty. Perhaps he cut it when he hit the floor, however right now all he wanted was sleep. He might still be getting paid by Her Majesty's Government, but he was on holiday and holidays meant not pushing himself past the limit.

~

Opening his eyes, he looked at the clock; 9.20 a.m. He touched his forehead. He could feel the lump under the congealed blood. Although his brain thumped, it was nothing like the bass drum someone had been banging inside it eight hours or so ago. Sitting up, his neck felt stiff but no more than that. He got up and twisted so he could just about see the back of it in the mirror. There was no sign of any bruising, but above his nose, there was the beginning of some severe discolouration around the seemingly deep one-inch cut.

He poured some tap water into the glass on the shelf by the washbasin. Unlike many hotels he'd stayed in, the water was genuinely cold and tasted good. Grateful Melanie hadn't chosen to undress him before treating his wound, he pulled off his clothes. He'd expected there to be some signs of blood on his shirt, but as far as he could see through his straining eyes, it was as clean as when he'd put it on.

The hot shower freshened him up and if he moved quickly, he'd still be in time for breakfast. He wasn't hungry, but he wanted to ask Melanie some questions.

'Sorry Mr Gallagher, 'er's not come in today. Mr Clegg has asked me to serve breakfast. What can I get you?' It was Grace, temporarily relieved of her cleaning duties.

'Just toast and coffee please Grace. Can't face anything heavy this morning.'

'Not surprised Mr Gallagher after your accident last night. Nasty cut you've got there.'

'You've heard?' She nodded. 'Slipped on the top stair apparently,' continued Brendon. 'I say apparently as I can't remember all the detail. Hit the fire extinguisher on the landing I'm afraid.'

'I don't think so Mr Gallagher,' she replied as she set off for his toast and coffee. 'I moved that over a month ago. It's in the left-hand corridor now.'

~

As she cleared up his dishes, Brendon asked Grace what had happened to Melanie.

'Can't help Mr Gallagher. I arrived to begin cleaning and Mr Clegg told me I was on breakfasts. Extra money, so I don't mind. Only three tables anyway, including

131

yourself. Other rooms are all businessmen so they'd had an early start.' She tutted. 'Not good going off to work on an empty stomach my mother always used to say. Now, if you'll excuse me, I must make a start on the bar before opening time.'

Brendon made his way gingerly up the stairs, the effects of his knock not completely cleared. Making an effort to recall the previous night's happenings, he dismissed paranoia; the stair carpet although slightly loose where it reached the landing wasn't dangerously so. As Grace had told him, the only fire extinguisher was in the corridor towards his room, although there was a faint, circular indentation in the carpet where it must have been located originally.

He looked to the left and right. The handles of the rooms between nine and five all jutted out from the doors, so perhaps if he stumbled after tripping, his head might have hit one of those. He inspected them all carefully; there was no sign of blood or hair. Room nine's was the same. He tried the handle; it was locked. Hearing footsteps he hurried back to the stairs.

'Ah Mr Gallagher.' It was Grace. 'Just on me way to get some clean tablecloths.'

'Hi again.' He glanced at the door to room two, opposite the top of the stairs. 'Grace?' he asked. 'How come the rooms going left from room nine are numbered one to eight rather than the other way around?'

She laughed. 'Nothing sinister Mr Gallagher. Seven and eight are extensions on the side of room five and when the owners renumbered the rooms, they wanted to keep room nine as 'tis, bearing in mind its history.'

'Which is?'

'Have to ask one of the locals. Jim and Pete would know the answer. Now then, if you'll excuse me— '

'So where're room ten and six?'

'Room ten's now used for storage so doesn't have a number and there's never been a room six.'

'Bit strange don't you think?' he asked automatically.

'No idea… before my time.' Keen to get on with her work, she took the cloths from the corridor cupboard and hurried off down the stairs.

Although eager to try room nine again, he decided to leave it until he knew Clegg was definitely out of the building. Instead, he'd ring the hospital and then touch base with McKenna.

'Still in a coma I'm afraid,' said a more friendly voice than the previous one, 'but doctor thinks she's improving and is hopeful she'll wake up soon.' She then added cautiously, 'But at the present he doesn't know how the injury will affect the brain.'

'Thanks,' replied Brendon. He rang McKenna.

'So how are you feeling after your fall? Hangover cleared yet?' joked McKenna after Brendon finished filling him in on last night's events.

'Three pints doesn't make me drunk,' Brendon responded indignantly. 'And anyway I wasn't at the top of the stairs when I fell, so I think someone decided to split my head to make it look like an accident.'

'Are you sure Brendon? Bit drastic. Concussion can do strange things.'

'I had the key to room nine and I'm certain I put it in the lock…' He hesitated. 'At least I think I did.' Suddenly

Brendon wasn't so confident. He began to feel faint. 'I'll ring you back Colin... not feeling so great... sorry.'

The knock at his bedroom door woke him.

'Come in.' He lifted himself off his bed.

'All right to come and do, Mr Gallagher?' asked Grace. 'I've left you to last.'

'Yes, yes, please do.' He glanced at his watch: Twelve-fifteen. He'd been asleep for an hour and a half.

'Are you all right sir?' She sounded genuinely concerned.

'Fine, just fine.' He looked out the window. 'Think I'll go and get some sun and fresh air Grace.'

'Good idea sir, 'tis a bootiful day.'

Once outside in the car park, he rang McKenna again. 'Sorry Colin, much better now. Any news on the gorge body?'

'Nothing yet Brendon and still unable to contact Ellie and Nathan,' McKenna advised him. 'Been allocated the four skeletons though. God knows where I start with them. Possible DNA might confirm it's the Hendersons, but after that... well... Johnson exhausted all avenues when they disappeared.'

'Perhaps the burial ground will throw up something.'

'I hope so Brendon. Forensics are still there, but the last I heard they'd found nothing of interest. Anyway, what are you up to?'

'Thought I might have a walk around the village this afternoon and then visit Caroline this evening. She's still in a coma, but... ' he sighed, 'you never know.'

'My fingers are still crossed Brendon. Let me know how it goes.'

'Will do.'

His head clearing, Brendon set off along the well-worn, tree-lined, unsurfaced lane running behind the pub. Used only by the occasional farm vehicle, off-road cyclists and walkers, tufts of grass and numerous weeds grew randomly between the rough, stony tracks. He passed an old granite outbuilding, its pitched roof missing several slates, the glass in the only window replaced by an ill-fitting piece of chipboard. Once used by the long gone, local butcher as a slaughter house, it was now relegated to just a good-sized storage shed. Peering through the gap between the padlocked, end wooden doors, Brendon saw old bits of furniture covered by torn sheets, the tears revealing settles and tables, perhaps either broken, or no longer required by the pub. After a couple more minutes, he reached an ancient spring, the water clear and refreshingly thirst quenching as, unruffled and untroubled, it burbled freely from the end of the short metal spout set in a half-metre-high stone. Climbing an overgrown and broken five-bar wooden gate he began following a narrow path running back parallel to the way he'd just walked.

Sprawling hazel and elder trees spread their branches over the rarely trodden path below the bank to the rear of the castle, while emerging stinging nettles, brambles and out of control blackthorn and hawthorn did their best to make passage impossible. As kids, he and his mates had often used this route to gain access to the gorge, not realising until they were in their teens, it was where the bodies of guilty prisoners, their innards crudely extracted, were thrown to the flea-ridden foxes and eager beaks of the crows.

As Brendon fought his way through the undergrowth, his jeans regularly snagging on the sharp prickles of the thorn, he covered his ears to the many imaginary hideous screams and pleas for mercy spewing from the mouths of the pitiless souls left dangling by the incompetent, inebriated hangman, as the executioner began sliding his rarely sharp knife down the length of their emaciated torsos.

Still feeling weak, his head beginning to pound incessantly, he scrambled fifty metres up the bracken infested earth bank from the path, as an enemy would have done if making an attack on the early Norman wooden stockade. Whereas an attacker would then have had to negotiate a ten-metre-deep ditch and timber rampart, in the twenty-first century, the defences were a boundary barbed wire fence and a sewerage works, where Jim and Gareth had often taken it in turns to ride the rotating arm as it emptied its contents over the stone filter bed, whilst Brendon and the others had watched, anxious not to go home smelling of effluent.

Crossing the sheep-grazed field between the church and the castle, he finally entered the churchyard through the wrought-iron gate. Sitting on the grass by a manicured yew tree, he heard no sounds, save those from the foraging ravens, carefully avoiding the unseen paths carved out by generations of living dead as they aimlessly wander in time, the endless rhythmic ticking of the watchmaker, beating the seconds from inside his tomb.

His peace restored, Brendon sat motionless, wondering when his final death would come.

CHAPTER THIRTEEN

Sat in the bar that evening, the heat from the log fire unnecessary, but the flames providing customers with the expected ambience of a cosy, country pub, Brendon watched Jim and Pete consume their normal excess of alcohol. His mind far away, he knew it would soon be time to go back. Once he did, he would probably lose Caroline forever, lost in another world, not one in which he could be part. He'd decided against visiting the hospital, realising there was little point. If she survived, he could stay with her for a while longer, but if she didn't wake up, then they would never meet. He would be close, but an unseen boundary would separate them for eternity. He desperately hoped she'd recover allowing him to enjoy her love one final time.

The door to the bar swung silently open.

''Ere vicar, what be having?' Jim asked immediately, as though responding to a senior officer's unexpected appearance in a subordinate's mess.

'Thanks Jim, but I'm not stopping.' David Soby flashed a glance towards Brendon. 'Just want to have a few words with Mr Gallagher. Catch up with you tomorrow.'

'As you likes then,' sneered Jim, turning his attention back to Pete. Soby crossed to where Brendon was sat in the corner.

'Mind if I join you?' he asked not waiting for an answer as he drew back the chair and sat down.

'Be my guest,' replied Brendon finishing his pint. 'Can I get you a drink?' Soby shook his head.

'Got to get back to church thanks. Meeting a couple to discuss their proposed marriage ceremony.' He smiled. 'Don't want to smell of alcohol.'

'Maybe next time?'

'Maybe.' Soby leaned forwards, his elbows on the table. He nodded towards Brendon's forehead. 'Nasty cut, an accident I assume?'

'Something like that.'

'Hmm, you want to be careful; could have been worse.'

'I'm sure you haven't sat down to discuss my medical condition.' Brendon was rapidly going off the clergyman.

'True.'

'So what do you want?'

'I hear you took the path behind the castle this afternoon.'

Brendon stared at him. 'News travels fast.'

'It's a small village Mr Gallagher, you should know that. Nothing much changes in a community like this.'

'Other than the vicar and the pub landlord,' offered Brendon, the hairs on the back of his neck beginning to rise.

Soby sat back. Choosing his words carefully, he held Brendon's eyes. 'Be that as it may, but what goes on here is best left to the locals.'

'Is that some sort of threat?'

The vicar leaned forwards again, his eyes still focused uncomfortably on Brendon's. He paused, then laughed. 'Only if you want it to be Mr Gallagher.' He rose from his seat. 'Alternatively, it could be a warning to ensure you come to no harm.' He pushed his chair under the table. 'Now then, if you'll excuse me, I must get back to my church, duty calls. Good evening.'

Brendon nodded. He watched Soby open the door, winking at Jim and Pete as he did so. They may have carried on their conversation, but Brendon was as sure as hell they'd heard every word the vicar had said.

'Enjoy your chat?' enquired Pete, as Brendon placed his glass on the bar. Ignoring him, he spoke to the landlord.

'Yes please Phil. One more before bed.'

'Sleepin' well are we, like a little puppy dog?' pressed Pete as the landlord pulled a pint.

'Now then Pete, I won't have you question the quality of my beds.' Phil's voice lacked any sign of humour. 'On the tab Mr Gallagher?' Brendon nodded.

'Not in room nine then?' asked Jim sarcastically.

'Wouldn't sleep well in that room whatever the bed was like,' sneered Pete. 'Not for all the tea in China or beer in Burton.' He turned his attention to his empty glass. 'At least one more before I go to bed please, Phil.' His tone was that of a young child. 'Don't want anything disturbing my night's sleep if you know what I mean.' He grinned, his nicotine-stained teeth matching the colour of the polished oak bar counter.

'Ever thought of teeth whitening? Dentists can do wonders these days,' retorted Brendon, his patience wearing thin. 'Perhaps you should go and see one.' Pete jumped to his feet but before he could say anything, he sensed Phil's piercing glare.

'I should go and have a fag Pete, it's a nice cool evening,' the landlord calmly suggested.

Pete glowered at Brendon through half-closed eyes. 'Good idea Phil, could do with getting away from this smart-arsed lump of shit.' Picking up his roll-ups and matches, he turned to his drinking partner. 'Coming Jim?' Jim obediently climbed off his stool. He looked at Brendon.

'You're not so clever Gallagher 'cos we've just seen a dentist.' The door closed noisily behind them.

'Sorry about that Mr Gallagher. They've been drinking since five.'

Brendon shrugged. 'Strange how friends can change Phil.' He stopped as he returned to his table. 'By the way Phil, what did Jim mean about seeing a dentist?'

The landlord smiled. 'David Soby, the vicar, used to be one before he turned to the cloth.' A well-dressed female approached from the large table by the fireplace where she was sat with four friends. 'Yes, my luv, what can I get you?'

CHAPTER FOURTEEN

12 May 2016

After his "friendly chats" with the vicar, Pete and Jim, Brendon suffered a restless night. Although worried about Caroline, the main reason for his lack of sleep was the screams emanating from the other end of the corridor.

His legitimate attempt to enter room nine had failed; however, the time would soon come when he would walk undetected past the portal but not just yet. He needed to find out more and he could only do that if he remained the person everyone in the village, plus McKenna and Pearson, thought him to be.

'Ah Melanie, nice to see you again.' She looked tired. Brendon saw the scratches on her neck had begun to fade. 'I thought you must have left us.'

She smiled as she poured his coffee. 'I was feeling poorly so I couldn't come in,' she explained. 'Mr Clegg wasn't too happy though.'

'Grace stood in for you. She said it wasn't too busy. Business people she said; all left early.' He noticed her enquiring expression. 'Is that not right then?'

'But I thought they were all workers from the railway. That's who were at dinner the night before. Surveyors and—'

A loud voice came from the swing door to the kitchen. It was Clegg. 'Now then Melanie, no time for gossiping. Plenty of washing up to do.' The landlord appeared around the partition obscuring direct vision into the kitchen. 'I'll see to Mr Gallagher.'

'Yes Mr Clegg.' She put down the coffee pot and hurried away.

'Poor girl; gets a bit confused at times. Something to do with a kick on her head from a horse she had as a child.' He picked up Brendon's empty cereal bowl. 'Now then Mr Gallagher, are you going to have a fried breakfast, only it's past ten and cook's keen to start preparing luncheons?' Brendon shook his head.

'I'm fine thanks,' he replied. 'Just finish my coffee and I'll be gone.' He rubbed his chin. 'Hmm, I thought the railway couldn't start until the dig had ended.'

'That's what I understand Mr Gallagher.' Tidying the serviettes in the glass on the breakfast stand, he continued, 'As I said Melanie gets a little confused. Now then, if that's all, I'll leave you to it.' He nodded and returned to the kitchen.

Brendon followed him, stopping when he reached the swing door. He leaned one ear towards it.

'I've told you girl, what goes on here is none of your business. I pay your wages, and a bit more besides for the extras you provide to keep the men happy.' Clegg sounded agitated. 'I've got enough on my plate without upsetting the locals. As far as Gallagher's concerned, we have businessmen staying here and that's that.'

'But… but… ' Brendon heard Melanie protesting.

'But nothing young lady. If you want to keep your job and earn the money you needs, you keep quiet, same as I, Grace and the others do. Understand?' Melanie must have understood as there were no further exchanges. Finishing his coffee, Brendon decided to ring the hospital from his room.

'She woke up last night sir,' a young nurse told him, 'but she doesn't remember anything. Doctor thinks she's got amnesia, you know, loss of memory.'

'Yes, yes I know what amnesia is,' acknowledged Brendon impatiently. 'Can I come and see her?'

'Just a minute.' She put him on hold. Three minutes later she confirmed it would be okay provided he didn't spend too long with her; she was still very weak.

~

'Hello young lady, how are you feeling?' It was a silly question but common enough when inhaling the clinical smell of a hospital ward.

She managed a smile. 'Been better thanks.' She held his outstretched hand. 'What happened Brendon? Why am I here?'

'Someone took a disliking to something you said or did. The police are trying to find out.' He sat on the edge of the bed, still holding her hand. In spite of the bruising to her face and forearms, underneath it all, she remained strikingly attractive. 'Can't you remember anything?'

She shook her head feebly. 'Nothing, nothing at all. I

can't even remember what time of day it was or what I was doing. They said I was still in my underwear.'

Looking at her laid back in the unflattering hospital gown, he recalled their afternoon together. She'd been wearing a red lace bra and matching panties and as she kissed his lips and nibbled his ear, she'd whispered, 'Gareth has never seen me in this, I saved it for a special occasion.' Sliding the straps over her shoulders, Brendon noticed how her breasts remained firm, her nipples large and erect. She'd looked after herself well.

'We think you must have been attacked immediately after getting out of bed, unless of course you like to do the housework in your underwear!' he joked, hoping to lighten the mood.

'Not usually,' she replied, her eyes intent on his. 'At least not unless you're helping me wash up.'

Managing to remain focused, he asked, 'Was anyone staying with you as there was no sign of forced entry?' He was grateful her answer was no.

'I'm sure I'd remember and I always lock the doors… sort of a night-time ritual.' She yawned. 'Sorry Brendon, I'm so tired.' Her eyes closing, she released the grip on his hand.

'No problem, my love. Rest, there's plenty of time for questions.' He kissed her gently on the forehead. 'We'll get whoever did this to you and I'll make sure they suffer.' Whether or not she heard him, he didn't know or care. He would get even before he left her world and those responsible would receive no mercy.

Sat in his car in the hospital car park, he rang McKenna.

'Caroline's awake but very tired,' he told him. 'She can't remember anything about the attack.'

'Nothing at all?' queried McKenna.

'No, not even the time of day it happened despite what she was wearing.'

'Bollocks!'

'Any joy with the bodies at the dig?' Brendon hoped there'd be some good news for the chief inspector.

'Based on their age and time the family disappeared, the pathologist thinks it's likely the bones belong to the Hendersons. Hopes to trace dental records today and confirm for sure.' He didn't mention the male adult had already been identified from his DNA. Brendon heard him sigh. 'Still nothing on the body in the gorge though. No identification, no one reported missing, no bloody anything to go on. My superintendent's not a happy bunny.'

Brendon felt sorry for him. He wanted to tell him he could help, that perhaps in time he would answer many of his questions, but not just yet. He needed Caroline to himself for a while longer.

'Something will turn up, it's bound to.' His attempt to reassure McKenna fell on stony ground.

'I wish I shared your confidence Brendon. Lingtree's had more than its share of unexplained deaths.' Someone in the background spoke to McKenna. 'Brendon, I'll be right back.' The line went dead.

It was another hour before McKenna rang, by which time Brendon had returned to Lingtree.

'It's the Hendersons. Dental records confirm it. Now I definitely have another four murders on my hands. Speak to you again later.'

~

Finishing his sandwich in the comfortable pub garden, the caringly manicured shrubs providing natural shelter from the slight north-westerly wind, Brendon decided to follow up on Melanie's comment about the railway workers. She wasn't serving lunches; Grace had stepped in to do that again.

'Poor old Melanie, not well again Phil tells me. He's getting a bit frustrated with 'er,' she'd said smiling as she served his food. 'Still, good for me pay packet. No new residents booked in again so can always do the beds in the afternoon after I've done the old man's dinner.' Scurrying back to the kitchen, she'd added, 'Lovely out here; enjoy the sunshine Mr Gallagher. Nice day for a walk if you ask me.'

'Thank you Grace, will do,' he shouted after her.

Bearing in mind the overheard conversation in the kitchen, Brendon wondered how much of what Grace had told him was true. He was beginning to think the only person he could trust was Caroline and just at the moment, there wasn't a lot she could do to help him.

Wiping his mouth, he screwed the red paper serviette into a ball and dropped it onto his empty plate. Fifteen minutes later, he could believe one thing Grace had said; it was indeed a lovely day. As he walked along the route of the Corpse Way, past where a small stream emerged from a temporary meandering underground, a much used place as a cycle water splash when he was a kid, he thought how tranquil and peaceful everything seemed, not like the Treforthamm he would have known in AD 996. It had been a horrendous battle and he, like his comrades, would have been tired and eager to get back to the ship moored some twenty miles or so away. He would not have been interested in leaving his seed in the fallen women, nor in pillaging the silver coins or burning the wooden church, but would have merely watched as brave men died defending everything they'd worked so hard to achieve. It was strange how a thousand years later the residents of Lingtree would invite a modern day Viking to mark the attack on their village by carving and erecting a runic stone for all to see. Later, a group of his fellow countrymen would re-enact the battle and join in the celebration of the deaths of so many. Had the current village residents witnessed the carnage and rape of that day in AD 996, their hatred would surely have lived on 'til eternity.

'Ah Mr Gallagher.' It was Frank Hatcher. 'I expect you know they've finished at last.'

Woken from his reverie and startled by his approach, Brendon gazed at him blankly. 'Hmm... sorry... what did you say?'

'The police forensic lot, they've gone.' Puzzled, Hatcher looked at him, as if studying a newly discovered artefact. 'Are you all right Mr Gallagher?' He appeared genuinely concerned.

'Yes, yes I'm fine. Just a bit tired that's all. My axe is very heavy.'

Hatcher looked at Brendon's hands, then back at his face. It was his turn to apologise. 'Not with you I'm afraid. Thought you said axe.'

Brendon shook his head clear. 'Facts, I mean. The facts are weighing very heavy.'

'Ah yes, of course, much to digest, bones and all I suppose. Sorry to be so nosy.'

Brendon shook his head. 'No, that's fine Mr Hatcher. Pleased to hear you can get on with your dig.'

'Good news, very good news. Much to do.' He glanced around him. 'Are you going far?'

'Only to look at the proposed railway siding.'

'I see…' Hatcher paused, shifted from one leg to the other. 'Well, 'err, perhaps I could show you. Could do with a break myself. How about it?'

A few minutes' walk from the water splash, they stopped in the lane by a recently installed, metal, double field gate on the left-hand side leading to an area cleared of trees and brush. Measuring approximately five acres in all, boundaries were marked with temporary wooden posts and red and white tape.

On the far side of the cleared area was the tree and bush-lined hedge of the once great GMR railway, neglected and dormant after the metal tracks and wooden sleepers were lifted by contractors forty plus years ago, the transport of freight and passengers considered to be more efficiently undertaken by lorry and car. In the distance, the tors of the moor provided an attractive backdrop, the clear blue sky adding to the feeling of an uninhabited and peaceful countryside. Approximately fifty metres away towards the viaduct was the archaeological dig, where no more than three men and two women were working diligently with their small trowels. However, the railway workforce consisted of only two men, one holding a black and white ranging pole, whilst another peered through a theodolite. It struck Brendon as rather quiet.

'So this is where the siding will be?' he asked, scanning the barren land.

'So I understand Mr Gallagher. Not really my concern; more interested in the burial site before they start bringing in their diggers and oversized lorries.'

Brendon noted how the quarry railway line could be joined to the defunct main line, although in doing so destroying a length of the Corpse Way. Reopening the old line, bearing in mind how much of it had been sold off to farmers and residents who had used the opportunity to extend their gardens, not to mention closing the popular cycle track, would be quite an undertaking. He assumed the price of tin would make it worthwhile.

'No, of course,' he replied. Seeing the luxurious static caravan over the hedge adjoining the site of the proposed siding, he asked Hatcher, 'Is that Simon Enscale's?'

Hatcher nodded. 'That's right. I'm told he won't move. Hasn't made a lot of difference to us. What we couldn't carry between us, we managed to bring up the lane in a Land Rover. It'll bugger up the construction lorries though if they can't get access.'

'Compulsory purchase perhaps?' suggested Brendon, shrugging his shoulders.

'Probably, but it's one thing to get an order on undeveloped land but another to get someone off it. Could take ages.' Hatcher looked at his watch. 'Now if there's nothing else I can do for you Mr Gallagher, it's time I got back to work. Bit short-staffed at the moment; sent them home because of the police work; might be difficult to get them back now.'

'No, that's fine Mr Hatcher, thanks for your help. I'll stay and have a look around if that's okay.'

'All right by me; as I said, the siding's not my responsibility.' He turned on his heel and headed for the dig, stopping abruptly as he heard Brendon ask:

'Have you started on the tunnel yet, you know the one from the gorge to the castle?'

Hatcher looked at Brendon sternly. 'It's not possible, too dangerous. Not worth the risk. Goodbye Mr Gallagher.'

Odd, thought Brendon as he climbed the gate and made his way to the man holding the theodolite.

'Hi... Brendon Gallagher.' He held out his hand. 'I'm staying locally. I know Caroline Pettit, the owner of the land next door.'

The man shook his head, shrugged his shoulders. 'So?' he asked brusquely.

Taken aback, Brendon withdrew his hand. 'So... I thought I'd say hello.' The man turned away.

'Goodbye,' he said. It was only one word, but Brendon immediately detected an accent. 'I'm busy and this is a construction site, not open to the public.' He picked up his instrument, closed the tripod and wandered off in the direction of his colleague. Brendon stood rooted to the spot, his brow furrowed. It hadn't been the reaction he'd expected and the reason for the small numbers working on the dig didn't add up either.

Would you really send people home for what was likely to be no more than two days at the most? he asked himself, eventually returning to the gateway where he and Hatcher had chatted. *Perhaps you do.* He wasn't convinced.

Rather than walk back the way he'd come, he

continued along the Corpse Way, passed under the viaduct, crossed the river by a narrow wooden footbridge, then after a short walk through a cutting formed by a tall field hedge and the edge of a wood adjoining Pete Grayson's property, he eventually met up with the lane leading towards Caroline's house.

The blue and white tape still ran across the front of the gate. There was no sign of any police presence, although he noticed the gate bore what looked like a brand new padlock.

Climbing the gate, he didn't really have any idea why he was there. It was as though something in his subconscious had summoned him. The house had been gone over by forensics; he'd had a quick look around when he'd discovered Caroline, as indeed had DS Pearson. However, something had drawn him to it and he had to know what. He checked the front door; locked, as were all the downstairs windows at the front.

There was an unlocked wrought-iron gate to one side leading to the back garden whilst the other side had double-width wooden field gates leading to the farmyard a further thirty metres or so to the rear of the house. These were also padlocked. From here he could see the various barns, an open one containing a four-wheel-drive John Deere tractor, whilst he knew the closed one contained a fully restored Series One Land Rover which Caroline had told him was Gareth's pride and joy and which he wouldn't let her drive. She'd have to sell it, but not for a while she'd told him the day they'd made love. He assumed the shed also contained her dark blue Nissan four-wheel-drive. The three large, partly enclosed cattle sheds were all empty, their winter occupants happily grazing the fresh spring grass. Several different farm implements were parked untidily around the yard, some partially covered by torn and soiled tarpaulin.

Brendon made his way back to the other side of the house and opened the small gate into the post and rail fenced garden. Immediately, he fell backwards, fortunate not to strike his head on the concrete path. The screams had been deafening, penetrating his brain like a dentist's drill burrowing into his ears.

'No, no, please stop.' It was the voice of a young woman. More screams followed. Brendon jumped to his feet, his eyes drawn to the open upstairs window. 'Please don't do it, please don...' As suddenly as the screams had started, they were just as quickly gone, the silence filled by the "whoop, whooping" of a pheasant wandering through the long grass in the fields beyond and the "keeow" of a buzzard circling for an early supper.

His head still full of the piercing scream, the natural sounds went unheard by Brendon. He rushed to the back door. It was locked. Without hesitating, he lunged against it with his shoulder. The pain seared down his arm.

'Fuck!' he exclaimed loudly, 'fucking solid doors.' Picking up a small piece of granite from the edge of the ornamental fish pond, he smashed one of the four small panes of glass in what he knew to be the toilet window. Reaching in, he managed to release the catch and squeezed through the narrow opening. Running up the uncarpeted stairs, he darted into the bedroom from where the screams had come. It was Ellie's and it was empty. He frantically checked the other two bedrooms, the en suite, the family bathroom, wardrobes, under the beds and the airing cupboard and he even stood on a landing chair and lifted the hatch to the loft. Nothing, nothing at all.

He carried out the same fruitless search downstairs. The front door was locked. Returning to the first bedroom, he stood motionless in the doorway; the window was closed, as were all the others in the house.

Sat in the lounge, he swallowed the very large Scotch he'd poured from the decanter on the dresser, images of Syria soiling his thoughts. He poured and drank another. Opposite him sat Caroline, her thin, see-through negligee covering her naked body. She smiled at him, pouting her lips. She tugged at the belt holding the edges of her robe together. Standing, she let it fall to the ground and took the two steps towards him. He welcomed her with open arms. Accepting his embrace, she placed one leg either side of his. He leaned forward to kiss her breasts, his eyes following his empty glass as it bounced on the carpet. Squeezing thin air, he wiped away his tears.

The broken window partially covered with a small wooden shelf he lifted off a wall in the utility room and the handle jammed with a metal ladle, he shut the front door behind him. Ensuring it had self-locked, he took one last sweep around the outside before starting his journey back to The Judge's Parlour still totally unaware of why he'd been summoned to the source of the screams.

His head continuing to swim, possibly from the effects of the Scotch but more likely from the heart-rending experience, he ordered a large malt.

'Bit warm for a spirit I would have thought Mr Gallagher.'

For a split second Brendon contemplated the landlord's remark, wondering if it was an intended pun. Regardless, he emptied the glass. 'Another please Phil.'

'Certainly, sir.' The glass replenished, the landlord leaned on the bar. He spoke quietly, not that there was anyone else there to overhear him. 'I don't mean to be rude Mr Gallagher, but you have run up a pretty large tab what with the accommodation, drinks and meals. I was just—'

'You mean you want money,' interrupted Brendon, his voice slurred. Downing the Scotch, he pulled his wallet out of the back pocket of his trousers and tossed his credit card at Phil. 'Take what you want; it won't be much good to me soon.' He looked at his empty glass. 'And put another double on it... and a pint... and one for you.'

'Thank you Mr Gallagher; much appreciated.'

Brendon was sat in his usual corner when Pete and Jim entered. Seeing their look of disdain, he couldn't help himself. 'Fuck off will you? Just fuck off.'

Pete and Jim looked at each other, then at the landlord. Phil shook his head. 'Leave it lads, I don't want any trouble.' They laughed.

'Right you are Phil. Sounds as though the little fella's had a bad day,' scoffed Pete. 'Must be missing his sweetheart, you know the one he shagged whilst her dead husband was still warm in his coffin.'

It took all of Phil's and Jim's strength to pull Brendon off Pete. He hadn't struck him, but Pete was gasping for breath as he lay on the floor. The way Brendon had grabbed his throat, it seemed for one moment Pete wouldn't be downing any more alcohol.

No words were exchanged. Brendon finished his beer and "chaser", took one last look at Pete as his mate Jim helped him to his feet then left by the front door. His head was clear. He'd gone into automatic pilot when Pete had made his jape. Let him call the police, let Phil kick him out; he didn't care. The time was close so what did it matter?

CHAPTER FIFTEEN

The landlord of The Judge's Parlour didn't kick him out; he didn't even tell him directly not to cause any more trouble. Either he needed the money, or he was on Brendon's side when it came to Pete and probably Jim for that matter. Whatever the reason, when Brendon returned much calmer after exchanging pleasantries with several walkers and horse riders as he strode purposely along "The China Clay Way", an eleven-mile tarmac-surfaced cycle route laid on the old railway line in the direction of Melkthorpe, Phil was more than helpful.

'I've put you in the corner, next to the fireplace Mr Gallagher. Best table in the restaurant.' It wasn't, but it was a nice gesture.

'Thank you Phil. I'm sorry about earlier.'

'No problem,' he replied. 'I'm sure it was just a one-off.'

'It was,' Brendon assured him.

'Good. Now then, I'll give Grace a call. She shouldn't be a moment.'

'Melanie no show again?' asked Brendon, disappointed he wouldn't get a chance to ask her about the railway workers.

'Hmm… err… Melanie's left us I'm afraid,' answered Phil, avoiding Brendon's enquiring look. 'Wasn't for her she said, found it all too much.' He picked up the menu. 'Liver and onions on the specials' board tonight; fresh from the butcher's this morning.'

Brendon shook his head. 'Not for me thanks Phil. I'll have a think.'

'Leave you to it then Mr Gallagher.'

'Bit quiet tonight,' said Brendon as the landlord turned to go. 'What's happened to all the businessmen?'

'Sometimes they eat up the road… at the posh guest house with the bistro… just for a change you see.' Wringing his hands, he left, brushing past Grace on his way to the public bar.

'Hi Grace, how are you?'

'Fine Mr Gallagher, thank you for asking,' she replied as she walked to his table. 'Have you decided what you'd like? Liver's good.'

Brendon smiled. 'No thanks, really not keen.' He lowered his voice. 'Grace, what's happened to Melanie?' he asked checking over his shoulder the landlord hadn't returned. Grace blushed.

'Gone to stay with her aunt I believe.'

'Did her mother and father live in the village?'

'Mother died at childbirth; not long after, her father left home. Brought up in care but been living with her boyfriend for a year or so now. 'eard they've fallen out though.' She glanced towards the bar. 'Now what would you like?' She shifted from one foot to the other.

'Probably the chicken with rice or… should I have the fish again?' Grace looked at her watch. Brendon waited a moment. Eventually he confirmed, 'Chicken, definitely.'

She grabbed the menu from him. 'Anything to drink sir?'

'Just water thanks Grace; I've had enough for one day.'

'Right, chicken and water it is.'

'Thanks Grace. Oh, one more thing.'

'And what will that be?'

'The railway workers who dined here last night; how many were there?' Brendon saw Grace's lips tighten.

'Railway workers, Mr Gallagher? I think you must have been dreaming.' Order taken, she wasted no time disappearing behind the kitchen partition.

~

Brendon sat in the garden, the red sunset forming a photographer's dream backdrop. Completely sober after his walk and meal he answered the call from McKenna.

'How are you Brendon?'

'Been better thanks Colin. How about you?'

'Why, what happened?' McKenna asked ignoring his question.

'Nothing to worry about Colin, just a slight misunderstanding between me and one of the locals.' He had no intention of telling McKenna what he'd heard at Caroline's house.

'One of your ex-friends?'

'Correct.'

'And Caroline?'

'I spoke to her a few minutes ago on the phone. She's still not there yet but much better.'

'Memory?'

'Nothing, sorry.'

'Shit, I was hoping things might be coming back to her.'

'Any news at your end?' enquired Brendon.

'Bugger all I'm afraid. Uniform have been doing the rounds of the village again but nobody knows anything. Bit of a closed shop if you ask me.'

'How did the Hendersons die?'

'Broken necks. Each skeleton had disrupted vertebrae; possibly caused by hanging.'

'Definitely murder then?' Stating the obvious however sarcastically wasn't normally Brendon's forte.

'Looks like it.' McKenna let out a deep sigh. 'What're your plans for tomorrow?'

'I'm going to visit Caroline around ten.'

'I'll meet you at the hospital. Sleep well.' The call ended.

Brendon didn't sleep well. He heard more screams. He lay awake, wanting to pray for Caroline to gain good health, but he practised no faith.

CHAPTER SIXTEEN

13 May 2016

Pulling into what appeared to be the only space left in the overburdened hospital car park, a few rows away, he saw McKenna leaning against the top of his car. As soon as he spotted Brendon, he pressed the remote and headed towards him.

'Morning Brendon.'

'Colin.'

Brendon entered his registration as though attempting to push every key through the machine's back plate, snatched his ticket, threw it on top of the dashboard and slammed the door.

'Are you okay Brendon? You seem a little agitated.'

'Not my best night, thanks Colin. Too much alcohol and... well... other things on my mind.' He attempted a smile. 'I'll be fine thanks; wishing I'd had breakfast though. C'mon, let's see how the invalid is progressing.'

'Hi Caroline.' She was sat up, her head propped against the pillows.

She returned Brendon's greeting before regarding McKenna suspiciously.

'It's all right, my love,' Brendon assured her. 'This is Detective Chief Inspector McKenna. He's an old friend and is investigating your assault.'

'I still don't remember anything,' Caroline apologised. 'Nothing seems to be coming back.'

'Not to worry Caroline,' comforted McKenna, hiding his frustration, 'these things take time.'

'Thank you Chief Inspector. I'm so sorry I can't be of any help.'

'No rush, no rush at all Caroline,' said Brendon. He took her hand. 'You concentrate on getting better, that's the most important thing.'

'Thank you Brendon, you've been so kind.' She frowned. 'Are Ellie and Nathan coming to see me?'

McKenna and Brendon exchanged glances. Caroline immediately picked up on their hesitation.

'They're not, are they?' Her head dropped.

'Umm… ' Brendon ran his hand through his hair. 'It's not that… ' He paused. 'It's just that… we just haven't been able to get hold of them yet. I'm sure they'll come as soon as they hear.'

Caroline's eyes watered; her lips tightening. 'What, neither of them?' she asked.

McKenna shook his head. 'One of my constables is on the case; she's doing her best at contacting them.' If he sounded confident, he didn't feel it. It had been a while since DS Pearson had first tried to get hold of them since when she'd instructed one of her subordinates to chase.

Caroline closed her eyes as tears ran down her cheeks. Brendon kissed her on the forehead.

'Ellie's in the back of beyond somewhere and Nathan's on secret manoeuvres,' he told her, his voice calm and gentle. 'They'll be here soon, you'll see.' He turned to McKenna. 'Best leave her I think.'

McKenna nodded. 'I'll meet you in the cafe Brendon; there's something I want to talk to you about.' After saying his farewell to Caroline, McKenna left them alone.

'Brendon.' Caroline's eyes opened. He stroked her head. 'It wasn't his fault,' she added.

He frowned. 'What wasn't, Caroline?' he queried, taken aback by her comment.

Her head turned to one side on the pillow, her eyes closing. 'Don't say anything to the detective,' she pleaded. She held his arm. 'Promise you won't say anything.'

'Of course I won't.'

'Promise me.'

'I promise.'

'Thank you Brendon.' Caroline began to breathe deeply. 'I always did love you Brendon,' she whispered before falling asleep.

~

The hospital cafe was busy, the chattering echoing around the sparsely furnished area tacked on to the side of the entrance hall.

'Sugar?'

'No thanks Colin.' Brendon stirred his coffee. He

hadn't mentioned Caroline's strange comment. 'Now, what is it you wanted to talk about?'

McKenna poured two sachets of sugar into his cappuccino. He leaned back. 'There's something I should have told you before I asked you to keep your eyes open.'

'Which is?' asked Brendon, sipping his drink.

'The reason the previous landlords left The Judge's Parlour.'

'You mean before Phil?'

McKenna nodded. Sitting forwards, he played with the milky froth. 'They weren't just a… shall we say… normal couple running a pub.'

'Sorry, not with you.'

McKenna looked up. 'They were undercover cops who'd received a crash course in pub management.'

Brendon laughed. 'You're having me on?' he said cynically, instantly dismissing McKenna's admission. However, McKenna's serious expression told him he wasn't. 'But for Christ's sake why?'

McKenna dropped his spoon into his saucer. 'Because of the Hendersons and Jess Withers.' He drank some cappuccino. 'We put Brenda Polson and her husband Graeme in just over eighteen months ago,' he explained. 'They'd met whilst on previous separate undercover jobs and saw the opportunity of running a pub as an apprenticeship for a role after retirement from the force.'

'And you think those deaths were connected?' asked Brendon, still somewhat disbelieving of McKenna's revelation. 'Enscale and the two neighbours must have happened on their watch, so how come they weren't able to prevent those?'

McKenna shrugged. 'You're right, but we weren't getting anywhere with any of our enquiries, that is my predecessors weren't and as you say, more deaths whilst they were there. When Gareth Pettit was found dead in the castle, it added to the frustration.'

'But your cops were gone before Gareth was found.'

'Correct.'

'But why were they pulled out?' Brendon shook his head. 'I mean if the other deaths weren't solved—'

'They weren't pulled out,' interrupted McKenna, 'they were driven out, or rather they ran out.' He stood up. 'I think I'd better get you another coffee before I tell you the full story.'

~

'I don't understand you, Brendon; I thought the one part of my saga you would think totally ridiculous would be what led to their virtual breakdowns.'

'You have to keep an open mind when it comes to ghost myths,' replied Brendon. 'But I am surprised your chief constable agreed to officers acting as pub landlords.'

McKenna looked at him and took a deep breath. 'It wasn't the chief,' he confessed, 'it was the Ministry of Defence.'

'Do what?' exclaimed Brendon, struggling to keep his voice down. 'What on earth have my employers got to do with local murders and ghouls in a haunted pub?' He shook his head. 'Come off it Colin, you're winding me up.'

'Not my style, you know that,' McKenna reassured

him. 'And it's not your employer, or rather it's not your department.'

'MI5?'

'Yep.'

'But how come?'

Brendon sat there, totally dumbfounded. McKenna's explanation of the Polsons' role had initially taken some believing and although totally ridiculous, the involvement of The Ministry had perhaps, made it sound a little more plausible.

DCI Johnson hit a total brick wall when it came to investigating the disappearance of the Hendersons. He knew it was most likely that after their car had become marooned in the snow, they would probably try and continue their journey on foot. They must have known Lingtree was not far from where they had ground to a halt.

Assuming they reached the village, the obvious place they would seek shelter and food would be the pub, but not one resident interviewed admitted to being in there and the landlords categorically denied serving anybody during the day or evening. They said it hadn't been worth opening but felt honour bound to do so. The lack of custom was hard to believe based on stories which came out later concerning how important the pub had been because of its large freezers and petrol generators.

Johnson never believed they'd fallen in the gorge but in the end, that's what he had to accept and that's obviously how it was left until the bodies were found at the archaeological dig.

Then came the death of Jess Withers. Exceptionally

successful businessman; built up his company from scratch working every hour God gave him according to the obituaries. Unmarried, assumed homosexual but kept his private life out of the limelight and decided to try his hand at letterboxing whilst staying at The Judge's Parlour. Our couple understood he got on reasonably well with both the previous landlords and the locals, particularly the heavy drinkers despite being a teetotaller, could have been your mates Brendon, and openly discussed his enterprise and how it depended on him for its success. Found dead in the mineshaft a few days after booking into the pub. Nothing to suggest it was anything other than an accident apart from the way his body had been pierced by the animal bone. Although not impossible, it was odd a broken thigh bone would be pointing vertically.

When I carried out our investigations into his death, a representative from the brewery which owns the pub told me that the present incumbents, two males, were being given notice as they weren't making any money, save that from local drinkers. Few diners, little income from letting the rooms, etc. and yet they appeared to be living an exceptional lifestyle and always met their rent commitment. Both had large, expensive estate cars, regular holidays abroad for which they had to pay for their own relief staff and apparently they built up a portfolio of rented properties whilst holding the tenancy.

That's when The Ministry had the idea of using our couple posing as seasoned landlords in the hope they could break into the community and throw some light on the two cases. We knew it would take some time but thought it was worth it. However, whilst they were there, Enscale died in a fire and Elliot and Collier allegedly died due to a faulty exhaust. As you know, nothing could be found to suggest foul play, not even by the Polsons. Unfortunately, having shown themselves to be naturals at the pub trade and actually building up a pretty reasonable all round business, for some unknown reason they started drinking heavily and liaising with them became more and more difficult.

Eventually, we had to get them out as our meetings stopped being briefings; rather they became weird confessions of ghostly encounters with some bearded, long-haired chap wearing a Viking-style helmet, sat in a corner of the main bar whilst upstairs they kept seeing mutilated hanging bodies in one of the bedrooms. It was driving them mad, so much so that they ended up spending time in a mental hospital.

It was decided that their presence hadn't achieved anything on behalf of the taxpayer, so they were replaced with a genuine tenant, the one who's there now.

McKenna went on to explain. 'Henderson, the father that is, had served in the military in Iraq and Afghanistan.'

'SAS you mean?' opined Brendon.

'Your words not mine. Anyway, he was retired with a leg injury, but was recruited by MI5. He was taking a break when he disappeared.'

'And the police thought, or more likely his employer thought, it was highly unlikely that someone with his intellect and past experience and training would simply let his family fall into the gorge and perish. Am I right?' asked Brendon, his eyes fixed on McKenna's.

McKenna nodded.

'And presumably Withers' death wasn't really much of a concern,' reasoned Brendon sarcastically.

McKenna shrugged his shoulders. 'Yep.'

'So why the fuck didn't you tell me this before Colin?'

The chief inspector leaned back in his seat, hands behind his head. 'It wasn't that I didn't trust you Brendon, it was—'

'Because you're a copper and I'm not,' interrupted Brendon.

'Something like that,' confirmed McKenna. 'I am sorry.'

Brendon sighed. 'Apology accepted, not that I have any choice; so what happens next?'

~

As he drove away from the hospital, Brendon's mind was saturated with the happenings of the last couple of days and he was finding it unusually difficult to take in.

The lack of numbers at the dig, the offhandedness of the two foreign-sounding workers on the site of the proposed railway siding, Caroline's comment about it not being *his* fault and the information McKenna had revealed about the Hendersons and Polsons. He was beginning to wish he hadn't come back.

Allowing Alan to die, to leave him there to the mercy of the wild dogs from the station, before persuading Gareth to return to the castle and then call the police, had betrayed his weakness, the same weakness that was to eventually return and let down his allies abroad, an act for which he would pay dearly. He should have done more but running was the only way he could cope.

Perhaps it was his parents' fault. Adopting him had been an act of kindness, his natural parents having died in a car crash; the hit-and-run driver never caught. But being adopted wasn't the same and before moving to Lingtree, he'd run away twice, desperate to avoid his policeman father's strict regime. In Lingtree, he'd been given so much freedom, freedom his father had felt it unsafe to give him in the criminal-ridden areas of the city. But for Brendon, it was too late; it was ingrained and would sadly come back to haunt him.

Thirty-eight years he'd served The Ministry: hard, character-building years. He'd hidden his instincts, desperate to be the man he dearly wished he was. In his time abroad he'd feared no one. Had it not been for the loss of Gareth and the opportunity to see Caroline again, he would never have returned to Lingtree Castle, the place where he pushed his best friend Alan to his death.

Sweating and shaking, he pulled the car into the lay-by on the windy, single-track moorland road a mile or so outside Lingtree. He'd decided to come back across the moors from the hospital to give himself time to reflect. The route had been quiet save for a few sheep and cattle. If only Caroline would recover, return to her home, he could comfort her and make love to her.

It was an hour later when he awoke, startled by the harsh knocking on the side window.

'Are you all right sir?' It was a uniformed police officer.

Brendon turned the ignition two clicks and then pressed the electric window button. 'Yes... yes... just a bit tired, that's all,' he replied rubbing his eyes. 'Thought I'd better pull over... safety and all that.'

'I see sir.' The policeman looked in the back. 'Would you mind getting out of the car please?'

'Yes, of course.' He climbed out. 'Have I done something wrong, Officer?'

'Not from around these parts are you?'

Brendon shook his head.

The policeman sniffed the air. 'Been drinking have we?'

'Certainly not, Officer. Well... err... not since yesterday.'

'Hmm, stays in the blood you know; takes time to work through.'

'Yes, I'm well aware of that thank you.' He pointed to his wallet lying on the front passenger seat. 'If you allow me to get that I can show you something that might help.'

The policeman's eyebrows rose. 'What are you suggesting sir?'

'Nothing,' he snapped indignantly, 'other than I have an identity card in there, it'll explain who I am.'

'All in good time, sir. Now then, bear with me one moment.' The policeman walked over to his unmarked car and came back with a breathalyser. 'Right, I'd like you to blow into this please.'

'But this is totally unnecessary, officer,' protested Brendon. 'If only you'd let me get my wallet.'

'One long blow please sir, no sucking in air.'

Realising he had no choice Brendon did as he was told. He watched as the policeman inspected the machine closely and he felt his stomach tighten as the uniformed officer's reaction suggested the reading was positive. However, two minutes later he was stood by his car, totally amazed as tyres squealing, the officer drove off.

'Let that be a lesson to you sir,' the policeman had said, 'I don't like criminals on my patch. Next time it'll be much worse. Good day.'

Shaking his head, Brendon got back into his car and started the engine. A conversation that evening with McKenna confirmed what he'd already realised once he was fully awake. As the imposter walked away from him, he'd noticed his cap, or at least the hair protruding from underneath it. Policemen don't have long hair and neither do they drive ten-year-old, Japanese four-wheel-drive vehicles.

'Brendon, somebody wants you out of there; for God's sake be careful.'

CHAPTER SEVENTEEN

There were still only half a dozen workers on the archaeological dig and no one to be seen on the proposed railway site. Hatcher was also absent.

Having had a sandwich for lunch, Brendon had walked there via the gorge bridge which was now fully reopened to the general public. There was still a police presence, but it consisted of one uniformed officer asking visitors if they'd been there in recent times and seen anything suspicious. As he walked up the hill the other side of the bridge, coming towards him was one of the two men he'd seen surveying the day before. The heavily-set man, with hair and a thick grey beard, nodded as he walked past, but ignored Brendon's verbal greeting. Brendon had considered following him, but presumed he was on his way to the pub for a pint or a late snack. However, on his return journey, he spotted the man coming out of the gorge car park. In recent times, the Trust had built a small cafe so perhaps he'd gone there for coffee, although he didn't look the sort who would enjoy afternoon tea and cakes.

The man stopped at the edge of the road and looked to

his left and right, as if expecting someone or something. As Brendon drew near, he heard the sound of a large truck approaching from ahead, its engine revving loudly as it overran its gears to help with braking around the curve down the twenty per cent gradient hill from the village. Reaching the bridge, the two-year-old seven-and-half-tonner accelerated noisily up the fifty metres to the car park. The man acknowledged its arrival and directed it in, then followed behind on foot. A moment later, the engine was switched off and all that could be heard was the sound of the thundering water from under the bridge.

Curious, Brendon crossed the road and strode quickly into the car park. The lorry was parked near a double gateway leading to the wood above the gorge. Casually, as if just another visitor, Brendon approached the vehicle; the cab was empty, the driver and his mate nowhere to be seen. Walking around to the back, he checked again for any sign of the pair before grabbing the handle on one of the back doors. There were a few people milling about the entrance hut and cafe, some picking up and putting back postcards from the revolving rack outside, but no one was showing any interest in the lorry. The door swung open and he climbed inside, easing it gently closed behind him.

Cellophane wrapped plastic bottles of water were stacked from floor to ceiling on one side whilst on the other were tins of food; corned beef, ham, baked beans, carrots, peas, various other vegetables together with cardboard boxes containing bottles of vodka and Swedish Crocodile beer. Squeezing between the boxes, Brendon found supplies of camping gaz and ten-litre petrol cans.

It didn't strike him as the sort of thing The Gorge Shop would offer visitors planning a stroll by the river.

For a brief moment he sat on one of the crates, trying to fathom out the reason for this delivery, when from outside he heard two voices speaking loudly in Swedish, his knowledge of the language sufficient to understand their conversation.

'That's better. I could have done with that about an hour ago,' said one of the men.

The other laughed. 'One day Erik, you will be able to afford a silver-lined toilet in your cab, plus a shower instead of just that shit-stained bed.'

'Ha,' said the other, 'if I can afford that, then I will pay someone else to do the driving whilst I drink vodka all day and fuck many women in gigantic silk-covered bed.'

'And what will your wife say about that?' joked the first man. 'Now then, we must move. I'll unlock the gates. It is dry enough to drive quite close.'

Brendon heard the cab door open and slam shut. As the engine turned over, he climbed out the back, closed the large door as silently as possible, then careful not to be visible in the truck's mirrors, walked nonchalantly in a straight line directly away from the vehicle as it slowly pulled forwards. A glance over his shoulder told him it was safe to turn and head towards the cafe. A group of elderly, chattering people, the three men sporting full grey beards, the four women wearing large, floppy sunhats and all seven dressed in walking boots and carrying small rucksacks and hiking poles, offered an instant screen for Brendon as they approached the turnstile pay booth. Over the top of their heads, he watched the Swede chain and padlock the gates before trotting after the lorry as it disappeared into the trees.

Puzzled by the vehicle's presence, he made his way to the side of the cafe and souvenir shop. Peering in the windows, he saw the staff casually serving customers, not one appearing to be interested in the delivery. Presumably to them, it must be an everyday normal occurrence however strange its cargo. With the public having daytime access, Brendon was debating whether or not to follow, when a sudden tap on his shoulder caused him to swing round.

'Mr Hatcher, what are you doing here?' he asked, surprised to see the archaeologist straying so far from the dig, although dressed in shorts and walking boots, he didn't look out of place.

'I thought I might ask you the same question,' he replied, as if talking to a truant schoolchild. 'I thought you might have seen enough of the gorge when you were growing up.'

'I'm sorry, how did you know I grew up here?' queried Brendon, surprised by this statement. He was sure he hadn't mentioned it before.

'Small village Mr Gallagher, a very small village indeed,' he mused. 'Everybody knows everything in a small village, wouldn't you agree?'

'Not entirely Mr Hatcher,' he said shaking his head. 'Anyway, for your information I was looking around the cafe and the shop; it wasn't here when I was growing up as you put it.'

'Ah yes, of course. The entrance was down on the bridge, where that body was found I understand.'

Hatcher's eyes were half closed. 'Do they know who it was yet?'

'Not that I am aware. You'll probably know as soon as I do.'

'I don't think so Mr Gallagher,' he sneered. 'After all, we don't all work for The Ministry do we?'

'I'm sorry, what did you say?'

'Small village Mr Gallagher, a very small village,' he said, holding Brendon's eye. 'Everybody knows everything. You have to be very careful in a small village, even those that grew up here. Don't want to upset the apple-cart do we?' He studied his watch. 'Now then, if you'll excuse me, I must get back. Good day Mr Gallagher.' He turned on his heel and strode off purposely to the car park exit, before stopping abruptly ten metres from Brendon. Half pirouetting, he spoke just loudly enough so as to be heard, 'Do be careful, we don't want any more accidents do we?'

Rooted to the spot, Brendon stared after him. A few more strides and he was gone. Brendon needed a drink and it wasn't a soft beverage from the cafe.

~

'A large malt please Phil.'

The landlord placed the bottle of Scotch on the bar, added a tumbler and removed the stopper.

'There's roughly ten measures left in there,' he told Brendon, 'probably slightly more. Help yourself, I'll charge you for six.'

Brendon eyed him suspiciously. He'd never thought of Phil as being generous with his drink or his food for that matter, but here he was turning down in excess of fifteen pounds of retail.

'Thanks Phil,' he said, pouring half a tumbler full, 'very generous; come up on the horses have we?'

The landlord laughed. 'Not a gambling man Mr Gallagher I'm afraid, but you look like someone who needs a drink. I've heard you've had a busy day.'

Swallowing his Scotch, Brendon picked up the bottle and glass and moved to his corner seat, Hatcher's words rumbling through his head. *Everybody knows everything. You have to be very careful in a small village.* He didn't reply to Phil. He was tired, even more so than yesterday and he had a job to do tonight. He poured a large measure. The Scotch tasted good, exceptionally good. When he woke in the morning, fully clothed on his bed, he wondered if he should have put something with it, unaware that somebody already had.

CHAPTER EIGHTEEN

The hand-drawn trailer moved silently along the well-trodden but no longer religiously revered path. Silhouetted against the pre-dawn cloudless sky, the three men pulling it spoke rarely, except when pausing occasionally to strengthen their grip on the unforgiving metal drawbar.

It was a warm, late spring/early summer's night and the sweat flowed freely from their brows. Many times they'd considered using a quad bike to tow the eight-foot barrow, laden with a small, but exceptionally heavy casket, but until someone invented the noiseless engine, the idea was quickly dispelled.

For the last three years, two of them made this trip seven times each summer, always commencing three hours before dawn so as to remain unnoticed by the many villagers who weren't in the know. For the other, it was only his second year. It wasn't the shortest route, but it avoided a short stretch of main road where, however unlikely, early morning police patrols might roam.

The helicopter could land in the dark, but waiting until first light ensured it would draw no attention; instead it would be thought of as part of an army exercise, night use of the moorland firing range having been banned by the National Park.

'Shit, that fuckin' hurt,' exclaimed the tallest of the three men, holding his wrist as he shook his partly numb hand. 'Watch out for the fuckin' lumps of granite.'

'Sorry, but the missus ain't fed I enough carrots to see in the dark,' joked the much shorter, stocky one.

'Keep your voice down, you idiot,' snapped the one with the posh non-local accent. 'Do you want to wake the dead?'

'Might be better company than you,' the tallest one chortled. 'Anyway, no bugger died on this route, unless they put 'em in their coffin still breathin'.'

''Ave you no respect?' asked the short one, his grin unseen in the dark. 'We only 'ave to yank this fuckin' cart three miles, not like the poor bastards in the old days. Some had journeys over seventeen miles if 'twas wet, poor sods.'

'Quit the history lesson,' chastised the posh one. '"The Way of the Dead" it might have been but not any longer. Now then, all together.'

For the next hour and a half, the three pulled hard. They passed under the disused granite railway viaduct, unconcerned by the threat of its possible revival to carry mineral-rich stone from the quarry.

'It'll never happen,' they'd said confidently as they'd sat drinking their pints, the posh one smiling as he read aloud the article in the parish magazine. 'Cost too fuckin' much to re-lay them rails.'

'Don't you believe it,' said the man sat at the table, unable to avoid overhearing their conversation. 'Would solve the flood problem on the other line at the same time I believe.'

They'd ignored the arsehole stranger, instead ordering another beer and changing the subject. However, a friend had later ensured the arsehole wouldn't interrupt them again.

Once clear of the arch, they stopped. As he'd done so many times before, the short one ran ahead to the Old Mill. There were no lights, no sign of the newcomers and fortunately no dog. He waved to the others. Downhill for a few hundred metres, they gathered their strength, preparing themselves for the short, steep incline on the other side of the valley, a high hedge on the left and an even higher tree-root-exposed bank on the right. The cart too wide for the bridge, they would have to cross the river first, soaking themselves to their knees, but grateful they no longer, as they would have done in days gone by, have to risk the slippery track along the edge of the water as it gathered speed before beginning its meandering route through the deep cleft of the gorge.

Clear of the valley, their task became easier, the route now following a rough, but reasonably level and much wider lane. They would bypass the farm owned by the now dead non-believer, instead crossing two fields before stopping short of the road to the moors, hidden by dry-stone walls built by French and American prisoners of war during their stay in the dank, isolated, granite moorland jail. Many died before their release, their ghosts allegedly still visible in the thick mists immersing their shallow, stone-covered graves.

'Road's all clear,' whispered the short one. Opening

the wooden gate, he looked up, his hand to his ear. 'It's coming; better get a move on, you knows they don't like 'anging around.'

With one final effort, they dragged the trailer across the road. The sun's rays began washing away the dark of the night as the noise of the helicopter's rotors broke the peace of the dawn. It would land in the dip, out of sight of the road, its rotors still spinning as the two people on board awaited the arrival of the small but valuable cargo.

'Give us a 'and,' shouted the tall one, 'it's a bit heavier this time.'

Both jumped out of the side door, eager to be gone. Neither spoke, their eyes unseen through their darkened helmet visors despite the waking light. Two minutes later, the rotors sped up and it was gone. The three on the ground straightened; there was no way the blades could harm them, but instinctively they covered their heads until the flying machine was just a bird-like spot in the sky.

'Right. I'm knackered. Could do with a pint,' said the posh one. The other two agreed and together they headed back the way they'd come. In a few more hours, the short one would collect the trailer and tow it back home with his truck. Forgetting it was nearly summer and the grass was fresh and green, no one not in the know would suspect he'd been doing anything other than feeding some cattle.

CHAPTER NINETEEN

14 May 2016

'Mr Gallagher... Mr Gallagher... are you all right?'

It was becoming a familiar question.

Brendon's head was thumping. Opening his eyes to the pain of the sunlight streaming through the undrawn curtains didn't help his cause.

'Thank God for that, I thought you was dead.' It was Grace. 'I hopes you don't mind me using my passkey, but Mr Clegg was concerned you hadn't been down for breakfast.' She noticed the empty whisky bottle on the bedside table. 'You wants to be a bit careful. It's what did for Mr and Mrs Polson in the end.'

He scrutinised the bottle. 'But... but I didn't drink all that.' He held his forehead. 'I'm sure I didn't.' He swung his legs over the side of the bed. 'What time is it Grace?'

'Gone half past ten Mr Gallagher.' She pointed to the tea tray on the dresser. 'Can I get you a coffee?' she asked.

Brendon nodded, immediately regretting it. 'Very strong please Grace.' He looked at his feet, then the rest of his body. He was fully dressed, save for his shoes which were placed neatly beside each other by the bedroom chair. 'How did I get here Grace?'

She switched on the kettle. 'Mr Clegg says you left the bar at about nine o'clock. You'd had several pints he said; bit the worse for wear. Apparently you insisted on buying the rest of the bottle of whisky to take to your room.' She opened two sachets of instant coffee. 'Says you didn't want to stay because your two old chums were there.'

'Pete and Jim?' he asked.

'Think so,' she replied. 'Sugar?'

'Two please Grace; hopefully it will do some good.' He closed his eyes, trying desperately to remember yesterday evening. He'd intended to go back to the gorge; to climb over the wall and find out what the lorry was doing with its load. He focused on his shoes. They were clean, no signs of mud. The small black plastic kettle clicked off. Even that was enough to stick a needle in his head.

'Thanks Grace.' He placed his cup and saucer on the bedside table. Standing up, he looked out the window at the village street. Other than a couple of parked cars, it was empty.

'Grace?'

'Yes Mr Gallagher.'

'What's going on here?' he asked, rubbing the back of his neck. 'Please tell me.'

'I don't knows what you mean sir,' she replied. 'Now then, if there's nothing else I'll leave you to it and come back later. There's no other rooms to do so I'll go help in the kitchen.'

'Of course. You must do your job.' He picked up the cup. 'What did happen to Melanie?'

There was no reply as the door latched automatically behind her.

A quick shave and a leisurely shower helped Brendon begin to recover. He still had no memory of any events after returning to the pub, but at least the pain was starting to fade. Pulling on a clean polo shirt and light green cargo trousers, he recalled what Grace had said about there being no other residents. As he walked down the stairs, he heard the sound of bottles clinking in the bar.

'Ah, you must be Mr Gallagher. Phil... sorry... Mr Clegg told me you were still upstairs. How are you feeling sir? A heavy night I hear.'

Brendon appraised the young, probably eighteen or nineteen, slim blue-eyed girl with short blonde hair, dressed in a V-neck sweater and tight denim jeans, restocking the chilled drinks cabinet. He shook his head. 'Sorry, have we met?'

She smiled, her face lighting up.

'I'm Melanie's replacement, Sue.' Her smile seemed effortless. 'Started today.'

'Well, pleased to meet you Sue.' He grinned. If only he was forty years younger. 'But please call me Brendon. I've been staying here long enough to qualify as one of the staff by now I should think. Where are you from?'

'I'm from Denmark.' She had no sign of an accent. 'Been travelling for nearly a year now, working my way round your wonderful country.' She shrugged. 'Ran out of money, heard there was a vacancy and hey... here I am.'

'I see. Well, welcome to this good old-fashioned English pub.' He heaved himself onto a bar stool. 'Between you and me it's haunted you know,' he whispered, 'especially in that corner.' He pointed behind him.

'Ha, you mean the old boy with the helmet? He won't harm you. I've already made his acquaintance. We've had a good long chat.' She saw Brendon's look of astonishment. 'Only joking Mr Gallagher... I mean Brendon. Mr Clegg told me all about the ghosts, particularly the ones in room nine. Said best not to go in there.' She winked, her eyebrows raised.

Grinning in recognition, Brendon grabbed his opportunity, totally forgetting his head felt as though it'd been split with an axe. 'Where's Mr Clegg?' he asked.

'Gone to the bank,' replied Sue, putting the last bottle in the cabinet. 'Said he'll be back around noon. Told me to unlock the front door at half eleven although he said it was unlikely we'd get any customers that early.'

'So, you're like me then Sue? I mean if someone says don't do something or don't go somewhere, it makes you want to do it even more?'

Biting her lower lip it was obvious it did. 'Brendon, are you suggesting I go upstairs with you?' For a teenager, she wasn't slow in coming forwards. Seeing his face redden, she assured him, 'Don't worry, I know what you meant. I might have lost my mum and dad in an aeroplane crash, but I'm not looking for a father figure just yet.' She laughed. 'C'mon, I'll get the key. You can hold my hand when I start screaming.'

If Brendon expected there to be anything other than just another bedroom, then his hopes were immediately dashed.

'There, I told you Brendon. He was just winding me

up.' She lay back on the four-poster. 'Lovely bed though. Come and join me.' She grinned, her face unaffected by adulthood. 'Only joking. Got to open the bar anyway.' Sitting up, a look of fear replaced her humour. She was staring at the bare stone fireplace opposite. 'I'm sorry, I must go.' Screaming, she pushed Brendon aside as she darted for the door.

Ignoring the urge to run after her and check she was okay, Brendon scoured the room. A small window, directly opposite the door, looked onto the road and car park. The four-poster, a small bedside table either side, was on the left, whilst on the right, was the end wall of the pub, on which was built the stone-faced fireplace which seemingly had scared Sue. To the left of it was a small dressing table, a small-screen old-style television, plus a tea and coffee tray. When fully open, the door to the room partly hid a dark, stained, small built-in double wardrobe.

Not really sure what he was looking for, but desperate to find something, Brendon walked all around, looked under the bed, up at the ceiling. About to leave, he noticed the wardrobe doors were slightly ajar. It was empty save for a mixture of half a dozen or so plastic and wire coat hangers. Seventy pounds a night didn't buy smooth, varnished wooden ones. As if examining a stage magician's box for the disappearing lady act, he tapped the inside of the sides and back. Although solid wood, the back sounded hollow. He shivered, the air feeling unexpectedly cold. About to explore further, he stopped abruptly as an anxious voice behind implored him to leave.

'Brendon, Phil's car has just pulled in; you must get out.' It was Sue. She looked shaken, but had managed to summon enough strength to warn him. At that moment it didn't occur to him to ask why she'd ran. She grabbed his hand. 'Quickly, I must get back to the bar.'

Reluctantly, he pulled the wardrobe doors together, took one last look around and locked the door as he left. Hurrying, he made his way back to his room. He'd worry about replacing the key later. Grace was still to make his bed, so rather than ring Caroline from here and have Grace overhear his conversation he set off to the garden. On his way down he heard Sue talking to Clegg.

'Yes Mr Clegg, all done. Cabinet's refilled, beer mats and cloths are all out and I've unlocked the front door. All we need now is some customers.' She sounded calm and confident.

'Thanks Sue. I'm sure you'll make a big contribution, particularly with the locals,' replied Clegg. 'Now then, if you'll excuse me I've got a couple of things to do in the office, so just give me a shout if you need me.'

'Will do Mr Clegg.' She saw Brendon stood at the foot of the stairs. 'Ah, you must be Mr Gallagher. I'm Sue, I've just taken over from Melanie.' She winked. 'If there's anything I can do to help, just let me know. Your room key, anything at all.'

Shit. He still had room nine's key and Clegg was now sat in his office. One look at the key rack and he'd be sure to notice.

'Thank you Sue, pleased to meet you. I could do with a glass of water if it's no trouble.' He followed her to the bar.

'Are you all right?' he asked. 'You looked scared out of your wits upstairs.'

'Sorry,' she apologised, passing him a glass full of ice

cubes. She picked up a water jug from under the counter. 'It's just that for a moment, I saw… ' she paused, looking around. 'At least I think I saw… somebody hanging from the ceiling.' She filled the glass. 'I'm sorry. It sounds as though I believe in ghosts… I know it's stupid.'

Brendon smiled; if only she knew. 'Don't worry,' he reassured her. 'It's the power of suggestion. You were expecting something, so you saw it. Nothing unusual.' He lowered his voice. 'The key… I've got to put it back.'

'Not a problem. I'll tell Clegg I need some help with one of the dispensers. When he comes out, you return the key.' She smiled her beautiful smile. 'Perfectly simple, you'll see.'

It was. He drank his water alone in the garden. Time to call Caroline.

'Hello Brendon… thanks for calling… yes, much better thank you… tomorrow they say… that's great. I'll give you a ring when they finally give me the okay.'

Their conversation was short. She hadn't asked about Ellie and Nathan. Perhaps she'd forgotten or perhaps they'd been in touch and she omitted to mention it. Either way, he'd find out tomorrow. He rang McKenna.

'There's something odd going on in the gorge Colin.' He told him about the lorry and how he was sure he'd been drugged.

'Anything to do with you intending to follow up on the truck?' asked McKenna.

'Possibly; big coincidence if not. Trouble is, how did anyone know I'd seen it? I mean, there was no one other than the landlord in the pub when I started drinking and

I certainly didn't say anything to him. I might not be able to remember everything but—'

'He must be involved,' interrupted McKenna, his voice rising an octave. 'That would make sense. He drugs you, stops you going back to the gorge and whatever is going on gets done.'

'But you said Phil Clegg hadn't been here long and things were already happening when your two coppers were *in situ*. Presumably he came through the brewery, so—'

'That's true,' conceded McKenna, his excitement waning. 'Bollocks.' The line went silent. Eventually he continued. 'I guess you're going to try the gorge again tonight?'

'Have to Colin. Caroline's back tomorrow, so I want to spend some hours with her before I… ' He stopped abruptly.

'Before you what Brendon?'

'Nothing, Colin.' Hurriedly he added, 'I might get called in for service at any time now and I'd have to go.' It was a lie, but his policeman friend believed it.

'Fair point Brendon, I understand.' His empathy was genuine. 'You've been a great help and I'm sure you'd like to see things through, but if duty calls… not a lot you can do I suppose. So what time tonight?'

'Ten o'clock.'

'Right, come and pick me up. You can say you're going out for the evening so no one will see us. Okay?'

'Okay,' agreed Brendon. 'At the police station?'

'Yep. Nine-thirty.' Another phone rang in the background. 'Brendon, I'm going to have to go… been expecting a call… might have got a lead on the body in the gorge… tell you more tonight.' The phone clicked.

'Excuse me.' The short-haired young man, dressed in T-shirt, jeans and sandals, was stood on the steps to the garden. Brendon guessed he was still in his late teens. 'Are you the landlord?' he asked.

'Sorry, just a guest. Phil Clegg's inside I think.'

The young man shook his head. 'No I've tried there. A girl said he'd gone somewhere, thought it might be the garden.'

'Not seen him I'm afraid. Can I help?' He didn't know how, but the young man looked distraught.

'I'm Melanie's boyfriend. She works here.'

'Ah yes. Not been well I hear. Is she any better?' The young man walked towards Brendon's table.

'I don't know; that's the problem. I haven't seen her since two days ago.'

'I thought she'd gone to stay with her aunt, at least that's what I've been told.'

'What aunt?' the young man asked angrily, his face flushing. 'I don't know of any aunt. Are you trying to wind me up?'

Brendon put his hands up in front of him. 'Steady. I'm only telling you what I heard. Perhaps if you go upstairs in the pub, you may be able to find a lady called Grace; she might be able to help.'

Whether or not she could, Brendon would never know.

After the young man had ungraciously thanked him for his help and headed for the back door, not wanting to raise any suspicion, Brendon drove his car to the small parking area on the edge of the moor approximately a mile from the centre of Lingtree. At one time, there was no restriction as to how far cars could venture off road, but in order to preserve the moorland only pedestrians, horse riders and farm vehicles were now permitted access.

Heeding the several police signs attached to fence posts warning people to protect their belongings against theft, he locked his wallet in the boot of his two-year-old Mercedes Coupe and headed towards the general area he understood Jess Withers' body had been found.

As he walked purposely along the well-worn stone track, yet to be shorn, sheep grazed around him on the tight, wiry grass, their spring lambs either sent off to market or added to the flock for breeding next year. As a youngster, there would have been one or two herds of Dartmoor ponies running free, but now, unwanted and unaffordable, many had been slaughtered for meat and there was just the odd one or two left to roam and forage for themselves.

On his left, he passed by the location of the Royal Observer Corp underground bunker, long redundant after the ending of the Cold War and subsequently filled in, the unnatural grass mound the only evidence that it ever existed. As a boy, he remembered the ventilation shafts and entrance hatch exposed above ground. Half a mile further he reached the wooden footbridge beside the ford and the large stepping stones someone many years ago had moved into place. It was a popular spot for picnickers with very young children, the shallow waters offering little danger. However, despite the brilliant sunshine, there was nobody else in sight.

A few hundred yards downriver was the pool where he'd swum, formed by years of river damming by those eager to cool off in the heat of the day. Since the early part of the twentieth century, the pool has been watched over by a wooden bench, together with a metal plaque secured to a large black granite rock in memory of an army captain killed in the First World War. It had been a popular summer "hang out" for Brendon and his mates in their early teens. On the other side of the river, rose one of the moors best-known tors, commonly known as Victory Tor, a granite-block cross erected at the top to commemorate the Golden Jubilee of Queen Victoria. To Brendon, the tor was simply called Vickers and many times he would race up it to dry off after a dip in the pool.

All of this now meant nothing to Brendon as he followed the river upstream before striding out along the old railway line leading to the disused Cranbrook arsenic works, trying to temporarily forget the fate which awaited him in the near future. He intended to walk for an hour before doubling back to his car. Having purposely not ordered dinner in the pub, he would snack in Chilstoke prior to meeting McKenna, safe in the knowledge that his absence from the village meant his planned visit to the gorge should go undiscovered.

Thirty minutes later, his head swimming in confusion, he sat down on a dilapidated wooden railway bridge over a stream. Head in hands, he closed his eyes.

'Why now?' he asked. 'Why here?'

Waking from his trance-like state, he examined the ground around him. There was nothing to suggest the cause of the sudden subconscious outburst. His head pounded like that of a blacksmith's hammer on an anvil. Picturing the bleeding, headless corpses, he vomited uncontrollably, his thoughts taken over by a clear image of Gareth's body, twitching, as if searching for its decapitated head.

His stomach empty of content, he retched violently. Struggling to his feet, he began retracing his route. The mind-numbing intensity of the last few moments receded and after five minutes, his head was clear and his stomach settled. Failing to see the young girl with short blonde hair, sat on a large lump of granite nearby, he followed the old railway line, eventually climbing a small, round-topped barren tor. Although dwarfed by its much taller 300-million-year-old rock and peat covered "brothers and sisters", the vantage point was still high enough for Brendon to see the village of Lingtree three miles to the north-west. Various houses, bungalows, roofs and farm buildings stood out clearly against the background of acres of The Forestry Commission's array of evergreen trees.

At the far end of the village proudly rose the church steeple, a lookout point in past eras, but now just housing the church bells, occasionally rung by a diminishing number of local campanologists to summon the village believers to the once-monthly Sunday evening service, or to celebrate a rare village wedding.

To most people, this view would have been one of tranquillity, of a place where a walker could anticipate refreshment or even a bed for the night after a long moorland trek or for a farmer to discuss his day over the pleasures of a pint, but for Brendon, it was not a vista he could enjoy, for rising above the church stood the unwelcoming, time-blackened granite walls of the castle, its secrets and history encased in memoriam. He hastily turned away, his thoughts of Alan and Gareth replaced by plans for his and McKenna's clandestine visit to the gorge.

CHAPTER TWENTY

'It looks like it might be an estate agent from one of the large, successful, posh London firms,' said McKenna after climbing into the car. 'We think he went missing a few weeks ago, but no one at his office thought to report it. Apparently his secretary was off sick and both his co-directors were on holiday.'

'Wife?'

'Not married and lived alone. Spent all his time building his business so he could float it on the stock exchange. By all accounts, kept himself to himself.'

'And the reason for being down here?'

'Undertaking a valuation for Gareth Pettit according to a member of staff. An email shows he booked an overnight stay in the pub.'

Shaking his head, Brendon recalled the open screen on Caroline's computer. Saying nothing to McKenna, he continued to drive. Caroline would no doubt explain tomorrow.

They approached the gorge from the opposite end to the village. It was the direction the Hendersons had been travelling on the night their lives ended so suddenly.

Brendon parked his car a few hundred metres up the lane which led to Caroline's farm and past Pete Grayson's house. Walking back to the road, he and McKenna passed under the old, narrow granite railway bridge before turning into a gateway set back off the road.

'Follow me Colin.' Brendon climbed over the gate into a field between the disbanded railway and the valley of the gorge. McKenna had turned up in jeans and walking boots, but even so, he cursed loudly as he landed in the partially dried cowpat.

'Shit,' he exclaimed.

'Very apt Colin,' jested Brendon, 'but best we keep conversation and loud expletives to a minimum.' He saw McKenna nod.

The day's light had faded and the sky having clouded over, meant there was only occasional help from moon or stars.

Running across the field, they passed behind a large house and its lodge, both in darkness, the occupants either out or retired for the night. Eventually they reached the fence bordering the gorge.

'Someone's gone to a load of trouble to keep out people not wishing to pay,' whispered McKenna, assessing the eight-foot-high, quality wire mesh with strands of barbed wire along the top. 'How the hell do we get over that? It's like a bloody prisoner of war camp.'

'We don't,' replied Brendon, taking a small pair of folding bolt cutters from the leg pocket of his trousers. 'I used to be a Boy Scout,' he joked as he made short work of the wire. 'Mind you, in recent times I normally only needed this tool to get out rather than get in. C'mon, even you can squeeze through the gap.'

Once in, Brendon led McKenna down a short, gentle earth and stone bank until they came to a deeply rutted track bordered on both sides by stumps of felled trees. After listening intently and scouring the immediate area McKenna switched on his torch. 'Tyre tracks; wide, truck ones I would think.'

They followed the once tree-lined track, stumbling at times on the uneven surface. In places, pitch black replaced what little light penetrated the thick, leafy shrub growth. Not knowing how close they were to the river and fearing tripping and disappearing into the gorge below, McKenna occasionally flashed on his torch. The path started to drop gradually, eventually reaching what appeared to be a vehicle turning area. From here, the path narrowed and fell steeply. The sound of the fast flowing water began making itself heard.

'I think this path must be higher than the one used by the public,' whispered McKenna. 'I don't recall anything so steep on this side of the river when we were recovering the body.'

'I don't remember it at all from when I played here as a kid,' confirmed Brendon. 'It must have been put in pretty recently judging by the length of the new shoots sprouting on the stumps.

Another fifty metres and the path ended.

Cautiously, McKenna shone his torch. No tracks, no footprints, no building, no cave, just nothing other than the trees and overgrown bushes.

'What the... ?' blurted Brendon. 'Doesn't make sense.'

'Shush,' snapped McKenna. 'Listen.'

Holding his breath, Brendon detected the slightest muffled hum of distant machinery. He looked at his feet. 'Pass me the torch Colin.' Kneeling, Brendon shone the light in front of him as he scraped at the dead foliage. They stared at the round, metre in diameter, metal manhole cover.

'So what now McKenna?' asked Brendon.

'You're the secret agent, Brendon, you tell me.'

~

Back in the car, McKenna rubbed his boot with a wet tissue wipe. Deciding it was probably not the best time to lift the cover, they'd brushed back the foliage and made their way up the path, repairing the wire fence as best they could.

On the return journey to Chilstoke, McKenna went into senior policeman mode and outlined his plans.

'Two armed response officers and four uniform should be enough,' he told Brendon.

'Bit over the top, Colin, and you'll have to get permission of the Trust; after all, it might be nothing and if you go bursting into one of their... well, one of their drains I suppose, then there could be hell to pay.'

'You know it's not just a drain Brendon,' he scoffed, 'but on reflection, I suppose you're right. Don't want to cause an unnecessary fuss on top of everything else and wreck the gorge as a profitable attraction. Can you imagine the public outcry from all the "do-gooders"?'

'And from the villagers,' added Brendon.

It's a small village, a very small village.

'I'll give you a ring as soon as I know what's happening,' McKenna told Brendon as he shut the passenger door. 'Thanks for the lift.'

Colin McKenna would never contact the Trust, nor would he organise a gorge visiting party. After being dropped off by Brendon, his impulsive decision to walk the half-mile home rather than drive proved to be his last. At first, he didn't take any notice of the car approaching from behind, the engine revs low, the lights extinguished. It was only after the engine began screaming and the tyres thudded over the kerb that he turned to see the bull bars of a large four-by-four a mere metre away. Any other type of vehicle and he may have been thrown onto the bonnet, but the aggressive, shiny-chromed tubular steel front ensured he was knocked to the ground. The two and a quarter tonnes of metal and rubber took care of the rest. One eyeball rolled across the pavement like a smoothly struck golfer's putt, as the noise of his skull cracking echoed around the concrete and masonry edifices. The wide off-road wheels reversed over him, not once but twice, just to make sure.

It was a drunken couple, their kebabs in hand, who found him and rang 999, but even if the ambulance had arrived within seconds, it would have been too late. Detective Chief Inspector Colin McKenna, loving husband of Sergeant Julie McKenna, née Ransom, was well and truly disposed of.

CHAPTER TWENTY-ONE

15 May 2016

'Oh my God, Jenny, I can't believe it. We were with each other last night.'

'Yes I know, Mr Gallagher. The guvnor kept me informed of what he was working on with you,' acknowledged DS Pearson.

'Have you any idea who's responsible and... and how's Julie coping?'

'We've nothing on the vehicle whatsoever, no witnesses, no tyre marks, no paint flecks; a very neat, clean hit-and-run job.' The clearly frustrated young woman on the end of the phone swallowed hard. 'Julie's got our welfare officer with her but as you can imagine she's—'

'Yes I can. I'm so sorry... ' He paused before asking, 'You said neat, clean job as if you think it was deliberate.'

'Chief Inspector McKenna was found in a twenty-mile-an-hour zone on a three-metre-wide pavement, the road was straight, nothing restricting vision; lends itself to intent.'

Brendon shook his head. Was it just a coincidence after their discovery in the gorge? If it was deliberate, why had McKenna been picked on and not him?

'Hello... hello... Mr Gallagher, are you still there?'

'Sorry Jenny, still here. Hard to take in, that's all. So what happens now, I mean about Colin's intention to pay...?' He stopped himself saying, "the gorge a visit". The detective sergeant hadn't mentioned having any detailed knowledge of last night's events.

'Pay, Mr Gallagher? I don't understand you,' queried a puzzled Jenny. 'Who was he going to pay?'

'Jenny, I've got to go.' It was a lie, but he would much prefer initially exploring the manhole cover without a police presence. 'Sorry, I'll come back to you as soon as I can. Please give my heartfelt condolences to Julie.'

'But Mr Gallagher... Mr Gallagher... we need to talk. Can we me—?'

He pressed the "off" button. He needed to speak with Caroline about Gareth instructing an estate agent and he needed to visit the gorge. He glanced at his watch; nine-twenty. Time for a shower, coffee and toast, by which time he hoped Caroline would be ready to leave the hospital.

'Good morning Mr Gallagher. How are you after last night's excitement?' The landlord's smile was strangely irritating.

'What excitement was that then Phil?' Brendon replied as he sat down at a breakfast table. 'Had a walk on the moors and then ate in Chilstoke for a change. Hopefully that's okay with you.'

'Why of course, no problem at all. Quiet at the

moment anyway; not worth turning on the chip pan.' His smile had become a smirk, even more irritating.

'No other residents Phil?' queried Brendon.

'Early start Mr Gallagher.'

'So what was last night's excitement? Did I miss out on something?'

'The accident in Chilstoke; a policeman was killed I understand.'

How Brendon wanted to smack that smile from the landlord's face. One good slap would do it. 'News travels fast Phil.'

'Small village Mr Gallagher, a very small village indeed.' At last he let go the smirk. 'Now then sir, what can I get you for breakfast?'

'Just coffee and toast please.'

'Right you are sir.' He headed for the kitchen. 'By the way, stuffed heart on the dinner menu tonight and some lovely smoked sausages, proper intestine wrapped, not like the ones you get from the supermarket. We've got an excellent butcher.' The kitchen door swung back and forwards behind him.

Breakfast done, Brendon sat in the garden. Last night's cloud had cleared and it promised to be yet another warm, sunny day. His mobile rang.

'Caroline… how are you…? That's great… what time…? Okay, I'll be there as quick as I can… looking forward to seeing you.'

~

'You look remarkably well,' he commented, helping her into the car. He put her bag in the boot.

'Feeling it if I'm honest,' she replied. 'Bruises haven't healed but my head feels fine.'

Brendon turned the ignition key. 'Have you heard from the kids yet?' he asked.

She shook her head. 'Not yet Brendon, although Detective Sergeant Pearson phoned me yesterday afternoon to confirm they'd been contacted. No need for them to worry now. What's happened has happened, so it's time to move on.'

Brendon pulled onto the main road. 'We'll... I mean... they'll catch the person who hurt you before long Caroline.' He almost added, 'It's a small village, a very small village.' She caught hold of his arm.

'I'd rather try and forget the whole thing.' Shaking her head, she laughed. 'That's silly, I can't remember it anyway.'

'But the marks, the scars; whoever did it deserves to be caught.' Her comment worried him. 'He might try and do it again.'

'I don't think so Brendon.' She sounded very confident. 'Anyway, enough about me, what have you been up to while I've been resting?'

'Let's wait until I get you home. Have you got much in the freezer?'

'Plenty Brendon. Remember, I'm... sorry... *was* a farmer's wife.' "Was" instead of "am" didn't seem to cause the slightest bit of concern.

After a brief walk around the house and outbuildings Caroline unpacked her bag while Brendon made some tea. Sat at the breakfast bar, he asked if she would be all right in the house. He'd forgotten about the gate having previously been padlocked as he climbed out of the driver's seat and pushed it open.

'Not a problem,' she replied. 'As I said, what is done is done and… ' she grinned, 'I can't be scared by something I can't remember, can I?'

'I suppose not.' He poured the tea.

'There're some biscuits in that barrel by the toaster.'

'I'm fine thanks, Caroline; you?'

'No, I just want to get back to healthy eating after all that hospital food. Most of it seems to get wasted.' The tea too hot to drink, she held her mug in two hands. 'I was sorry to hear about your policeman friend Mr McKenna. He seemed quite a nice man.'

Brendon looked at her, trying to recall if he'd mentioned it on the journey home. He was certain he hadn't. 'Yes, very nasty. Hit and run I understand. The police are hopeful of finding the driver pretty quickly though.'

Sipping her tea, she replied, 'Most unlikely I should think.' He could almost hear her saying, "Small village Brendon, a very small village indeed!" She looked at the fridge. 'Right, let's see what I can find for lunch, I'm starving. Not very exciting I'm afraid. I'll go into town and do some shopping tomorrow.'

Having a freezer full of meat was fine, but the only "cook from frozen" items were battered cod, oven chips and peas.

'All good thanks Caroline, bit of a fan if I'm honest; makes a change from sandwiches.'

They chatted freely as they ate, but Brendon didn't mention his visit to the gorge with McKenna.

Sitting back in his chair, he wiped his mouth with a paper napkin. Eventually he asked, 'Did Gareth instruct someone to value the quarry site?'

She eyed him curiously. 'Not as far as I know, why do you ask?'

'Because McKenna told me they thought the body found in the gorge was an estate agent from London who'd been employed by Gareth.' Caroline put her plate on top of his and rose from the table.

'Well, if he did, he didn't tell me.' She picked up the kettle. 'More tea?'

'Yes please.' He rubbed the back of his neck. 'Is it… sorry… *was* it unusual for Gareth to do things without telling you? I mean getting someone from far away seems strange when you've got many experienced farm agents in the area.'

Caroline sat back down, fiddled with the vinegar bottle for a moment then met Brendon's eyes. 'Brendon, do you remember what I told you the afternoon we made love, you know about how Gareth had changed in recent times?' He nodded. 'Well, part of the change was the way he stopped including me in any of the farm decisions.' The kettle clicked *off.* Automatically she got up to make tea.

Her back towards him, she continued, 'We'd always discussed everything; when to sell the cattle, when to cut the hay, even when to buy a new tractor.' Covering the teapot with a cosy she turned towards him. 'Then I'd find that things had been done without any consultation. It wouldn't have changed anything, I would have agreed with him anyway, but he was leaving me out and I didn't like it.'

'Did you discuss it with him?'

She shook her head. 'Gareth wasn't the sort to discuss things if they were personal.'

'Did you tell Ellie and Nathan?'

She shrugged. 'You really don't know do you?' She poured the tea and milk.

'Know what Caroline?' he asked, totally bewildered by her question.

Placing his mug in front of him, she answered, 'They hated him, absolutely hated him, ever since he started… '

She crossed to the window; Brendon heard sobbing. He jumped up to comfort her. His arm around her shoulders, he asked, 'Started what Caroline?'

Tears running down her face, she looked up at him. 'Abusing Ellie.'

He held her tightly, initially unable to take in what she'd told him. Finally he managed, 'When?'

She swallowed hard. 'She was twelve when he started.'

'And you knew?' Shaking his head in disbelief, he released his hold.

She nodded. She tore off some kitchen roll from the dispenser beside the fridge and began dabbing her eyes. 'I didn't believe Ellie at first when she came to me crying, nor Nathan when he said he'd walked in on his father and he was… was… touching his sister.' She took a deep breath. 'But then I came home earlier than expected and…' she pushed Brendon away.

'And what, Caroline, what?'

'I heard screams from the upstairs window. Ellie was telling him to stop.' She gazed at the ceiling, sobbing uncontrollably. Brendon recalled his own experience.

'But what did you do?' She didn't reply. Facing her, he held her shoulders. 'Caroline, what did you do?' He felt an urge to shake her. 'Caroline, what did you do?'

She put her head in her hands. 'Nothing Brendon, I didn't do anything.' Unexpectedly, her body went limp. Catching her before she hit the ground, he carried her upstairs and laid her on her bed. Sat in the rocking chair, uncertain how he felt, he watched her sleep.

CHAPTER TWENTY-TWO

Closing the farm gate behind him, he remembered the padlock; it was nowhere to be seen. Perhaps the police had put it there and since retrieved it. Trying to collect his thoughts he stopped in the lane. He'd sat with Caroline for an hour whilst she slept. On waking, she seemed very vague about the things she'd told him, initially disbelieving his recounting of her story.

'I shouldn't have said those things; they were a long time ago, not to be discussed with… with anyone inside or outside the family.' She looked angry. 'It wasn't Gareth's fault, he didn't know any different.'

'You mean he was abused as a child?' She didn't answer his question, choosing instead to get off the bed and go to the bathroom. On her return, her face was flushed.

'I think it's time for you to leave Brendon; I need to be alone.'

Respecting her wishes, he'd kissed her cheek and left. Now sat in his car, he tried to get his head around her outburst. He had no recall of Gareth being abused as a child. It wouldn't have been something his friend would want to talk about but surely it would have been obvious?

They'd all played many times at Gareth's parents' farm, stayed for tea, watched television. Gareth's father had a great sense of humour; his jokes weren't always funny, but he was always laughing. Brendon couldn't imagine he would have molested his son. Brendon tried to put it to the back of his mind; he had other things to do.

Jim and Pete were sat in front of the pub. Walking from the car park, there was no way he could avoid them.

'How's your lover then little weaner; did you manage to make her come?' gibed Jim as Brendon approached.

'Not able to get it up perhaps,' joined in Pete.

Brendon ignored them, desperate to end both their lives. Everybody knew his slightest move and he'd had enough.

'Sorry to hear your Detective Chief Inspector friend is no longer with us, just as you were getting on so well too. A nasty business,' chortled Jim.

'A very nasty business indeed,' chimed in Pete. 'You want to be very careful mister MI6 person.'

'Very careful indeed I should say. We don't wants anything happening to you now do we?' taunted Jim.

'Don't know about that Jim,' sniggered Pete. 'Wouldn't worry me none. Another pint?'

'Love one Pete.'

They got up, leaving Brendon motionless in the middle of the road, his fists clenched. He had to stay disciplined, at least for the time being.

~

In an attempt not to be followed or seen, after donning walking boots, he left the pub by the back entrance and followed the lane leading past the ancient spring and headed for Lingtree Forest, the dogging spot where the bodies of Harry Elliot and Linda Collier had been discovered. It was roughly a four-mile-walk, two miles of which was on an unclassified, poorly maintained tarmac road. No doubt at some time in the future the council would fill in the potholes, finances permitting. Two or three cars passed him, but he didn't recognise them or their occupants as any vehicle or person he'd seen in the village.

Leaving the road, he walked half a mile along an unmade but well-used farm track, before entering Lingtree Forest, the name given to five hundred acres of Forestry Commission land. A small sign attached to one of the tall conifers reminded members of the public they were welcome, provided they kept their dogs under control and avoided dropping any litter or burning cigarette butts. The trees stood upright and tall like line after line of warriors preparing to go into battle. Fifty metres into the woods, a rough, pitted area approximately half the size of a football pitch had been cleared of trees and designated a car park. Due to its concealed location from the road, in recent years it had been a popular venue with night-time courting couples and those wanting to share their sexual pleasures and delights with both voyeurs and other keen participants.

Two steps into the open area, without warning, Brendon's head became swamped with a feeling of giddiness so strong that immediately his stomach retched, the bile engulfing his throat and his mouth. Unable to resist an overwhelming sense of foreboding, unceremoniously he collapsed to the ground. For a few seconds he lay there face up, jagged rocks enforcing their intent to leave deep depressions in his back and his head. He saw the tops of the pines begin swaying viciously in a wind unfelt on the ground. He imagined their green sharp-pointed needles raining down on him like Anglo-Saxon arrows protecting their warriors' enclave and instinctively he covered his eyes. Unable to move, he lay there, holding his throbbing head, the pain as sharp as that caused by the screams from Caroline's bedroom window. He wanted to sleep, to return to sanctity, but there would be no peace, no solitude, for in the distance, he heard the sound of an engine.

Straining to open his eyes, he saw day had become night and his fingers felt numb, stretched out where they rested on the ice-surfaced puddle. The rattle of a worn diesel engine filled his ears and he watched as a large Volvo Estate entered the clearing, closely followed by a four-by-four with bull bars and spotlights.

A hooded man climbed out of the Volvo, moving quickly to the four-by-four to help its driver drag first one, then a second body from the back. They didn't speak, but noiselessly executed what was obviously a well-rehearsed plan. Laying the smaller of the two limp bodies face down on the bonnet of the Volvo, the man supported the other lifeless victim whilst his cohort carefully removed all of its clothing. Tossing the clothes through the Volvo's open front door, they effortlessly manoeuvred the male onto the empty back seat.

After undressing the second body, the silhouette of generous breasts revealing its sex, they manipulated it gently but deliberately astride the male. Winding down a rear window a couple of inches, one of them took a thick pipe from the four-by-four and secured an end around the Volvo's exhaust, before pushing the other through the partially open window. Acknowledging the man's wave of his hand, the accomplice climbed in and started the engine, revving it viciously several times, before clambering out and slamming the door closed.

Even with his vision distorted, Brendon could see the Volvo's engine wasn't the most efficient, as thick, possibly oil-tainted smoke filled the interior. The fumes penetrating every inch of the passenger compartment, the two figures watched silently, occasionally jumping up and down and flapping their arms vigorously in an effort to keep warm.

After twenty minutes or so, they nodded to each other, extracted the pipe from the window and yanked it off the exhaust. As one threw it in the boot of the four-by-four, the other opened the door of the Volvo and forcefully shook the two bodies, then reached gently for the necks. A "thumbs up" signal to his mate suggested they'd achieved their result. The Volvo's engine still running, the four-by-four pulled out of the car park. Gingerly rising to his feet, Brendon's vision and pain began to clear in the return of the warm, welcome sunlight.

He stared at the empty car park. He knew this was how it would be, but still it had shocked him, the way the screams at Caroline's house had done. For now, he had no choice but to continue with his journey for who would believe he had seen the dumping of the bodies. Had he been able to identify the two men at least that might have led to them being questioned, but there was no evidence to prosecute, so what was the point? As he continued along the path as it curved and descended its way to the far end of the gorge, he wondered if the same pair was responsible for the deaths of Jess Withers, the Hendersons and Michael Enscale. If there was time, he would find out, but then again, what would it achieve?

Forty-five minutes later Brendon clambered over a broken, three-strand barbed wire fence. Another two-hundred metres and he would be where the gorge ended its pouring through narrow chasms and cauldrons and where visitors could gain access as an alternative to the village entrance. It was here, that the Vikings had rested after the destruction of Treforthamm, making camp under the "Silver Lady" waterfall created by a second moorland river ending its journey cascading from thirty metres above the gorge. In the lee of the forest trees, they'd celebrated their victory and ill-gotten spoils by getting drunk on the stolen mead and wine.

Wanting to explore the opposite bank to where he and McKenna had found the manhole cover, Brendon took the left-hand path leading from the base of the waterfall and headed in the direction of the cafe where the lorry had entered. Should there be anyone guarding whatever operation was being undertaken, he sensed there would be less chance of being challenged on this side.

Scrambling twenty metres up the gently sloping, grass and bracken covered bank, he reached the tree line, grateful for the protection it provided. At this point, the gorge below contained little more than a placid, meandering river, but further upstream, it would change into the thundering, fast-flowing waters from where rescue would be dangerous and in places, impossible.

He sat quietly, eager to get bearings. It was difficult to gauge exactly where he and McKenna had discovered the manhole cover, but he clearly remembered being able to hear the river, so it must be some distance from where he was sat. Making his way stealthily through the trees and bushes, unexpectedly he heard it, the humming sound they'd detected last night, only much louder than on the other side. It was coming from under his feet. After a quick check to confirm he was alone, he knelt down, his ear to the ground. As well as the hum, he could hear a tapping sound, like somebody hammering in a nail, only much louder and heavier.

Crawling where the undergrowth allowed it, he tracked the tapping, following it to a small clearing amongst the trees, the noise appearing to be at its most intense here; any further and it began to fade. After another quick scan around, he dropped back to his hands and knees, scrabbling and searching for any sign of a manhole cover, trap door, drain or air duct. He found nothing and yet the hum and tapping were so clear. Twenty minutes later, his hands and knees sore from the constant probing by last autumn's fallen pine cones and needles, together with occasional pricks from half-hidden brambles and stings from innocuous looking nettles, he decided to call a halt to his fruitless search. There had to be something down there, but here wasn't its entrance.

Feeling his only hope of solving the underground mystery lay on the other side, he stumbled and slid from his position high on the valley to the river below. Controlled by the new growth of flora, at first his progress was slow; however, nearing the carved-out footpath, greenery gave way to earth and loose stone. Resorting to a sitting position to stop himself tumbling, he travelled a further ten metres before managing to land feet first on the path. Hastily rubbing his backside, he apologised profusely to the elderly couple he'd startled by his unexpected arrival. His apology obviously inadequate, they stared at him in disgust before continuing on their way. Once they were out of sight, Brendon descended far more elegantly the five metres to where the river temporarily widened and the water shallowed.

'Brendon, what are you doing?' a female voice shouted from above. It was Caroline, but she wasn't alone.

'Caroline. Hi.' He looked at the vicar, somewhat out of place in dog collar and sports jacket. 'Reverend Soby.'

'I said, whatever are you doing?' she asked irritably.

Brendon smiled. 'Um… just… checking what fish are here. I was wondering if it was still brown trout.' He knew his answer was ridiculously incredulous, but despite an hour passing since he'd observed the bodies being supposedly poisoned by carbon monoxide, his brain was faintly foggy and disorientated and it was the best he could do. 'Anyway, what brings you to the gorge; I thought you were tired.'

'I was, but then David called to see how I was feeling and suggested fresh air might do me good.'

Brendon hoisted himself back onto the path. 'I see, and did it?'

'Yes thank you.' She looked at him sternly. 'Now, are you going to tell me what you were really doing? Anyone in the pub would have told you, you shouldn't go fishing in the gorge, it's owned by the Trust.'

He was fishing certainly, but not for trout.

'All right, you win. Wanted to cool off, that's all. I walked the long way around, you know... via the woods. Got a bit sweaty and...' he shrugged, fully aware neither Caroline nor her companion were convinced, 'was thinking of going for a drink in the cafe. Perhaps you two would like to join me.'

The vicar and Caroline exchanged glances.

'Okay,' she accepted, 'but we'll take the conventional route.'

'Fine by me.'

~

The cafe was busy, full of visitors, no doubt many retired, chattering loudly as they enjoyed sharing their experiences of the gorge, passing around digital cameras and hastily purchased postcards. Some had to shout at their half-deaf companions and the general hubbub of conversation, together with rattling tea cups and saucers echoed continuously in the high ceilinged building.

'So Brendon, when... will you definitely... be leaving us?' spluttered the vicar, his mouth full of the last bite of teacake.

'I'm not sure, Vicar. I have no rush to go back, although it might be sooner than I hoped. Why do you ask?'

'No reason in particular, although it might be in your best interest.'

Caroline avoided Brendon's eyes, her hands cuddling her cup.

'Anything to do with our brief conversation in the pub the other evening?' enquired Brendon.

'That's for you to decide.' The vicar wiped his mouth, screwed up the napkin and stood up. 'Now then, if you will excuse me.' He pushed his chair under the table. 'Thank you for the refreshments Mr Gallagher.' He turned to Caroline. 'Take care of yourself young lady. We don't want anything else happening to you.'

Brendon watched him closely as he left. 'Nice man. Why do you have anything to do with him?' he asked sarcastically.

Caroline's attention still focused on her cup, she sipped the tea, deliberated for a moment then pleaded, 'Please do as he said Brendon, for all our sakes.'

Shaking his head, his brow furrowed, he demanded, 'But… but why Caroline, why would you say that? I thought you liked me here.'

Her eyes watered. 'I do Brendon, truly I do, but I also care about you.'

'Then I don't understand.' He looked away, confused by her reaction.

She touched his hand. 'I told you how I felt. I've never forgotten you but things have… have moved on since you left the village.'

It's a small village, a very small village indeed!

'How do you mean?' He turned back, his eyes narrowed. 'Are you talking about the murders, Gareth's death, your attack, what?'

'Haven't you noticed?' she snapped, surprisingly

217

loud enough for even the hardest of hearing customer to catch. The room fell silent, the elderly patrons hoping for something more exciting than their own conversations. 'I've got to go.' Red faced, she pulled her purse from her jeans' pocket and threw a twenty-pound note on the table. 'There, that should cover it. Keep the change.' She rose. He grabbed her arm, the interest from the curious busybodies beginning to wane.

'Please explain,' he begged. Then lowering his head, he added, 'I need to know before it's too late. I have to put something right, make up for the wrong doing. Please Caroline, please tell me.' She pulled away.

He jumped up, reigniting the attention of the audience as he rushed after her. The unseen girl with the short blonde hair sat by the door continued sucking her cola through a straw. She could tell him there was still plenty of time, if only he remained patient.

CHAPTER TWENTY-THREE

Caroline's car had been parked by the double gates leading into the woods. At first, she'd rejected his plea to open the passenger door, but after starting the engine and engaging first, she'd relented. Neither spoke as she drove to her farm. Brendon opened and closed the gate, then walked up the drive behind her.

He reached the front door just as she was unlocking it. He followed her in, accepting the silence. Taking his hand, she led him up the stairs and into the bedroom. Facing him, she slowly undid the six buttons on his shirt, pushing it over his shoulders. Kneeling, she wrenched undone the laces of his boots. Once removed, she reached for his belt, button and zip and eased his trousers and boxers down to his ankles. He sighed and held her shoulders.

Pushing him onto the bed, her eyes fixed on his, she lifted her blouse over her head, exposing her black, deep-cut bra. She kicked off her shoes, unbuttoned her jeans and suggestively slid down the zip. Stepping out of her jeans, she stood like a beautiful sculpture, her matching panty briefs highlighting her slim hips and shapely thighs. Licking her top lip, she ran a finger down her crotch.

His cock hardened as she undid her bra. One strap at a time slipped down her arm. He stared at her breasts, so firm and unspoilt. She rolled the nipples between her fingers and thumbs and she saw how much he wanted her. Free of her panties, she lifted her knees onto the bed, eased herself forward and encouraged his hand to explore her moistness. She gasped as he found and caressed her sensitive place. Panting, she guided his hand away, rubbed his erection lovingly then pushed it inside. They sighed together. Lifting his hips, he pushed in deep, gently fondling her breasts as she pressed then lifted. Her head went back, she mouthed his name, exchanging their love without words. Finally he passed out.

Feeling satisfied, he walked back along the lane towards the gorge, intending to locate the source of the noise. He had regained consciousness within a few minutes, awaking to find Caroline had already got out of bed and was showering. Seemingly relieved he was okay, they'd said their goodbyes. It wouldn't be the last time he saw her, but it would be the last time they made love.

'Ah Mr Gallagher; there you are.'

As always, the unexpected appearance of this man in shorts, socks, work boots and gold-rimmed spectacles made Brendon jump. He wondered if he'd been hiding in the bushes.

'Mr Hatcher. Sorry, were you looking for me?'

'Yes indeed,' he replied in his nonchalant manner. 'Thought you were still in the gorge; wondered if you'd found anything.'

Puzzled Brendon asked, 'Forgive me Mr Hatcher, but what makes you think I was looking for anything?'

It's a small village, a very small village indeed.

'Ah yes, I see.' He pointed the way Brendon was heading. 'I was going the same way; is it all right to walk with you?'

Brendon nodded. Setting a pace not much faster than a Zimmer-frame user, Hatcher explained his reason for asking.

'Well, Mr Gallagher, you know I said we were originally intending to explore the tunnel, or rather the supposed tunnel?'

'Yes I remember,' acknowledged Brendon. 'I believe you decided it was too dangerous.'

'That is correct... well, for others that is. However, based on recent information, I believe it's important to—'

Brendon never heard the moderatored shot above Hatcher's words, but the warm sensation trickling down the back of his neck stopped him in his tracks. Examining the body lying face down on the ground just behind him, he saw the bullet hole in the back of the head just above the nape of the neck. His first reaction should have been to take cover, lest the gunman's next shot was for him; however, as at least fifteen seconds had elapsed since he'd turned round, he assumed that whoever had pulled the trigger, hadn't wanted him dead as well.

Rolling the body over, he saw Hatcher's face was partially ripped open, the bullet tearing at the bridge of the nose and forehead as it exited. Had it taken a deflection, Brendon realised he could have been its second victim. Hatcher's wide-open eyes stared quizzically at Brendon, the gold-rimmed glasses, one lens shattered, hanging from one ear. Pointlessly checking the pulse confirmed Hatcher had left this world. Squinting in the low sunlight, Brendon scanned every angle, although unless the dead man had been facing any direction other than straight ahead as he talked, the bullet must have come from behind them, the lane back to the farm.

His first instinct was to call DS Pearson, but that would mean the cops swarming all over the area preventing him from exploring the gorge without interference. Crouched by the motionless corpse, Hatcher's interrupted last words ran through his mind.

So *why was the tunnel important and what was the recent information?*

After another quick look around and in intelligence officer autopilot, he lifted Hatcher onto his shoulder. Staggering under the not unsubstantial weight, he managed to force a way into the rhododendron bushes bordering the lane. After five metres, he lowered the body carefully onto the ground and positioned it, as far as he could recall, in the way it had fallen. He had no idea why someone would want to kill Hatcher, but for the time being he had other things on his mind. Once he finished his visit to the gorge, he would ring Pearson and tell her he'd discovered a body in the bushes. He would say that after leaving Caroline's he'd walked along the Corpse Way to the archaeological dig, had a look round and then on his way back, found the body. That way, time of death would fit in with his story.

He wiped the drying blood and small piece of Hatcher's flesh from his neck; there was nothing he could do about the sticky feeling on the back of his shirt. As he continued to the gorge, he began to recall his time in bed with Caroline. It was still unclear, as if he'd been a drunken voyeur rather than a participant. Before entering her, his mind had been fine. Okay, so they'd not spoken, although that had somehow added to the excitement, but as he'd ejaculated, he'd become confused and uncertain, as though something had been cast out. He was still feeling unsettled as he climbed through the reopened gap he'd cut in the wire fence the previous night. It was now just after seven and the gorge was closed for the day.

Arriving at the turning area, he followed the path but instead of it ending fifty metres later, it continued all the way down to the river. Retracing his steps, he tried different ways of leaving the clearing, but the routes either led to overgrown dead ends or to other paths back to the top of the valley.

Realising he was getting nowhere and time was passing rapidly, he reluctantly hurried back to where he'd left Hatcher's body. Switching his phone off "silent", he ignored the bleeping advising him he had "missed calls". Although the light was fading, it didn't explain why he couldn't find the dead man. There were signs of activity where he'd deposited Hatcher, but once the trail of flattened grass reached the lane, there was nothing obvious to follow. Perhaps daylight would show tracks, blood, footprints, anything to indicate how and in which direction it had been removed, presumably by the assassin.

Cursing, he checked his phone. Six missed calls from a number he anticipated being DS Pearson's. He pressed "call". It rang once.

'Mr Gallagher, where have you been? I've been trying to get hold of you since you cut me off,' she snapped.

'Er... h'mm... I'm really sorry,' he replied, guilty and uncomfortable. 'I must have been without a signal.'

'Your phone rang sir,' she snapped, this time sarcastically.

'Well, I'm sorry DS Pearson,' he retaliated, 'I can't be at your beck and call all the time. Anyway, I'm here now,' he continued, calming down. 'How can I help?'

'No, you're right, I apologise.' DS Pearson paused.

Brendon sensed her gathering her thoughts.

'I know Colin... DCI McKenna held you in high regard and I guess I was relying on you helping me and his replacement in the same way. Having someone in Lingtree I can trust is very important to me... to us both.'

Brendon felt his gut tighten. 'Of course you can trust me,' he lied, rubbing the back of his neck.

'Thanks, I really appreciate it.' She sighed deeply. 'The body we found in the gorge is definitely that of sixty-three-year-old John Wakeham, a wealthy and highly respected...' she sniggered, 'sorry... land agent from London. Apparently he received instructions from Gareth Pettit to value some land, the site of the proposed sidings to service the quarry.'

'I see,' acknowledged Brendon. 'Any idea why he was killed?'

'That we don't know... well... ' She hesitated. 'At least we're not sure if it's relevant but— '

'What is?' he interrupted impatiently.

'Well, before he was killed, he emailed his office requesting details of the compulsory purchase order.'

'So?'

'There is no compulsory order; in fact, there're not

even any plans for a quarry,' Jenny explained, 'nor a reopening of the railway line.'

Brendon fell silent.

'Mr Gallagher?'

'I'm still here Jenny.' Another silence. Finally Brendon broke it. 'So why does everybody believe there are plans and who are the workmen?'

'No idea at the moment I'm afraid. Also, I need to have a word with the archaeologist. I understand it's a Mr... Mr...'

'Frank Hatcher,' Brendon informed her.

'Yes, that's it... Mr Hatcher. Have you seen him lately?'

His guilt returned. 'I think we'd better meet up Jenny, there's something I need to talk to you about.'

'Can it wait until the morning, only it's been a very long day?'

'You're telling me,' Brendon agreed, 'but I'm afraid it's not over yet. I'll meet you about half a mile up the lane which leads to Caroline Pettit's farm, you know where—'

'Yes, I know,' the detective sergeant replied. 'Twenty minutes then.' She hung up.

CHAPTER TWENTY-FOUR

'And this is definitely where you found the body?' DS Pearson shone her torch on the undergrowth to where Brendon had moved Hatcher.

'That's right. I saw some marks in the lane, sort of dragging marks and so I followed them into the bushes and there it was.' Lying came easy to Brendon; it had been part of his job.

'How long ago?'

'One and a half, maybe two hours. I tried to ring but the battery was dead.'

Brendon could just make out her frown.

'So how did you charge it so quickly?' she asked.

'Spare battery back in the car... it was still in the pub car park.' Although uncomfortable, he didn't want her to know about the gorge, at least not yet.

'I see. And when you returned, the body had gone.'

'Correct.' He knew she wasn't totally fooled, but so what.

Pushing back the branches of the rhododendron bushes, she battled her way to the lane.

'Forensics please,' she said once her phone call had

been answered. 'And do you know if DI Eversden has finished on the Jones' case...? Okay... can you ask him to contact me as soon as possible please...? Yes, I do know what time it is thank you... cheers for you help.' She shook her head. 'Bloody young upstarts... ah, Henry, I need your team out at Lingtree... we've lost a body.' She gave Henry directions.

'Does Mrs Pettit know about this? I assume that's why you were here,' she enquired, switching her attention to Brendon.

'No. I'd left her at the farm and was walking back to the pub.'

'Perhaps we ought to go and tell her what's going on,' suggested Pearson. 'She's likely to hear the van engine and see the arc lights; she might be concerned, especially after what happened to her.'

'I don't think that'll be necessary,' he said hastily. 'She was very tired, still recovering from her ordeal; I'm sure she'll sleep through.' Thinking quickly, he added, 'That's why I didn't use her phone.'

Pearson stroked her chin. 'Okay... fair enough... perhaps you're right. By the way, we haven't been able to get hold of her kids yet either.'

'Sorry?' exclaimed Brendon incredulously.

'I said we haven't been able to get hold of her two kids,' repeated Pearson. 'One of my DCs keeps trying, but it's as if they're avoiding her.' Shining the torch at him, she regarded Brendon closely. 'You seem surprised.'

'No... no... not at all,' he replied, wondering why the hell Caroline had told him otherwise. 'I'm sure there must be a good reason why.'

'Yes, that's probably true,' she mused, lowering the torch and changing the subject. 'Forensics should be here in fifteen…' Looking at him quizzically in the dark, she paused abruptly. 'Where were you when you rang me Mr Gallagher?'

'At my car of course,' Brendon replied confidently. 'Why do you ask?'

'No reason, just wondered that's all.'

'You mean, how did I get here so quickly bearing in mind you took a quarter of an hour from Chilstoke and the pub's a good forty minutes' walk away?'

'Your words not mine.'

'I keep myself very fit even at my age; I have to; it helps me stay alive.'

She'd already noticed his shape confirmed it.

'I ran all the way; in fact I sprinted the last two hundred metres.'

'That's fine.'

Brendon hated the word "fine" when used by the female fraternity. So what if she didn't believe him, he wouldn't be around much longer.

'So Mr Gallagher.'

'Please call me Brendon, Jenny.'

'So Brendon. You say Mr Hatcher had been shot in the head.'

'From behind.'

'And the blood on your shirt?' She'd noticed it in the torchlight.

He wanted to say "fuck".

'I fell, knocked my nose.'

Fuck, fuck, fuck, fuck, fuck.

'I see, so you won't mind if we twist your head around the right way, or perhaps you had your shirt on back to front,' she remarked. Sighing, she continued, 'I may only be a sergeant Brendon, but contrary to what you may think, I'm not stupid. Now, do you want to tell me the truth, like why didn't you drive back here and how come it took you an hour and a half to fetch your battery?'

Sighing loudly, he shook his head. 'I'm sorry Jenny, you're right.' He took a few moments to think. 'Look, if I tell you what really happened to Hatcher, will you give me space to tidy up a matter or two before you start interviewing every Tom, Dick and Harry?'

'You are joking?' she quipped. 'I'm the copper remember?'

'No, I'm not. In fact I've never been more serious. I suppose I could plead the protection of the Official Secrets Act.'

'And I could plead insanity to my DI,' she retorted.

Pleading wasn't something he ever liked resorting to, but this was important.

'Okay, until close of play tomorrow,' relented DS Pearson, 'but only because of Colin. For now, the body was where you showed me.'

'Thanks Jenny, you won't regret it.'

'I hope not Brendon because I have no intention of remaining a sergeant.'

At that moment, she could not possibly have known that, despite her ambitions, sadly fate would prove her wrong.

He explained where and how Hatcher had been shot, the fact that no one had taken a second shot at him, but not the reason he'd moved the body.

'And that's it? ' She sighed. 'C'mon Brendon, I think you owe me more than that. You realise you have to be my prime suspect?'

'You know I'm not involved… with the shooting that is. Look… give me the time I've asked for and I promise I will fill you in with all the details. There are things I have to see to which at the present only I can sort out and that's not being sexist.'

'Sounds like it to me,' she said, disgruntled with his explanation. 'And also, who was Colin going to pay… you remember you were in the middle of explaining when we were conveniently cut off?'

'It will all come clear and when it does, you'll be promoted to inspector.' He couldn't really see flattery working and he was right.

'It won't be that simple; born with the wrong bits you see.'

The headlights of the forensics van appeared, jiggling up and down as the vehicle sped towards them along the potholed lane.

'Henry, how are you?' she asked, as a six-foot-plus, somewhat overweight man with a thick, untidy beard, strode up to her, his not insubstantial outline casting a long shadow in the light from the van.

'Unimpressed at this time of night,' he responded. 'So what have we got?'

'This is Brendon Gallagher. He's… shall we say… with the Government.'

'A spy, eh?' He crushed, rather than shook Brendon's hand. 'Colin was a good friend as well as a colleague. He spoke highly of you.'

'Thank you Henry. It was a tragic loss.' It was, but it wasn't the first work colleague to depart Brendon's company prematurely.

Henry nodded his agreement then pointed to the much shorter, much leaner, much younger, clean-shaven lad, approaching from behind. He was carrying a large attaché case. 'This is Liam, who is... shall we say... my assistant.'

'Pleased to meet you Liam.'

He rejected Brendon's offered hand. 'So what's to do?' he asked, eager to get started. Jenny led him to the area in the rhododendrons.

'Not much,' she explained, 'but a body was dumped here and then removed. Seal it off and then see if you can get anything useful.'

'Lights will probably be the only useful thing here. Looks like this has been well trodden; you realise it was a crime scene?' Liam was very sure of himself after just four months in forensics.

'Just do as the lady asks.' It was Henry's booming voice. Casting his eye around the trampled undergrowth with a high-powered torch he tutted. 'He's right though, Jenny; does look a bit messy. Have you and Brendon been having a bit of a secret tumble?' He laughed heartily as they made their way out of the bushes. 'Time you got yourself a man. Living on your own makes you bitter.'

'Very funny Henry, I'm sure you're right. Anyway, until I do, just get on with it and also it might be worth having a shufti on this bit of the lane.' She shone her torch to where Brendon had told her Hatcher collapsed.

'How come?'

'Just a hunch, nothing more.'

Henry tutted again. 'Bloody difficult; not really sure what I'm looking for,' he moaned, picking up the light batteries from the rear of the van. 'Could have been home watching the end of *Silent Witness* on one of those old-fashioned channels. Different if there'd been a bleedin' body.'

'Now you know you don't mean that.' She speed-dialled a number on her mobile. 'I'll get uniform to park up alongside. Can't think there'll be much point, but I don't want to lose any bits of my body for not following procedure.'

'Thought you said you had the wrong bits,' chirped Brendon.

'Nice one.' She put the mobile to her ear. 'Better bugger off before I change my mind. Ten o'clock tomorrow. If not, you'll be arrested.'

Brendon kissed her on the cheek. Unaware she was blushing, he told her she wouldn't regret it and set off back to the gorge. He hadn't finished there yet.

As he disappeared down the lane, DS Pearson opened the boot of her car and picked up the pair of trainers. Henry could sort out uniform when they arrived and whatever Brendon thought, she wasn't stupid.

CHAPTER TWENTY-FIVE

It was almost 11 p.m. when Brendon walked up the steep road from the gorge to The Judge's Parlour, his boots covered in a thick layer of mud and the knees of his jeans muddied and grass stained. As he approached the pub, Jim and Pete were sat opposite each other on small single bench seats sank into either side of the porch walls. It was Jim who started.

'Been playing by the river have we?' he gibed as Brendon approached. 'Find much did we?'

'Funny time of night to go fishing I would have thought, 'less you was poaching,' chipped in Pete. 'Could fall down a big drain hole in the dark if you're not careful.'

Brendon stared at them. How they knew his every move no longer bothered him. If they intended him any harm, he was certain it would have happened before now. He was mentally and physically drained and in no mood for a discussion.

'For fuck's sake, go and get a life will you and let others get on with theirs,' he replied heading towards the front door. Jim immediately jumped up and blocked his way.

'Not a very nice way to speak to an old friend,' he

said, leaning against the front door. 'We was only being polite… you know, passing the time of day.' He looked up at the stars in the cloudless sky. 'Or should I say night?'

Pete got up and leaned against Jim. 'Definitely night Jim,' he smirked. 'Been a long day Mr Gallagher… sorry, Brendon, wouldn't you agree?'

Brendon had no intention of agreeing, but instead made to push past. Jim and Pete straightened.

'In a bit of a hurry are we?' asked Jim, his face no more than a half-metre from Brendon's. His breath stunk of booze and stale rollies.

'Out of my way,' demanded Brendon, not dropping his eyes from Jim's.

'That's definitely not a very nice way to speak to an old friend,' repeated Pete, ''specially as we've been looking out for you. Wouldn't want you to end up like that old fart the archaeologist now would we?' He smiled, his pursed lips covering his teeth. 'After all, can't eat without your teeth now, can you?'

'That's enough.' It was an order, not a statement. Immediately Jim and Pete took a half step back. Brendon turned to see the vicar, minus his dog collar, stood behind him. His authoritative voice continued, 'Time you lads went home, don't you think?'

'Yes Mr Soby, of course,' they agreed. 'Sorry.' They pushed past Brendon, Jim eyeballing him and deliberately belching, causing Brendon to turn his head away. 'We'd finished with him anyway.'

Brendon watched as they made off towards the village.

'Thank you Vicar,' he said, 'I can do without all this hassle.'

'Then why don't you leave? There's nothing here for you Mr Gallagher. The village is what the village is.'

'And what's that?'

'A place for the locals and visitors passing through; not for long-term busybodies,' he informed Brendon, his face emotionless. 'I would suggest you leave while you're still able.'

'Threatening me again Vicar?' enquired Brendon, unperturbed by the clergyman's attitude.

'As you like Mr Gallagher. Now then, if you'll excuse me it's time for my bed and final prayers of the day. Goodnight.' Picking up a small holdall, he turned on his heel and was gone, but not towards the dormer bungalow "new" rectory opposite the church. Instead, he set a good pace in the same direction taken by Jim and Pete. Brendon let Soby put two hundred metres between him and the pub and then followed, sticking as close to the hedge and gateways as possible.

A few houses had lights on, the windows lit up by the flickering of television screens, but most were in darkness, the upstairs' curtains drawn. As he passed the property on the right with the wooden veranda, once the post office with a bright red telephone kiosk outside, he heard a man and woman shouting, perhaps arguing after an evening flirting in the pub, or the state of their bank balance or even why the bed wasn't made. As a kid, Brendon and his friends had sometimes sheltered under the veranda when "hanging out" on wet, winter nights, making nuisance calls without spending the four old pence required to connect the telephone line. The kiosk had at some time in the past been relocated to the lay-by in front of the village hall and was no doubt little used in an era of mobile technology.

Seeing Soby glance over his shoulder, Brendon ducked into one of the several old Anglo-Saxon narrow roads which ran off at right angles from what was now the main village street. Presumably not spotting his pursuer, Soby forked to the right, taking the lane which it was thought originally led to the village mint, where silver dug laboriously from the edge of the gorge was hand stamped into coins. It was also the end of the old Corpse Way. About to cross the road to follow him, Brendon's vision became enveloped in a sepia cloud, his head throbbed and the horrific screams coming from the house in the middle of the fork resonated like church bells in his ears. As flames, initially held back by the windows, started to sweep up the front of the building, shattered and splintered glass shot into the gardens and roads and the all too familiar smell of burning and melting flesh began to fill his nostrils.

He saw a diminutive figure jump over the low railings and run at speed down the lane opposite the front of the now fire-engulfed house. Brendon ran to the front door, covering his face with his arms. He reached for the handle, but however hard he stretched, it remained beyond his grasp. The screams and strained cries for help were becoming more and more harrowing and he could hear banging on the other side of what had become a solid, impassable wooden barrier.

Unseen, he watched helplessly as people ran up the road from the pub. No one attempted to enter the building; it was all they could do to stand within thirty metres of the heat. There were no more screams, just the crackle of burning wood and the smell of Sunday roast. He didn't see the fire engines arrive and put out the flames which took Michael Enscale's life and neither did he see the vicar again that night.

His pursuit having been brought to an unwanted abrupt end by the vision of the past, he left the boarded-up property and walked slowly back to the pub. The lights were still on in the public bar. Entering by the rear door, he saw Sue taking a tray of freshly washed, steaming glasses out of the washer in the restaurant bar. Hearing him, she looked up and smiled. 'Someone's had a hard day; would a brandy or Scotch be in order?'

Grateful, he acknowledged her smile. 'A large malt would go down a treat please Sue and one for you as well.'

'I shouldn't, but seeing as the boss has retired for the night, I will join you.' Stretching, she carefully took the bottle from the top shelf and poured two generous, unmeasured Scotches into tumblers.

Putting her finger to her lips she said, 'If you don't tell, I won't.' She grinned, opened the counter flap and offered him a bar stool. Wearily, he sat down. She pulled up another beside him.

'Cheers Brendon. Here's to old wrongs being righted.' Seeing his puzzled expression, she added, 'I thought that's what secret agents did.'

'Sometimes,' he replied, although slightly surprised by her comment. 'Cheers.'

They took large gulps.

'Sometimes they cause even more wrongs,' he said ruefully, 'at least to other countries.'

'That's politics for you I guess,' she responded

offhandedly. 'Nothing's changed in the last eleven-hundred years.' She topped up their glasses. 'On the house... matey boy can afford it.'

'Trade that good then?' inquired Brendon, accepting an even larger measure than the first. 'Never seems that busy.'

'Appearances can be deceptive. I accidentally saw the contents of his safe. Stacked high with foreign currency; Krona I think.'

Brendon lowered his glass. 'Really, are you sure?'

'As sure as Scotch is malt and mead is honey,' she replied, smacking her lips as she enjoyed the last little drop. 'Hardly room for the till tray.'

'Interesting.' He drained his glass. 'My shout.'

CHAPTER TWENTY-SIX

16 May 2016

After showering and shaving, it was nearly 2 a.m. before Brendon lay on his bed, naked save for his underpants. Sue had proved to be great company. They'd emptied the bottle of malt. Although she was confident Phil wouldn't notice it hadn't been put through the till, Brendon insisted she add a certain number of measures to his bill, even if it wasn't the full amount. They chatted about nothing, but at times Brendon thought her conversation was very personal, as if she knew him well and understood his feelings. He felt comfortable in her company and immediately trusted her totally.

Despite this, he hadn't mentioned his discovery in the gorge, nor his involvement with the shooting of Hatcher. There was no one he could tell yet, but he had until the end of the day to come up with something concrete for DS Pearson, although after his lack of success on his return visit to the gorge, he wasn't sure he'd be able to fulfil his promise.

After leaving Pearson, he'd intended to find the drain,

but bizarrely, he'd still not been able to locate it. He'd followed the path, which even in the dark he was confident was the one he'd first discovered with McKenna.

Retracing his steps, he'd tried leaving in different directions from the hole in the fence in the hope that earlier events had muddled his memory, but after an hour and a half, he'd realised searching in the dark was like looking for the proverbial needle in a haystack, so reluctantly, he'd decided to wait until dawn. Closing his eyes, he began wishing he hadn't been distracted by the beautiful Sue.

Before sleep took over, he wondered where the vicar was going and more importantly why? The fire at Michael Enscale's house he knew was just another experience, like the one in the "dogging" car park but for a moment it had fooled him into trying to help and, like the previous episode, he'd been unable to identify who was responsible for the murder, as murder it obviously was.

In the two hours before his alarm rudely awoke him, he dreamed of Sue, the sensitive nape of her long neck responding to his touch as facing away, she crouched naked astride him, his swollen cock deep inside her moist, welcoming fanny. With one final thrust, they came together, their moans and sighs breaking the silence. As she collapsed by his side, he stretched out his arm, instinctively pressing the "off" key on his mobile's alarm.

Undeterred by his lack of sleep and forgetting his dream and guilt towards Caroline, he lay there for a minute, listening for any activity either inside or outside the building. As the sun began to rise in the cloudless sky, a few birds started their early choruses. A cock crowed from behind the house opposite his window, but no sound of human life interrupted the sense of solitude.

As he crept sock-footed along the corridor to the stairs, aware the floorboards would probably creak regardless of whether or not he was wearing the boots he was carrying, he paused, head tilted. He could swear he heard several faint voices coming from the end of the corridor in the direction of room nine, but as he stood perfectly still, a few seconds later he accepted he was not fully awake.

Unlocking then locking the back door with his resident's key, he bent down and slipped on his boots. Not wanting to risk being seen walking down the hill to the gorge, he crossed the lane and climbed through the three-strand wire perimeter fence of the castle. As he straightened, he stopped, certain he could hear distant, muffled voices, but after looking round, he saw nobody. Crossing the recently mown, grass-covered former bailey, he forced his way through an overgrown gap in the dry-stone wall and picked his way down the bank, as ever, the brambles and bracken seemingly eager to halt his journey by tearing at the cloth covering his legs and his arms. His thoughts became entangled as he sensed the mutilated and maggot-ridden corpses lying everywhere, some on top of others, some decapitated, eyes picked out by the crows. All had guts removed, the bloody entrails and organs randomly stacked in snake-like heaps. Brendon covered his nose and mouth, eventually letting out a sigh of relief as he reached the sanctity of the hospitable flowing water of the small stream, which after half a mile, trickled happily into the gorge. Gradually his head began to clear.

The path alongside the stream was in places a

wilderness, with yet more brambles, nettles and the early beginnings of seasonal parsley grass and bracken. Rotted fallen trees occasionally caused minor detours, but after much effort, he eventually reached a part of the gorge where the river spread wide, its depth reduced as if needing a rest, before once again narrowing and restarting its never-ending breakneck journey to the sea. Here, the waters could be crossed by wading up to the knees. Sitting down, he undid his laces and removing his boots and socks, he rubbed the scratches caused by his battle with the undergrowth. Sharp stones on the riverbed would also take their toll, but it was better than exploring in wet, creaking leather footwear.

Tucking his socks inside his boots, he jumped at the sound of a breaking stick. Instantly turning and rising, hands to the ready, he was relieved to see the curious and startled face of a young muntjac deer. Frozen, it stared at him. Brendon stared back, admiring its beauty and innocence, until it finally managed to regain control of its instincts and run off into the cover and protection of the trees and the hedgerows.

Cursing incessantly under his breath as he tentatively felt his way across, the clear water cold but not uncomfortably so, his feet slipping on smooth, time-worn rocks, he managed to reach the other side without a drenching or a jagged cut to his feet. Tying his laces, he glanced around for signs of animal or human life. It appeared he was alone. An hour later, he was still unable to find the manhole cover, despite his certainty the path he took from the hole in the fence was, as last night, the right one.

There was no sound, no tracks, no broken branches; no indication whatsoever the path ever led to a drain or potentially an underground works' access. There was nothing for it but to try and discover an opening on the other side where he'd heard the sounds of the hammering as well as the humming. About to make his way to the shallows, he became aware of voices approaching from the gorge entrance. Lying prone, he hid in the thick undergrowth. Thirty seconds later and he could clearly hear their conversation in Swedish.

'It is here Erik, under this hazel tree.'

'Ah yes, it works well.'

From where he was lying, Brendon could only guess what the two men were doing, but the grunts and cursing suggested they were lifting and moving something reasonably heavy.

'All this just to keep out nosy policemen; it would be much easier to shoot them instead.'

'And women,' suggested the one addressed as Erik, 'then she definitely wouldn't come back.'

His friend laughed. 'It is most unlikely anyway.'

Brendon heard the sound of metal being dragged across the stone.

'Come Erik, we will not be long. We can move the tree back when we leave but remind me to bring a tyre lever next time, my fingers are raw.'

A moment later, another dragging noise was followed by a loud "clunk".

Lifting his head cautiously, Brendon checked the two had dropped into the drain. A two-metre-high hazel tree, its trunk mounted on a round, turf-shrouded wooden base, was blocking and obscuring the path to the river. Placed on top of the cover, the path was clear to continue. It was the reason he hadn't been able to locate the entrance; a pile of loose dead bracken and brambles adding to the deception.

Brushing himself off, he caught hold of the metal cover. Fortunately, having just been moved from its sunken spot, it lifted more easily than he'd expected and with much effort, he gradually managed to haul it clear. A small amount of light shone out from what appeared to be a deep drain. The faint humming could be heard, but no hammering. Metal rungs, like those attached to a tall industrial chimney ran down into the depths. Avoiding a rope pulley mechanism, he carefully lowered himself in. About to manoeuvre the cover across above him, he heard voices below.

Clumsily scrambling out, he hauled the cover back into place, using his foot to prevent it slamming shut. Hiding in the bushes, another thirty minutes passed and still there was no sign of the two men emerging from their underground haunt. He looked at his watch, it was ten past eight. He rang Caroline.

'Caroline... we need to talk... can I come round?'

~

The scene of Hatcher's murder was sealed off with blue and white tape, but surprisingly there was no police officer in attendance. A small dark area on the surface of the lane had been ringed with red aerosol paint.

Brendon entered the bushes where he'd laid the

body, but apart from the flattened grass and broken rhododendron branches, there was no sign of any forensic activity. He could only assume Henry and his assistant had completed their examination and as there wasn't a body, had decided there was no point in protecting the crime scene. Either that, or DS Pearson had doubted him.

He opened the gate to Caroline's and as he knocked on her door, he noticed a padlock lying on the ground beneath a downstairs window. He couldn't be sure, but it was similar, if not the actual one which had been put on the gate while Caroline was in hospital.

Good of the police to leave it behind, he thought as the door swung open.

'Come in Brendon.' There was no hug, kiss or any other show of affection. 'Coffee?'

'Yes please, Caroline, and if you have any bread, I could murder some toast.'

She threw a couple of slices of white in the stainless-steel-sided toaster. He sat at the breakfast bar, not quite sure what to say. It was Caroline who started the conversation.

'What happened when you left here yesterday?' she asked, her face deadpan.

'Hatcher was shot,' he replied nonchalantly. 'I'm surprised you didn't know.'

She poured hot water into the mugs. 'I wondered what it was.' No surprise, no shock, no horror in her voice. She added the milk and passed him his coffee.

'Aren't you curious as to why?' enquired Brendon, studying her closely.

She shrugged. He followed her to the lounge; she

made herself comfortable in one of the armchairs while he sat on the sofa.

'A lot has gone on here recently Brendon,' she said, contemplating her coffee. 'After awhile you become oblivious to it.'

He could understand her words if she did his job, but in a small village like Lingtree?

She sensed him staring at her and she met his eyes. 'You think I'm odd don't you?' she asked.

'A little,' he replied.

She got up, gazed out of the window at the garden. 'Lingtree's not the place you remember Brendon. It's changed, the people have changed; nobody cares anymore.'

'That can't be true,' he protested. 'Okay, I agree Jim and Pete have become weird, the landlord of the pub is... is... well, kind of different, some of...' He began to struggle. '... Some of the locals... perhaps most of the... ' *Fuck,* he thought. She's right. Apart from Jim, Pete and Grace, he hadn't spoken to anyone who lived in the village. There was the vicar, but he hadn't been here long nor had Sue and as for the other two waitresses, they weren't around long enough to get to know.

She faced him. 'You see, what did I say? You've been lucky Brendon. How lucky you don't know, but luck runs out... eventually. Before it does Brendon, it would be best for you to go... to go home... now.'

He shook his head. 'I will be very soon Caroline, but not yet, there are things I have to do first.' He couldn't fathom out where she was coming from. She seemed so different since her attack, so distant. 'For one thing, I need to find out who hurt you, what is— '

Putting her mug on the table, she knelt down in front of him. 'You never will Brendon, it's impossible.' She glanced at the window. 'You'll end up like Hatcher, like John Wakeham, Michael Enscale, Linda Collier, Harry Elliot and— '

'Jess Withers?' he interrupted.

She sighed, her clasped hands covering her mouth. 'No, that was different, that was an accide...'

Brendon jumped up, his coffee spilling on the tan woollen carpet. 'You mean you know they were murdered?' he asked angrily. 'Tell me Caroline, did you know?' He grabbed her arms, hauled her to her feet. Her head dropped. 'Tell me, please,' he pleaded.

She pulled away, her eyes full of tears. Wiping them off her cheeks with the back of her hand, she looked up at the ceiling.

'Go while you can Brendon, forget everything you've seen. Go and don't come back, it's not the same anymore.' She shook her head. 'I'm so sorry.' After a moment's silence, unable to face him, she ran up the stairs.

Confused, hurt, angry, scared, frustrated, anxious, all these emotions swept through him as he stood motionless, his legs unable, or more likely unwilling to respond to his brain's instructions. The one person he'd felt he could totally trust and rely upon had rejected him, was again telling him to leave. The first time he'd thought it was because the vicar had suggested he go, but now alone together, why? What did she mean Withers' death had been an accident but not any of the others? He knew that, but he was different, could see things others couldn't; but not Caroline.

Finally he managed to move to the bottom of the stairs. He'd heard Caroline slam her bedroom door, shutting him out of her life. He needed to know more. At the top of the stairs he stopped. He'd expected to hear sobbing, but not voices.

'Yes I know, I'm sorry, but I can't.' It was Caroline.

'It's the only way, there's no alternative.' It was David Soby, the vicar.

What the hell's he doing in her room?

Brendon grasped the door handle; pushed firmly as he wrenched it down. The door remained shut, locked on the inside. He thumped it hard with his fist.

'Caroline, what the fuck's going on? Let me in.' He kicked the lower panel. 'Now,' he ranted.

The key turned. Caroline opened the door. 'Go away Brendon, this has nothing to do with you.'

'I think it does.' He muscled his way in, ready to confront the vicar.

'Where is he?' he shouted. 'Where's the fucking vicar?' The en suite was empty, the wardrobe contained just clothes and shoes and he could see under the bed. Rushing to the window, he looked in the garden.

'Brendon, what's the matter with you? There's nobody here.'

'There is, I heard you talking to the vicar. Where the fuck is he?' His head was thumping. He raced down the stairs, out the front door. Still he saw no one.

'Brendon, you're imagining things.' Caroline was stood behind him, her tears forgotten. 'You look tired. Did you not sleep well last night?'

He confronted her. 'What makes you say that?' he

snapped, wondering how she knew he'd only had a couple of hours.

She stepped back. 'Because of the bags under your eyes, why else would I ask?'

Sighing loudly, his head sunk into his hands.

Caroline put her arm around his waist. 'Is this the reason you're on holiday?' she asked tenderly.

He shook his head. 'I've got to go; there are things I've got to see to.' He kissed her forehead then ran up the drive.

Caroline waited until he'd closed the gate before going back indoors.

'Has he definitely gone this time?' asked the man.

'Yes David, he's gone.'

Brendon hadn't notice the storage cupboard in the en suite, nor the unmade bed in Ellie's vacated bedroom.

CHAPTER TWENTY-SEVEN

'DS Pearson, please.' Her mobile had gone straight to "Message saver".

'Who's calling please?'

'Brendon Gallagher. I've been helping her with some enquiries.'

'Just a minute please Mr Gallagher.' He was put on hold. Thirty seconds passed before the voice returned.

'Sorry Mr Gallagher, she's off sick today.'

'Why, what's wrong with her?' She was fine when he'd left her last night.

'I can't tell you that I'm afraid. You'll have to ask her friend, the one who rang in,' the voice on the end explained politely.

'Is Henry from forensics there please?'

'I'll find out.' Forty seconds later, Henry came on the line.

'How can I help?' He was polite but curt.

'Last night… Jenny Pearson… was she all right when she left you?'

'I thought she was with you,' he replied in a matter-of-fact way. 'Chased after you then texted me to say that once

I was finished, to tell the uniform officer not to bother staying. Said her inspector had told her resources were too stretched to have someone guard an unconfirmed crime scene.'

'And that's what you did?' Brendon asked somewhat cynically.

'I beg your pardon Mr Gallagher? You might be some fancy government employee but that doesn't mean you can tell me what to do.' Henry wasn't impressed by Brendon's tone. 'Now then, if we're done, I've got important police business to attend to.'

'Sorry Henry, I shouldn't have snapped,' Brendon conceded. 'You've been very helpful, thank you.' He hung up.

Why the hell did she follow me? he asked himself as he hurried down the lane. He tried her mobile again; it went straight to "Message Saver".

A thought struck him. If Hatcher was dead, what was happening at the archaeological dig? Wouldn't someone be missing him, reporting his absence to the police? He branched off where the Corpse Way left the lane.

There was no one at the dig and neither was there anyone at the quarry site. All of the archaeologists' tents were gone and the exposed ancient graves had been filled in. Although the Hendersons' graves were still open and taped off, there was no police officer on duty. Presumably the bodies had been buried too long for there to be anything further to be gained by forensics and the remains of the two adults and two children would now be with the pathologist.

Brendon continued along the Corpse Way. About half

a mile outside the village, he was greeted by a young, long-haired male in his early twenties, who'd pitched a "one man" tent on the grass verge beside an overgrown gateway.

The young man greeted him. 'Morning.'

Not in the mood for social niceties, Brendon nodded his response as he continued past.

'Excuse me?' insisted the young male.

'Yes, what is it?' Brendon asked, eager to keep walking.

Sensing his interruption wasn't welcome, the man apologised. 'Sorry, I don't want to be a pain, but do you know what's happening at the site of the Iron Age dig?' he asked hurriedly.

Shaking his head, Brendon let out a loud sigh. 'Sorry, not a problem; it's me that should apologise; been a bad day.' Curious to find out the reason for the question, he held out his hand. 'Brendon Gallagher.'

'Larry Henshaw,' replied the man, smiling as he shook. 'Budding archaeologist. I understood there was a dig going on and I thought I could help out during my holiday, but there doesn't seem to be any signs of life other than four empty graves, several filled in holes and some police tape.'

'I'm as mystified as you I'm afraid,' replied Brendon. 'They had to stop for awhile due to finding a few bodies which were… shall we say… somewhat more recent than anticipated, but it seems as though they haven't come back.' Puzzled, he asked, 'How did you learn about it?'

'H'mm… a friend put it on social media, said they were looking for help.'

'Nothing official then? I mean, wasn't in any archaeological magazines or anything?'

Pursing his lips, Larry rubbed his chin. 'No, not that I saw and I read all of them.' He looked embarrassed. 'Bit of a geek, my girlfriend says.'

'Did your friend say who was organising it?' Brendon had no idea how these things worked, but imagined some mention would have been made.

Larry wrenched his mobile out of the front pocket of his tight denims. 'Now then, let me see.' He pressed a few keys. 'Ah, here we are. It was a... Mr... David Soby. He lives locally and has an interest in... '

Brendon grabbed the handset, reading the details for himself.

'Hey, do you mind?' objected Larry. 'I only just got that. Forty quid a month.'

'Sorry,' said Brendon, handing it back. Larry hastily replaced it in his pocket. 'Did your friend mention any other name at any time?'

'Not in his post. Just what I told you. Is there something wrong? Have I been wound up?' He swore under his breath. 'Sort of fucking stupid thing that bastard would do.'

'No, you haven't been wound up,' Brendon reassured him, 'at least no more than anyone else.'

Larry's face dropped. 'So there isn't a dig?'

'Seems that way I'm afraid.' Brendon grinned. 'I should enjoy your holiday if I was you. Now, if you'll excuse me, I must go. Good luck.'

'Thanks.' Larry sat down in front of his tent, grabbed a beer from a rucksack and swore quietly.

So who was Hatcher? wondered Brendon as he left Larry behind.

The public bar was empty. Phil was busy tidying up the shelves and cleaning the mirror behind the optics. 'Ah, Mr Gallagher, missed you at breakfast. Thought you must have died in the night.' It didn't sound like a joke. 'Gather you kept my new barmaid up.'

'Been for a walk Phil and yes, she's a good listener.'

'That's good. Nice to know my staff are accommodating. Now, can I get you a drink?'

'No thanks; had enough last night.' He pulled up a stool. 'What happened at the dig? I thought they were there for a few weeks.'

'Found all they needed apparently.' He wiped the gin bottle. 'Right, must get to the kitchen, see what's on today's menu. Don't think we've got any fresh offal just yet, so might have to dig deep into the freezer until we hear from the butcher.' He scurried off.

After leaving Larry, Brendon had tried DS Pearson's phone again; as before, it went straight to "Message Saver". Sat at the bar, he pondered his next course of action. At some stage, he would have to contact the detective sergeant's superior and fill him in on everything he'd gleaned. However, first he had to sort out a few answers himself. He linked his mobile into the pub's free Wi-Fi and searched Frank Hatcher.

Frank Hatcher, born 12/08/1953 Retired Ministry of Defence Officer. Widowed, no known children. See "Hatcher Associates".

Brendon clicked on the underlined name.

Hatcher Associates, Private Investigators, 28 Madley Avenue, London. Appointments by referral only.

The information was on a free directory of

investigators. There was no Hatcher Associates website, no telephone number, no details of partners, no mention of any trade body memberships. Searching the address on his "Maps App" proved fruitless.

'So who in hell employed him and why did he say he was an archaeologist?' Brendon said aloud.

'First sign of madness Mr Gallagher; talking to yourself that is.'

The landlord was stood in the doorway to the lounge bar.

'What's the second one?' *Mind your own business* is what Brendon really meant.

'Never got that far, left school before then,' Phil retorted. 'If you want anything, give Sue a shout, she's helping in the kitchen. I've got business to attend to.' The landlord left by the backdoor. A few seconds later, Brendon watched him drive off past the front window. Now was his chance.

Leaning through the reception hatch, he lifted the key to room nine off the rack. The pub was quiet, save for radio music emanating from the kitchen. There was no one upstairs. Turning the key, he checked over his shoulder and gently pushed the door; it swung open to his right. Stepping inside, he looked to his left. Stars flickered in front of his eyes as he fell to the ground, this time blood spurting from a cut on the back of his head. The blow with the hammer didn't kill him, but it was another forty minutes before his eyes opened and another five before they were able to focus clearly on Caroline's.

CHAPTER TWENTY-EIGHT

Not for the first time in recent days, Brendon's head felt as though it had been used as a football by players wearing steel-capped boots, only this time he wasn't lying on a bed. Instead, he was sat on a wooden dining chair, but should dinner be served on the mahogany table in front of him, he would have been unable to eat. His hands were tied tightly behind him presumably with the same blue nylon rope he could see binding his ankles. Attempts to wriggle his wrists free merely caused painful abrasions.

He looked round the windowless room. On two sides were a set of bunk beds, on which were several rolled-up sleeping bags, whilst against another wall was a small stove and sink and an open door to an en suite. Next to a closed door in the fourth wall was a low wooden cabinet supporting a flat-screen television, mini hi-fi system and several scattered CDs and glossy magazines. Above the table, hung posters of naked women, all with long blonde hair.

On two of the three other chairs sat Caroline and David Soby. The woman with whom he thought he had been in love, stared blankly at him, her eyes cold and free of any signs of emotion. It was the vicar who spoke.

'I warned you Mr Gallagher, but like the people who wouldn't listen to Noah, you will pay the price.' Brendon noticed the slightest twitch of Caroline's lips.

'The price being?'

The vicar smiled. 'I'm sure you don't need me to remind you of the scriptures Mr Gallagher.'

'Not a religious man I'm afraid Vic.' Brendon turned to Caroline. 'And what do you think of this Noah story, my love?' At times like this, he found sarcasm and humour a helpful coping mechanism.

She turned away.

'Caroline does as she must,' replied the vicar. 'She enjoys the rewards too much not to.'

'And what are those rewards?' Brendon felt sick. His head hurt, his vision was blurred and he was desperate to smash the face of this man of the cloth with the heaviest object he could manage.

'You will reap yours in heaven, the same as the others, regardless of your lack of faith. God always forgives.'

'And does he forgive the murderers of Withers, Enscale, Collier, Elliot, Wakeham and Hatcher?'

The vicar leaned back, his arms folded. 'Of course. All but Withers were a hindrance. They were killed for the greater good of the village.' He shrugged. 'Our friend Mr Withers shouldn't have listened to Pete. If he hadn't of done, he wouldn't have bought the long-out-of-date guidebook, or should I say the one with the easily removed appendix? Pete and Mr Withers was a personal thing, nothing to do with the organisation.'

'It wasn't just the shares he made a killing on then?' quipped Brendon.

'Very funny Mr Gallagher, good to see you are able to maintain a sense of humour, especially as you are as guilty as anyone.'

'I carry no guilt for doing my job,' argued Brendon.

'And Alan, your best friend; do you carry guilt for him?'

His mouth falling open, Brendon glowered at him through half-closed eyes. The vicar leaned forwards, pleasure written all over his face, the same one Brendon would now like to make totally unrecognisable with one of the cutlery knives lying by the sink.

'Yes I know all about it Mr Gallagher. You thought Gareth was searching the castle grounds while you were... shall we say... encouraging Alan to walk around the top of the wall.' He grinned, his eyes reflecting the pleasure of his put down. 'He even heard you say, "get on with it or I'll have to push you". Am I right?'

Brendon shook his head, tears filtering down his cheeks. He tried to wipe them away with his shoulders, but the knots restricted even the slightest movement. 'It wasn't like that. When I saw him sat on top of the wall he asked me to climb up and help; wanted to show me how he wasn't scared to walk around to the front. As I pushed him forward, he tried to turn back; lost his balance.' He looked at Caroline, begging for forgiveness. At last she spoke, totally emotionless.

'I knew years ago Brendon. Gareth told me not long after we started going out with each other. He told me how he saw you on top of the wall, holding Alan's shoulders, pushing him backwards, how you—'

'That's not true,' pleaded Brendon. 'He asked me to help; said I mustn't let him turn back. I thought I was helping.' He stopped as he realised. 'Is that why you chose Gareth over me?' The tears ceased.

She shrugged. 'And the dogs, the strays you didn't try to chase off, what about them?'

'There was nothing I could do.' He shook his head. 'They were vicious. You never saw them.' His speech was becoming faster and faster, like a child trying to justify a wrongdoing. 'They used to chase us through the gorge sometimes. We reckoned they were owned by the odd bloke who lived near the station, the one with the boarded-up windows and old rusting cars in the garden. Most of the time they were locked up in a shed so nobody knew they were there. You have to believe me Caroline; have to believe me... please.' Had he not been tied to the chair, he'd have been on his knees.

'Enough,' interrupted the vicar. 'No more begging for forgiveness, the Lord will see to that.' He got to his feet. 'Come Caroline, Sven will sort out your lover boy when he returns. In the meantime, we have to decide what accident befell the policewoman; after all, they'll soon be looking for her.' He held the door open.

'What have you done to her, you bastard?' screamed Brendon, hysteria creeping in. 'She didn't know anything.'

'Ah, but she would have done, just like her boss.'

Brendon tried to get up.

'There, there Mr Gallagher. I can assure you Caroline is far more expert at tying knots than those two overpaid buffoons who messed up on Wakeham. Bashing people on the head and lighting fires are all they're good for.' The vicar winked at Caroline, a wry smile on his face. 'Perhaps you can do the rope honours with Mr Hatcher my dear; his body's too old for any other purpose. Nothing left to inflate so he should stay sunk.'

Caroline avoided any acknowledgment of the vicar's request. Instead, she kissed Brendon on the forehead as she made for the exit.

'We tried to warn you Brendon. I'm so sorry, I really am, but I have too much to lose. I told Gareth the same, but he insisted he was going to sell up, start a new life.'

'But the quarry, the railway, the dig, they're all lies. Wakeham found that out,' replied Brendon.

'And that's why I killed him,' she boasted, 'the same as that interfering prat of a part-time archaeologist Hatcher, the one who entered the tunnel. We had no idea it was just a hobby to him. Ellie had met him at a party; said he was discreet and in need of some cash. Both he and the arsehole of an estate agent discovered the plans were just a front to keep away nosy, interfering villagers not in the know.' She shrugged. 'We are so close to finishing. If Harry Elliot had kept his mouth shut instead of blurting out one night when he was pissed that he hadn't seen any plans in his office, then he and his tart of a lover would still be here now.'

'And Michael Enscale?' challenged Brendon.

'The stupid idiot had dementia and genuinely believed the story. Simon, his son, said he was going to see an estate agent and sell his land privately. Who knows what would have come to light.'

David Soby touched her arm. 'You've said more than enough Caroline.'

Like a wild animal eyeing its prey, she smiled longingly at Brendon as the vicar closed the door behind her.

Brendon's attempts at loosening his hands merely increased the discomfort. The vicar was right; Caroline had become very adept at tying knots during her work on the farm.

He looked around. Presumably the room was the bedroom Grace said was no longer used for anything other than storage. Perhaps she'd told him the truth but, if she hadn't, then she must be working with the vicar and Caroline as well as the landlord. He wondered who the hell else was in on it. Some of the villagers must be as well. He also wondered if Jenny Pearson was already dead. However, whatever the answers, more pressing at the moment was where the fuck was Sven and what did he have in mind.

Brendon looked at the knife by the sink. It wouldn't be very sharp, but with patience it might do the trick. Rocking the chair, he attempted to manoeuvre towards it. He'd managed half a metre before losing balance and crashing over.

'Fuck, fuck, fuck, fuck!' he exclaimed, his already pain-ridden head feeling the full force of the solid wooden table leg. He lay unmoving, regathering his breath. He tried rolling, but the chair resisted his efforts. He tried to push against the table leg which had inflicted the hurt, but although the table was heavy, so was he. Confirming "for every action, there's a reaction" meaning the table made more progress than the chair, he slowly began to accept the hopelessness of the situation. He would have to wait until Sven showed his hand before any further possible escape plans, that is provided Sven untied him prior to doing his worst.

Although Brendon's vision through tired eyes and nauseated mind was blurred and partially distorted, it was still sufficiently clear to watch a hatch in the floor rise up in front of the en-suite doorway. Certain he was about to meet Sven, his heart thumped, his palms became clammy and he could sense the hairs on the back of his neck responding instinctively. His body tensed as the distinctive blonde hair of a Swedish head rose above the uncarpeted boards. A split second later, the tension was immediately replaced by surprise, as the face under the long blonde tresses introduced itself as Sue the barmaid.

'Ah, there you are Brendon; I've been looking for you. Are you all right?'

It crossed his mind to say, "Yes I'm absolutely fine thank you Sue. Lying on the floor tied to a chair with dried blood in my hair, is my fucking way of relaxing," but instead he replied, 'Does it fucking look like it?'

'There, there Brendon, no need to be sarcastic.' She lifted herself out of the hatch, closing the lid down carefully. 'Now, let's see.'

'There's a knife.' He pointed with his head to the sink. 'It might do the job.'

'Not as well as this little rascal,' gloated Sue, pulling a four-inch switchblade from the side pocket of her combat trousers. She knelt down beside Brendon.

'Do you always carry that with you?' he asked, apprehensive she might be a little heavy-handed cutting the rope.

'Only at times like this. There, that's your feet, now then hold still.' He had every intention of doing so.

Sat upright on the floor, he rubbed his wrists, his fingers tingling as the blood flowed back. The sight of Sue, rather than his expected executioner, had temporarily relieved his agonising headache. Her youthful light-heartedness bolstered his mood.

'Silly question, but what were you doing down there?' he asked. 'Clegg said you were in the kitchen.'

'All in good time Brendon,' she replied, offering her hand and hauling him to his feet. 'Cleggy doesn't know me as well as he thinks he does. Anyway, first things first though.'

'Which are?'

'To get the fuck out of here I would suggest.'

'Fair point,' he agreed trying the door handle. 'Locked.'

'I could have told you that; room ten always is. The passkey doesn't work either; discovered that when I first came here. I'm surprised you hadn't as well,' she said, shaking her head superiorly. 'Not much chance of breaking it down without gaining the attention of anyone in the pub, so I guess it's going to be back the way I came in. Here, give me a hand.' Together they lifted the hatch.

'So where does this go "little Miss Know-It-All"?' asked Brendon, peering into a dimly lit hole approximately seven-metres deep. A steep wooden ladder gave access to the bottom.

'C'mon, I'll show you, but keep your voice down. The first part passes behind a false wall in the beer store before dropping down to a cellar.' Sue put a foot on the top rung of the ladder. 'Follow me and shut the hatch after you.'

Having done as he was told, he looked around the cellar, a room roughly six metres by six metres, hewn out of the natural rock, probably granite. A small electric lantern hung from the ceiling, providing sufficient light to see the rack of coat hooks on one wall and shelves on another. Two pairs of work boots sat on one of the shelves, together with several pairs of heavy "riggers" gloves. A shovel leant against an uncluttered wall, whilst a tunnel led off from the fourth.

'This way,' instructed Sue, grabbing his arm and leading him to the tunnel. 'The floor's a bit uneven, but there's just about enough light to see by.' Brendon looked up at the electric wire hanging loosely from the roof, to which were attached low wattage light bulbs every five metres or so.

Although the passage was just about high enough to cater for people over six-feet tall, in places the width meant turning sideways to negotiate large lumps of damp rock sticking out from the sides. It smelt dank, reminding him of some of the men's urinals he'd encountered on his travels. Occasionally, he swore as he kicked off the rats from his feet.

After about forty metres, Sue pointed to a second tunnel branching off at an acute angle to the right. 'I haven't been in there yet but I have a feeling it leads into the castle.'

'So straight ahead leads to the gorge?' asked Brendon, amazed by the thought.

'Correct. Not only to, but under the river and up the other side,' she replied matter of factly, as if to say, "Why wouldn't it?"

'But… but… I thought that was just a myth, something made up by the Normans.'

'Well, I can personally assure you it isn't and that's not all. Wait until…' She stuck out her arm, pushing Brendon back into the castle tunnel.

'What the…?'

'Voices, coming towards us,' she whispered, covering Brendon's mouth with her hand. 'Quick, in you go.'

Stumbling on the rougher surface, he struck his shoulder against the wall. 'Fuck, that hurt,' he exclaimed under his breath.

'Shush. Get a bloody move on.' She encouraged him up a short flight of bumpy steps. The light from the main tunnel faded rapidly. 'That's far enough,' instructed Sue. They stopped. The voices came closer.

'How are you going to do it this time, Sven?' The question was asked in Swedish.

'Much easier than the last, Erik. According to the boss he has no ties… is on an extended holiday. No one will miss him for some time and when they do… we will be gone.'

'Ha,' exclaimed the one called Erik, 'let's hope the river never dries up.'

'If it does, it will be like the dig, full of old bones plus a few rusty cars.'

Their enthusiastic laughter faded as they passed the end of the tunnel.

'We've got to get out of here, Sue. Once they discover I'm gone they'll be back,' stressed Brendon.

'Okay, okay, don't you think I know that?' She ran up the tunnel towards the castle. She was back within a matter of seconds. 'It's bricked up; we'll have to go to the gorge.'

'Is that wise?'

'Have we a choice? C'mon, get your arse into gear.'

Brendon was grateful for her leadership. His meeting with Caroline and the vicar had left him confused as to whom he could believe and more importantly, as to whether there was anyone he could trust. At the moment, he had to put Sue in the category of saviour. Also, his head had returned to feeling like a bomb had gone off inside, the shrapnel piercing each and every brain cell. Left alone, his decision-making would have been bereft of instinct and ideas.

They made their way along the tunnel, stopping every now and again to listen for approaching life. It descended gently at first, then the gradient steepened; eventually steps led them down towards the humming and hammering noise Brendon had heard from the surface, only much louder. The light became brighter. Sue held up one hand, signalling Brendon to halt, one finger on the other touching her lips.

Peering over Sue's shoulder, Brendon saw they were at the entrance to a cavern roughly the size of a tennis court. Down one side were stacked boxes, possibly some of those Brendon had seen on the lorry in the car park. A large generator, its exhaust pipe disappearing into a hole in the ceiling was sat idle in one corner, whilst an electric motor hummed constantly, sourcing its power from a bank of batteries, presumably charged by the generator when required. On the opposite wall to the boxes, three men were busy hammering at the shimmering rock with pickaxes, whilst another loaded what Brendon assumed was unwanted spoil into a small truck mounted on a narrow-gauge railway line. In the bright light, he could see the track headed off into another tunnel at right angles to the one in which he and Sue were now stood.

She beckoned him to follow. Hidden from the workmen by the boxes, she led him to their escape route, a tunnel which a few seconds later, he realised from the thundering noise above, crossed under the river. After three minutes of painstakingly cautious progress, they reached the base of the drain, presumably the one he'd located with McKenna.

He climbed the metal rungs first, trusting his strength would be sufficient to raise the manhole cover, with or without its camouflage tree. It took his best adrenaline-fuelled effort, but he managed to raise it enough to make sliding it to one side a possibility. He offered his hand to Sue, who gratefully, but he sensed unnecessarily, accepted his help to clamber out. Together, they put back the cover and replaced the toppled tree.

After passing through the hole in the fence, they sat together, both breathing heavily, the copse of hazel trees in full leaf obscuring them from the gorge and the road.

'Now then young lady, as much as I appreciate your help… in fact, probably in saving my life, I think we have to have a chat, don't you?'

Sue lay back on the grass, relaxed and uninhibited. 'You remember when we first spoke?' she asked. 'You know the time we went to room nine and I spooked?'

'Yep, very well. You saved me from an embarrassing

encounter with our pub landlord.' He smiled graciously. 'Seems like saving me is becoming a habit.'

'Think nothing of it,' she graciously acknowledged. 'Anyway, after that I thought it was time to grow up and get on with some investigating of my own.' She propped herself on one elbow. 'Well, next day I went back to room nine with the key but couldn't open it; it was as if it was bolted on the other side. The key turned but that was it, I couldn't budge it. Strangely, neither could I enter any other way.'

Brendon assumed she meant by the window.

She continued, 'So, I decided to try room ten which is on the other side of the corridor, around the corner from the other bedrooms. I found the door wide open and that's when I discovered it wasn't any ordinary bedroom.'

'That was the one in which you found me?'

'You've got it. It's right above the beer store. Anyway, I had a good look around and other than what you've seen, there was nothing else. Only later, when I was getting some bottles for stocking the bar, it dawned on me the store seemed smaller than the room above it.'

'Hence the ladder.'

'Correct.' She sat upright. 'I didn't think any more about it, just assumed the side wall of the store had been blocked off for some reason; perhaps it had been used as a cupboard in the past. However, the next morning when I was in there, I heard footsteps going up the wall.' She grinned. 'Nearly spooked again.'

'Understandable,' empathised Brendon. 'Go on.'

'Well, brain kicked in and later I went back to the room and found the hatchway.'

'The door was open again?' he asked, rather surprised.

Sue bit her lip. 'Guess I was lucky,' she answered sheepishly.

'You obviously were.' Now wasn't a time to doubt her. 'And you climbed down?'

She nodded. 'Followed the passage to the mine; I think it's silver by the way, and then on to the drain where we just got out, which I believe might be access for some of the supplies they need; you know, the ones it would look strange delivering to the pub.'

'Makes a lot of sense. That would explain the lorry load of goods I saw arrive in the gorge car park.' Raising an eyebrow he asked, 'So what were you doing in there again today?'

She went back to one elbow. 'Do you remember how long room nine was from the door to the window?'

He shrugged. 'About fourish metres give or take.'

'And the end wall of the pub, from outside that is?'

'Never thought about it… ' He stared at her, open mouthed. 'Of course, what a fool.'

'You or me?' she smirked.

'Room six? You were looking for room six?'

'Got it in one.'

'And?'

'Nothing; no other passage, no doorway, no hatch, basically no way of getting in.'

His eyes lit up. 'The wardrobe in room nine,' surmised Brendon. 'There's got to be a way in from there.'

'Perhaps you're not so dumb after all.'

'Why thank you ma'am. But how do we get in there?'

Sue got to her feet. Brushing off her back and legs she

said, 'Sorry warrior, you'll have to work that one out, I can't do all the thinking.' She offered her hand. Taking it, he hauled himself up. She added, 'I've got to get back to the pub or Phil will want to know where I've been. Not a good time to get the sack.'

'Okay. Perhaps we can speak later. Are you working this evening?'

She nodded. Checking around, she asked, 'Are you coming with me?'

Brendon shook his head. 'No, I've got someone to surprise first, but there is one thing.'

'And what's that?'

'Are the guys doing the mining all Swedish?'

'Yes, I think so. Why?'

'No reason.' Rubbing his chin he asked, 'Do they sleep in room ten?'

She nodded. 'Possibly, although they sometimes use the other bedrooms I'm guessing and occasionally eat in the restaurant or up at the bistro.' She headed for the gate to the road.

'So that's why Melanie thought they were railway workers.' He helped her over the top bar. Very quietly, he murmured, 'So Grace must definitely be in on it too. Shit and I started off trusting her.'

As he walked up the lane to Caroline's, he wondered if he could trust Sue and reasonably confident he could, he asked himself, *so who the hell is she.*

CHAPTER TWENTY-NINE

Anxiously looking around as if help in the form of the vicar would be standing behind her, Caroline stared at him as he locked the back door and put the key in his pocket.

'I know you're alone Caroline; I've been watching you for the last twenty minutes.'

She stayed silent, her feet glued to the kitchen floor. Grim faced, he stepped forwards. Grabbing her hair, he jerked her head back hard, causing her to scream. He ignored her pleas to let go.

'I think we've got some talking to do, don't you?'

She met his eyes, her own filling with tears. Still she didn't speak.

'The lounge will be much more comfortable, don't you think?' He tightened his grip. She winced, but her mouth stayed shut, her head unable to move. He dragged her to the front door, turned the key, pocketed it and then ignoring her resistance, half dragged, half pushed her into the lounge and spun her forcefully onto the sofa. She rubbed her eyes with her sleeve.

'What... what... what do you want?' she implored,

her voice shaking. He made himself comfortable in one of the armchairs.

'What the hell do you think I want; another meaningless fuck in your late husband's bed?' He sat forwards, his controlling eyes cold, his body rigid, his hands grasping the arms of the chair. 'I want an explanation, that's what I want and I want it now.' It was a different Brendon to the one she'd always loved.

Her head dropped to her hands. 'I'm so, so sorry Brendon. I... I... I had no choice. It was you or the operation. I couldn't let everyone down.'

It's a small village, a very small village indeed.

Through piercing eyes, he snapped. 'By everyone, I assume you mean your vicar friend and his cohorts?'

She used her other sleeve. Barely able to see through her salt-blurred vision she uttered, 'And my children.'

The mention of his godchild temporarily weakened his professional resolve. Nathan wasn't important. 'Ellie, what about Ellie? What the fuck's she got to do with anything?'

Caroline shook her head. 'She's the one behind it all.'

~

Slumped in a churchyard hedge, the gravestones casting shadows over the unmown grass, Brendon needed a drink, but returning to the pub wasn't on his agenda just yet. What Caroline had told him was still crashing around in his head, like some mad bull trying to escape its fate in the ring. At first, it had seemed like a story he'd read many times as a kid, but in the child's version, no one ever died in an Enid Blyton novel. However, Caroline's tale wasn't for kids; it was the grown-up version and it wasn't something he'd want to read over and over again.

At first, it had seemed like she was trying to fob him off, but once she admitted to not just shooting John Wakeham in the back of the head, but had done so whilst he knelt blindfolded in front of her, he began to realise hers was no fairy story. Afraid she might climb out of a window or make a call on her mobile, he'd gone with her to her bedroom for a box of tissues. He'd even stood by the en-suite door as she'd emptied her bladder. He could have done with relieving himself, but unless he'd tied her up before doing so, there was no way he was going to trust her not to try to get away or summon help. On leaving the house, the lane had proved an acceptable and welcome toilet.

Returning to the lounge, she'd managed to compose herself sufficiently to explain the reasons for leaving him to the attentions of Sven and his friend.

~

'One day whilst still in their teens, Ellie and Nathan were playing in the gorge when they discovered three silver coins in a cave on the castle side of the river. They rushed home to tell Gareth and me, but in Gareth's usual dull and unexcitable way, he dismissed the find as having any possible value. He said there were several coins, or Lingtree pennies as they were known, on display in The Judge's Parlour and many more in museums in Sweden, probably taken there by the Vikings after being given them as protection money, or "Dangelds" as it was called at the time. Gareth told the kids not to visit the cave again as it was probably dangerous. Whether or not they did go back, I don't know, as they would have been afraid to say in case their father found out.

'Several years later, after Ellie had studied geology at university and then completed a course in gemmology at a jewellery school in the States, she met up with a Swedish student who shared the same interest in valuable gems and minerals. She brought him back home for a holiday, told him about the cave where she and Nathan had found the coins and yes, they went to look for it. They didn't find any more, but they did find what they believed to be substantial silver deposits, the cave possibly being the site of the mine for the pennies.

'Sigurd, her friend, she insisted that's all he was, blabbed on the phone to his family back home, although it was some years afterwards before two Swedish geologists turned up on the doorstep wanting to explore the possible source of the silver contained in the pennies in the Stockholm Museum. They confirmed the deposits were indeed silver and also, having cleared a roof fall in the cave, they discovered the tunnel leading from the gorge to the castle which until then was just a rumour. Not only did it lead to the castle, but a narrow passage continued to a cellar under The Judge's Parlour; possibly a hideaway for the King's men during the Civil War.

'Anyway, a year or so after the silver deposits were confirmed, things snowballed. Sigurd told Ellie that he'd found some Swedish miners who would be prepared to come and secretly work in return for cash from the sale of the silver, thus avoiding declaring any knowledge of the mine to the owners of the mineral rights. Originally it was thought it would take four years to dig out the tunnel and extract the deposits, but then it was realised that getting supplies in and the metal out couldn't be done from the castle side of the river. Too many villagers and visitors would see what was going on and get suspicious. Consequently, a tunnel had to be dug to the other side of the gorge. Ellie had grown up with the manageress of the cafe and for a... shall we say... generous commission from the silver proceeds, she agreed to keep quiet and to warn us when senior employees or maintenance workers were due to visit. If so, work would stop. It had been these maintenance people who, when installing handrails some years ago, had cleared the path to where we decided to locate the access drain. The cafe and entrance employees were told that lorries containing fencing materials, cement, sand... that sort of thing, would be using the gates. That's why nobody takes any notice when a delivery of petrol for the generator and beer, vodka and snack foods is made every now and again.

'It took two years to dig the new tunnel. All the spoil is dumped in the river via small railway trucks using the original cave entrance which, as it emerges under the path through the gorge, it's unlikely you would find.

'Fred and Bernard, the two gays, were running the pub at the time it all started and as Gareth and I got on quite well with them, it was easy to convince them to let the miners use their rooms free of charge in return for a share of the eventual financial gains.

'Unfortunately, because the majority of rooms and

the restaurant were constantly in use and not producing any income, pub profits weren't good. However, Bernard had inherited a substantial amount from the death of his parents and therefore he and Fred lived a very comfortable lifestyle, which basically upset the brewery. Eventually enough was enough and Fred and Bernard were given the push. That's when the Polsons took over. They turned out to be straight in more ways than one. The miners then had to live underground, which didn't go down very well.

'David Soby, the new vicar, struck Gareth and me as a very reasonable sort and one night after a few drinks, we told him everything that was going on. His stipend and dentist's pension weren't much so he was more than keen to offer his non-religious services in return for the prospect of earning a lot of cash. It seems that after a drunken session with Jim and Pete, during which they confessed to how the Hendersons had helped solve a food shortage during the big freeze, he hit upon the idea of scaring the Polsons into leaving. All it took was regular use of hallucinogenic drugs in their drinks, a large doll dressed as an old man in a helmet and a couple of pig carcasses and entrails. The plan worked so well that they were taken to a mental home.

'Phil, their replacement, took little convincing, especially as by now the mine was producing substantial amounts of silver and the profits were at last beginning to filter into the pockets of the villagers in the know. The silver is processed in this country and then sold to a company run by Sigurd's uncle, a man with few ethics when it comes to cash transactions. It takes a while to turn it round, but the rewards are obviously worth the wait.

'Unlike Fred and Bernard, Phil was sensible enough to put some of his share of the earnings through his books as pub receipts, which meant the brewery stayed off his back.

'Just under two years ago, an allegedly wealthy investment banker from London stayed at the pub and told anyone who would listen that he was prepared to buy land and would pay an above market rate for it as he was keen to move his family to this part of the world and try his hand at hobby farming. You can imagine there were several interested farmers who would happily sell at the right price and clear their debts with their bank. I say allegedly, because after a bit of 'googling' by me and a couple of others, we discovered that this so-called investment banker was in fact a director of a large firm of house builders and was in conversation with the National Park regarding building sustainable and eco-friendly housing on the edge of the village, something we'd always been under the impression would never be allowed to happen. However, Lingtree is apparently a borderline case as far as the National Park is concerned.

'Were people to sell, our route for transporting the silver would be compromised, plus the fact that to those who had lived in the village all their lives, it would mean the virtual disappearance of a large section of the Corpse Way, something which even today they regard as sacred. Fortunately, market uncertainty must have scared the developers and eventually the housing plans were shelved.

'However, on hearing about the building plans and afraid someone else might come along, including the council, David Soby came up with the idea of the story about the quarry and later the archaeological dig as a defensive tactic. The silver deposits were nearing their viable end and once mining was finished, as far as some were concerned, they could build whatever they liked, not a view shared by all of us of course.'

'Is that when you had to dispose of Michael Enscale, Harry Elliot and Linda Collier?' Brendon had asked. She'd nodded.

'It was a shame, but Michael would have stirred up a hornet's nest if he started to follow things through and found the rumours to be false and as for Harry; well, we tried to buy his silence but it was too late. Linda Collier was regrettably an innocent bystander in the plot to dispose of Harry.'

'And Gareth?'

'Having cleared an area to look as though a quarry and siding were actually happening, for some reason, Gareth started to get cold feet; said the mining was all wrong and the underhandedness was against all his family principles. It didn't help when I started laughing at his change of mind and said without the money from the silver, we'd have gone under a year or so ago. That was it. He said we could pay our way by selling the land being used as the fake siding site to another farmer. I told the vicar and he must have told Jim and Pete as the next day they paid us a visit. Said they weren't particularly happy with Gareth's plans and if he did sell, it would definitely cause all kinds of problems, which wouldn't be acceptable to the others in the know.

'Naturally, Gareth told them to go away in no uncertain terms, but the damage was done. Three weeks later he was found in the castle.'

'Did you know what would happen to him?' She'd turned away.

'I told you I no longer loved him and David, the vicar, said it was the only way. A day after he'd made up his mind to sell, I found him looking at farms for sale on the Internet and a day after that, the estate agent bloke Wakeham appeared on the doorstep. I rang David. He said leave it to him.'

'So why did you have to pull the trigger to kill Wakeham?'

'It was a necessity. Jim and Pete had caught him sniffing around the site of the dig. They tied him up, the same as we tied you up. Dumped him in my field. David called round; said they intended to bury Wakeham near the Hendersons. He gave me the gun he'd allegedly got from a friend just to threaten Wakeham with, while he, Jim and Pete sorted out some tools. But they didn't tie the knots very well.' She'd screwed up her eyes. 'I believe they did that on purpose, perhaps to test my commitment and I panicked.'

Bereft of tears, her eyes had filled with hatred.

'Wakeham tried to get to his knees. I thought he was getting free, so I put the barrel to his head, told him to lie down.' Her face had lit up. 'He wouldn't listen. If only he had.'

'Would he still be alive if he had?'

She'd smiled, knowing his question to be rhetorical.

'And Soby removed his teeth, cut off his hands and instead of burying him they threw him in the gorge.'

'They said they'd changed their minds; the ground would be too hard. He wasn't meant to float, but Jim and

Pete cocked up their knots and the rocks fell off when he hit the water… splash.'

She'd laughed, as though savouring the thought of the body sinking to its intended grave.

'And Hatcher?'

'He was talking too much; he was talking to you. He'd found the tunnel, he had to be quietened. I still had the gun and I felt really confident when I took aim and squeezed the trigger. After all, I didn't want to hit you by mistake.' Smiling, she'd added, 'It was so good when he fell like a stunned cow in the abattoir. I was alive, free of Gareth's control and this time I made sure the empty bullet casing was safe in my pocket. I picked it up when you carried the crumpled Hatcher into the bushes. I wasn't going to drop it again.'

He'd led her back to Gareth. 'So what happened to Gareth, your husband?'

'I told you, he got cold feet.' She'd then squawked like a witch casting a spell in a bubbling cauldron. 'Ha, the whole of him is feeling the cold now, even his head.' Her top lip had drawn back over her teeth. 'They sewed it back on you know, for the funeral, not that anyone could see him once the lid was on.'

Brendon had struggled with this strangely weird and uncaring person sat on the sofa. It wasn't the Caroline he thought he knew, but she'd seemed so natural when she spoke, that he'd started to wonder if this was the real her.

'His head wasn't supposed to come off you know.'

He'd shaken his own head in amazement. 'Sorry, what did you say?'

'I said, his head... it wasn't supposed to have come off. It sort of... well... it kind of broke off when they hung him from the railings on the metal landing in the castle. Of course he was dead already,' she'd explained matter of factly. 'Jim had seen to that, but apparently the rope was too long so he fell further than intended before it yanked him back. Pete said it made a horrible cracking noise, a bit like a whiplash. At least Gareth didn't know anything about it, having already smashed his skull falling down the stairs; got into an argument in the pub in the early hours of the morning. Phil enjoys the occasional "lock-in" you see. Hanging was just to make sure they said, before the foxes got him. They said he shouldn't have followed them to somewhere he swore he'd never go again. Perhaps it was an omen.' She'd glanced at the ceiling. 'I hadn't thought of that before. Perhaps he never wanted to go back because he knew he'd end up like Alan, you know the best friend you pushed off the top.'

She'd then fallen silent. Struggling to come to terms with believing this was the same person he'd made love to not many days ago, Brendon's muddled thoughts had been interrupted by the ringtone of his mobile. He'd looked at the number; recognised it as the one Colin had sometimes called him on.

'Hello, Brendon Gallagher... oh, hi Sally... sorry, can you repeat that? ... But you don't know which one? ... No longer employed... okay, thanks oh Sally, have you heard from DS Pearson? ... Still sick her friend says... okay, thanks again... bye.' His mobile back in his pocket, he'd turned his attention to Caroline who, throughout his telephone conversation, had just stared vacantly at him.

'And what would have happened to me… after you and the vicar left?' She hadn't asked him how he'd got free. At that point her cocky demeanour had drained from her body and she seemed more like the Caroline he'd thought he'd known.

'I don't know Brendon; I don't ask what the Swedes do to their enemies. I didn't want it… honestly.' She'd sounded almost believable.

'Is that how you see me… as an enemy?' Despite everything she'd said, he couldn't forget how she'd responded when he'd entered her and thrust deep into her moistness.

She'd shaken her head.

'No Brendon, you could never be that, but… but I have to look after the friends I've made since you left—'

The words had run through his mind. *It's a small village, a very small village indeed!*

'Perhaps if you'd never left things would have been so different.'

For a moment, he'd wanted to hold her, to kiss her, to feel her warmth and softness, forget all her insane words, but then he'd remembered the telephone call he'd just had with DC Sally Smith.

'Who attacked you Caroline? Was it Nathan?'

She'd slumped back in her chair.

'How do you know?'

'The police forensics analysed the blood in the kitchen again. Most of it matched your DNA, but some in the sink only contained half a match. I'm guessing it's Nathan's. The police are checking with the RAF; hope to have the results shortly.'

His words had hit home; she'd taken a deep breath, run her fingers through her hair.

'He was still in the house when we made love the morning after the funeral. He was drunk, drunk from the night before and drunk from the Scotch he drank for breakfast. He thought I'd told you everything. He didn't care that we were in bed together, he hated his father, but he cared about the silver and he didn't want it ruined.'

'So he's involved as well?' Brendon had exclaimed, more and more shocked by Caroline's revelations.

'He flies the helicopter; the one which takes the silver to the processors.'

'I don't understand,' he'd confessed. 'How would the RAF let him use a helicopter?'

'It doesn't. He was kicked out four years ago. Ungentlemanly conduct; made a pass at another officer, a male one. Blamed his dad for fucking him up as he put it. Said Gareth never let him do anything he wanted. Wouldn't let him out to play until after he'd done all the farm work and school homework. Wouldn't let him go to dances in the village and spend time with the opposite sex unless we were with him. Blamed me for that. Said because I got pregnant before Gareth and I married, then we were afraid of him going the same way. He felt that whatever he did was never good enough for his dad. So who could blame him when he took it out on Ellie?'

He'd stared at her, lips tight, eyes half closed. 'You mean it was Nathan who assaulted Ellie, not Gareth?' She'd nodded.

'Ellie seemed to deal with it and we thought Nathan was all right when he joined the RAF and then got married.

But he never forgave himself for what he did to Ellie. Always drank heavily from the day he moved away but in recent times it got out of control. Money from the silver funded the drink, that's why he could stay sober when he needed to fly the chartered helicopter. Lives on his own in Brighton. We rarely see him. Eventually Gareth started to blame himself, felt he should share Nathan's guilt. Said he should have reported his son to the authorities years ago. It began to depress him.'

Caroline was no longer the confident, couldn't "give a shit" female she had been a few minutes ago. She was now just an ashamed mother, ashamed of her late husband, ashamed of her latent gay alcoholic son and ashamed of herself.

Inwardly and outwardly shaken by the disgusting revelation, Brendon had taken a while to temporarily put it to one side before asking his next question.

'But the police said the RAF told them he was on manoeuvres.'

'He had good male friends in his squadron despite his behaviour; promised never to let on. Whenever you ring, if you speak to the right people, he'll always be on manoeuvres.'

It was then Caroline had asked the inevitable question.

'What are you going to do now Brendon?'

~

He didn't know the answer then and sat in the hedge, he didn't know the answer now. He thought about all the lies Caroline had told him since the funeral. However, blaming her own husband, a childhood friend of his, for abusing their daughter, his godchild, was worse than any lies about her love for him, the mine, her so-called loss of memory about her attacker, the killings, her son's employment, the sale of the land, in fact everything she'd decided to tell him. He didn't even know if Ellie's employment was genuine.

Prior to leaving Caroline's, he'd ripped out her landline cord and stamped on her mobile. She might drive straight to the vicar's, taking the long route from the farm, although there again, if she did actually love him, perhaps that was the reason he'd been given several chances to live. They were probably already searching for him, unless of course, Sven had thought the vicar had let him go, but he doubted it.

It's a very small village, a very small village indeed!

Whatever he did, it wouldn't bring any of the dead back to life. It was how it was in AD 996 and it was no different now. He pictured the vicar sat opposite him in the pub.

Nothing much changes in a community like this Mr Gallagher, but what goes on here is best left to the locals.

Perhaps the vicar was right; perhaps he, Felman the "man from the mountains", owed the village that much. People were happy here in their own miniscule way.

'Brendon.'

He should have been startled, as he had been many times in the past when unaware of another human's unexpected approach, but now... now nothing surprised him any more. Instead of reacting defensively, he slowly lifted his head. 'Sue,' he said casually, shielding his eyes from the sun. 'I thought you were working.'

'I am, but Phil has gone out for the rest of the day. It's time for us to enter room six.'

He looked at her; she seemed different. 'Who the hell are you?' he asked, tired and confused. 'I feel we've met before but... my mind... it's all over the place.'

'All in good time Brendon. I'm here to help you make peace with yourself, which is all you need to know. Come, we must go.'

Rejuvenated a little by her sudden appearance, he took her hand, followed her to the pub. There was no Jim, no Pete, no landlord, no Grace; it was empty, ghostly quiet. Perhaps Arnold had fallen asleep in the kitchen. Although she alone wouldn't have needed it, Sue took the key to room nine from the board.

~

Sue shivered, the bitterly cold air from the almost silent air conditioning unit penetrating her thin white T-shirt. She grasped Brendon's hand as they stared at the three dangling naked bodies, their throats pierced by meat hooks attached to ropes hanging from the solid oak ceiling beam. Jan and Melanie hadn't moved away and DS Pearson wasn't ill. Under each pair of feet were plastic buckets, partially filled with blood. Several areas of the pallid, ashen skin bore scratches, as though someone had taken pleasure in making their presence felt. A pile of dried bloodstained clothes lay in one corner of the room, whilst in another was a knife rack, its contents worthy of a top-class butchers.

Like animal carcasses in a deep freeze, the torsos

had been split open from throat to groin, the organs and entrails removed. Incredibly, there was no smell of rotting flesh, no flies or maggots. From the colour of the wide-eyed, distant faces, Brendon guessed they'd been treated with some sort of embalming oil.

Brendon and Sue had entered this windowless room via nine's wardrobe, the back sliding in two parts to one side. Sue had seemed surprised when the key had turned in the lock of room nine.

'That's odd,' she'd exclaimed. 'Something's left here.'

Brendon stared at the corpses. 'This explains the screaming,' he mumbled, filling with guilt that he hadn't done more. He turned to Sue. 'Let's at least cut them down and cover them with blankets; they deserve some respect.'

Sue dragged the duvet and undersheet from the four-poster in room nine, while Brendon used one of the knives to cut the rope, careful to take the weight of each body as individual threads gave up their load. Laying the empty cadavers side by side on the floor, they conscientiously spread the bedding over them.

'There's nothing more we can do Brendon; it's time for us to leave,' Sue whispered, her voice gentle and calm.

He nodded. Taking one last look around the room, he spotted a mobile phone half hidden by the clothes. He scrolled through the texts. The last one read;

Sorry. Jenny has asked me to let you know she's still unwell. Hopes to be back soon. Her good friend.

'Bastards, fucking bastards.' He threw the handset down, selected the cleaver and saw from the rack. 'There are a couple of things I must do.' He stormed out through the wardrobe. The onslaught of wind knocked first him and then Sue to the ground. The room darkened, a vision like a laser-projected image appeared in the suddenly formed mist.

~

The door hinges still creaking, Ian Henderson turned away, vomiting bile over his wife's stricken body as she collapsed, unrestrained, face down on the blood-ridden floor.

'Not my kids; please not my kids!' he shouted.

He sunk to his knees.

Crying hysterically, he dug his fingers into the vile-smelling entrails, uncontrollably spreading them apart. Above, the bodies of two beautiful children, their torsos savagely torn open, swung slowly in the draught from the door.

Tears flowing freely, he pleaded;

'Where are the livers? I can't see the livers.'

~

The mist clearing, Brendon studied Sue's terror-ridden face. 'You saw it too,' he snapped, 'you saw the Hendersons.' She met his eyes. 'Who the fucking hell are you? Tell me.'

He pushed her onto her back, kneeling astride her. 'Who are you...? For God's sake tell me,' he bellowed, pinning her arms to the well-worn, dust-ridden carpet.

She looked at him contemptuously then spat in

his face. He wiped the saliva from his cheek, tasting its saltiness as he'd done so a thousand years before.

After a moment's hesitation, he laughed, more heartily than at any time in the past. He slid to her side.

There was no anger in his voice as he asked, 'Tell me girl, what is your name, for I wish you no harm?'

She smiled. 'I am Sunniva, "the gift from the sun".'

Propped up on his elbow, he stroked her forehead, ran his hand through her beautiful blonde hair. 'Indeed you are. I thought of you that night after the burning of the church and I thought of you for many nights more. Why are you here?'

'You spared me that day the Vikings came to my village. I ran far away. From the hills I watched the church burn. I slept with the sheep then returned the next morning. Many were slain, but many were saved. I helped with the injured. It took numerous years, but we rebuilt our lives, bred children, replenished the livestock and eventually replaced the stolen silver.' She sat up against the wall. 'I have never forgotten you, Felman. I have looked out for you.'

'So you have to go back?'

'Yes, like you, I was given one chance, but whereas Felman, "the man from the mountains" worshipped Freya and entered Folkvang, the field of the people, Balder, my god of immortality, would not allow me to travel the Earth in the way in which you have done. Instead, for nearly a thousand years I have walked the lanes and hills of Lingtree, unseen except by the undead, until you, my saviour returned.

'When Balder saw you were in dire danger, he allowed me one week. Once my time is expired, I must return.' She laughed. 'It is strange that I, Sunniva, an ancestor of the Anglo-Saxons am helping you, a Dane, from the rule of the Vikings.' She put up her fists. 'Perhaps we should fight instead.'

'No time young lady,' replied Brendon gaining his feet and helping Sue to hers. 'We have unfinished business.'

'Lead on my warrior chief,' she joked. 'I will let you live as you did me.'

'Very funny.' He gathered the cleaver and butcher's saw. Reluctantly re-entering room six, he picked up a coil of unused rope. Pointing to the en suite in room nine he instructed, 'Bring that container of toilet bleach please, I've got a bit of "social cleansing" to do.'

The door to room nine had swung shut. Although as an immortal, Sue would have been able to pass through without hindrance, the same as she had done with room ten, nonetheless she opened it, for Brendon was still a traveller from the field of the people.

The bar and restaurant were deserted. Lunch was over two hours ago and it was too early for the first evening drinkers. Scribbling his PIN on a food-order notepad, Brendon tossed his credit card onto the shelf beside the card machine.

'He can take what he wants; it's no good to me.'

Checking there was no one outside he crossed the car park, unlocked his car and dropped the keys on the front seat.

'Whoever wants it can have it.' He slammed the door. 'Right young lady, I need your help with this rope.' She followed him through the pedestrian gate to the castle, any fear he had as Brendon, no longer affecting Felman.

CHAPTER THIRTY

At four forty-five that afternoon, Jim Evans and Pete Grayson ordered their last pint.

'Busy day Arnie me boy?' asked Pete as the tussled-haired, spotty youth pulled Pete's pint.

Arnold yawned. 'Not very Mr Grayson.'

'Managed to stay awake then?' chirped Jim, rolling a fag.

'Just about,' Arnold retorted. He pulled a second pint. 'On the tab Mr Evans?'

Jim nodded.

'Better pay it sometime Jim,' suggested Pete. 'Phil will be getting fucking pissed off else.'

'Bollocks. He's got enough cash to last him a lifetime. He's got fuck all to spend his money on,' sneered Jim.

'Not like you with a bitch of a wife who spends everything you gets paid,' smirked Pete, sipping his beer. 'Bloody lovely pint today Arnie.' Arnold managed a grunt.

'And if you didn't spend all your money on they fuckin' rent boys, you'd be even fuckin' richer you pervert.' Jim looked pleased with his comment, although it was one he'd made many times before, particularly when Pete had returned from the gents, his zip unfastened.

'You be careful what you say Jim Evans, 'specially in front of young Arnie here; you're making him jealous.' Arnold grunted again, a little more loudly this time.

'Couldn't give one,' retorted Jim. He slipped off his stool. 'Time for a smoke you old faggot?'

'Lead the way arsehole.'

Jim jokingly held one hand over his buttocks as they walked outside. Leaving the cover of the porch, Jim's sudden halt caused Pete to spill his beer.

''Ere, steady on you—'

'Good evening gentlemen, lovely weather for the time of year don't you think?'

'What the fuck are you doing sat on our bench Gallagher?' snorted Jim.

Brendon raised himself up, pretending to examine the seat. 'Sorry gents, can't see a reserved sign anywhere on it.'

'And what's more, why are you still alive?' Pete appeared genuinely puzzled and for once, less sure of himself.

'Sorry, should I be dead? I do apologise.' For the first time since their initial reunion, Brendon was enjoying their conversation. The two locals exchanged glances.

'S'pose we could put things right,' suggested Pete.

'Vicar would be pleased,' agreed Jim. They put their drinks on the table.

'Oh my God, what are you going to do?' asked Brendon sarcastically. His arrogance hit home.

'Right you little bastard. You might have put one of us on the floor but you won't fuckin' manage two of us,' snapped Pete. Without warning, he planted his fist in Brendon's face. Startled, Brendon fell to the ground. 'Grab him Jim,' shouted an excited Pete as his Doc Martin sunk deep into Brendon's groin. They each grasped one of his arms. Attempting to pull himself free by clutching onto the table, Brendon knocked over their half full glasses.

'You'll fuckin' pay for that,' declared Pete, his knee catching the end of Brendon's chin. 'Almost full those glasses were.'

'Okay, okay. I'm too tired to struggle.' Brendon wiped the back of his hand over his nose, studied the blood then admitted, 'I've had enough. I was leaving anyway. I can't take any more. Do what you want, but please make it quick.'

'Told you he ain't so fuckin' hard Pete,' exclaimed Jim, causing Brendon to fold double as he landed one in his solar plexus. Grinning widely, Jim lifted Brendon's head by the hair. Staring into his eyes, Jim's forehead made contact with the bridge of Brendon's nose, causing his partially healed cut to reopen. Satisfied for the moment, Jim turned to his drinking partner. 'Fuck Phil, we should have taken him the last time.'

Nodding, Pete surveyed the village street. It was quiet, except for the yapping of a distant dog.

'Right you little fucker, you're going to share the same fate as our good friend—'

'Not in the end he weren't,' interrupted Jim, his lips forming a sickly sneer.

'—Gareth,' finished Pete.

Dragging Brendon between them, they slowly manoeuvred him into the castle grounds and up the well-trodden path worn into one side of the mound. On reaching the entrance to the keep, now no longer the dreaded doorway to Brendon's nemesis, they thrust him forward onto the metal landing. Brendon fell heavily, scraping his forehead on the tarmac surface.

'Right you bastard.' Jim pulled a six-inch blade from a sheath on his belt. The two of them stepped forwards. 'I've being looking forward to this for years. I never really liked you as a smart-arsed kid and now... now... I fuckin' hate your guts.'

'Funny you should use that word,' mocked Sue as she brought the cleaver down forcefully on first Jim's head and then Pete's, 'as I was thinking exactly the same.'

The two men thumped to the floor, blood spurting from the wide gashes in the top of their skulls.

'Perfect young lady,' congratulated Brendon, wiping his graze and nose with his handkerchief. 'Hopefully you haven't killed them... completely, shall we say?'

'Don't think so,' replied Sue, running her finger along the bloodstained edge of the cleaver. 'It's not that sharp.' She seemed unperturbed by the act of violence.

'Excellent.' Brendon looked down at the fallen duo; their wide, unbelieving eyes stared back at him, their lips quivering but unable to form words. 'Pass me the saw please Sue.'

The sun having dropped below the top of the castle walls, the fading light added a certain supernatural eeriness to the proceedings. With Sue holding the arms of his victims to prevent any reflex response, Brendon cut slowly and methodically through each wrist bone, savouring the mouthed, but silent cries of pain as more and more blood pulsed from their ulnar arteries. Unable to form a fist, the fingers twitched weakly as he severed the tendons. Tossing the hands unceremoniously over the railings, they made a sickly "splatting" noise as they landed palm down on the damp floor below.

Once done, he lifted Jim by the armpits and bumped him carefully down the spiral staircase.

'Don't want you to die yet old friend,' he remarked as he placed the body on the dungeon floor. Still able to respond, Jim's terrified eyes followed Brendon's as Jim made his final journey.

'Is that about the right length?' shouted Sue from the landing. 'Not too long?'

'No, that's fine Sue,' he replied, inspecting the two lengths of rope, the nooses roughly five feet from the floor. He gave them a tug. 'Perfect.'

Sue followed him down the stairs as he dragged Pete, finding his lighter body easier to manage. 'Must have caught what his partner died of,' he commented as he stepped off the bottom rung. 'Could be a welcome departure for you old friend.' He half carried, half hauled Pete to below one of the nooses. 'I'll hold him up; you put it round his neck.'

Once Sue had done as asked, he let the limp body go. Pete's feet were still on the ground making the way he hung, knees bent, arms loose by his sides, face white and lifeless, even more abhorrent. An arm began to rise, pointing the exposed bone and dripping flesh towards Sue. She reached out, as if to shake hands. The arm dropped back instantly.

'Fair enough,' she said. 'I wasn't particularly pleased to meet you either.'

'When you've quite finished canoodling madam,'

joked Brendon, 'give me some help with this fatter heap of shit.'

Once both Jim and Pete were comfortably hanging, Brendon fetched the bottle of bleach from the landing.

'Now then, who wants to go first?' He saw Pete's eyes flicker. 'I'll take that to mean you then.'

Holding the bottle directly in front of Pete's face, he nonchalantly unscrewed the top.

'Cheers,' he said as if to take a swig. Lifting the bottle above the hanging man's head, he slowly tipped half the contents into the open split in his skull.

Pete's mouth formed a scream, his eyes trying to blink out the bleach, reddening as the ammonia hit home.

'Who's a nice clean boy then?' asked Brendon in a childlike voice. 'That should wash away any nasty diseases. Mummy would be pleased.' He turned to Jim. 'Your go now Jim; we don't want you left out.'

Jim managed a high-pitched screech of agony, as the bleach entered deep into his wound. Brendon took Jim's knife from Sue. Partly appalled, partly enthralled by Brendon's torture of his childhood friends, she'd comforted herself by reverting to Sunniva. Growing up, witnessing attacks by the men from the far west of Dumnonia, she was hardened to the ways of the warriors and their rituals after defeat of the enemy. Before Felman began his pursuit, she had not been afraid to use a discarded sword to end the suffering of a fallen Viking, his leg barely attached by the sinews.

Holding the knife in both hands, Brendon inserted it into the neck of Jim's shirt. With one movement, he ripped through the cloth, exposing Jim's hairy, palpitating belly. Taking three steps back, he shouted, 'This is for Gareth, McKenna, Pearson, Hatcher and those I never met.' Rushing forwards, he plunged the blade into his victim's throat, splitting open the chest, the stomach and the abdomen. The intestines fell loose, the reddened eyes widened and bloody bile trickled from the rotten-teeth-filled mouth. Any remaining signs of Jim Evans' physical being had gone.

Brendon saw Pete try to summon up strength, in some ridiculous hope that he could avoid the wrath of his hate-driven assailant. The corners of Brendon's mouth curled. 'Now my old friend, it is your turn to pay the price.'

Despite the skinniness of Pete's frame, the knife did not cut so easily. Brendon had to work it up and down, like a butcher cutting through tough gristle. Penetrated by the point of the knife, air hissed from Pete's belly, the front of his trousers gradually soaked by a bladder no longer controlled by an alcohol-rotted sphincter. The smell of evacuated bowels was filling the air as Sunniva clutched Felman's arm.

'Come my love, it is now time. We can tarry no longer.'

Felman dropped the knife. Taking one final look at the carcasses, he spat in both faces. One thought filled his mind as he followed Sunniva to the site of the runic stone, the place where their return would be made complete.

I wonder what fresh offal will be on the menu tonight!

CHAPTER THIRTY-ONE

'Pete and Jim not in?' enquired David Soby as he closed the public bar door.

'Not seen them yet Vicar,' replied Phil, turning a page of *The Daily Telegraph*. 'Pint is it?'

'Yes please Phil; put it on Jim's tab will you; he owes me a couple.'

'Will do.' The beer pump pulled easily towards him, a frothy mass squirting into the glass. 'Sorry, just got to change the barrel first; won't be a jiffy.' Phil threw the cloudy dregs into the sink under the counter and headed for the beer store. While he waited, David Soby glanced at the open paper. A short headline on page four grabbed his attention.

BODY OF TORTURED GOVERNMENT EMPLOYEE RECOVERED FROM BOMBED-OUT RUINS IDENTIFIED

He read on;

The Ministry of Defence yesterday confirmed the body of its employee discovered six weeks ago in Aleppo, is that of Brendon Gallagher, aged sixty years. During the seven months before his unexplained disappearance, it is understood he had been undertaking an intelligence mission on behalf of the British Government. He was due to retire in June. No further information has been released.

The colour already vacated from his face, shaking uncontrollably, the vicar leaned over the bar and wrapped his fingers around the bottle of Scotch set to replace the all but empty one on the optic. Just managing to maintain his grip, he undid the screw top and lifted the neck to his lips. By the time Phil Clegg returned, David Soby lay writhing on the floor, part of the spilt amber liquid bleaching his light-blue clerical shirt. Half the neat, undiluted contents of the bottle had already burned the lining of his throat and stomach. In the far corner of the bar, the thick-set, tussled-haired, bearded man raised his tankard, drained the last of his ale then picked up his helmet. Leaving the empty plastic container of pipe cleaning fluid on the table, he made his way unseen past the vicar and landlord. Passing silently through the door, he turned, a smile as broad as any longboat adorning his face.